I could feel someone standing very near

I told myself it was an illusion; there could not possibly be anyone in my room. For the past two nights I had not only locked the bedroom door, I had dragged the heavy boudoir chair in front of it. Nevertheless, I felt a presence, the same horrible presence that had dogged my recurrent dreams.

Don't let him know you're awake! cautioned that inner voice. My skin crawled but I didn't open my eyes. I was strangling on fear. Apparently satisfied that I still slept, the person moved. I heard a faint scraping sound near my right shoulder. He or she or it was at the bedside table. Then I sensed, rather than heard, motion. I felt the presence recede. I drew a long, deep breath, gathering courage, opened my eyes, and looked to the foot of my bed.

A shape was there—a huge, dark shape....

ABOUT THE AUTHOR

Madelyn Sanders raised two sons and worked as a hospital administrator before she began to do what she had always wanted to do: write novels. She says reading and writing are her tools of survival—and fun, besides. Madelyn lives in North Carolina.

Under Venice
Madelyn Sanders

Harlequin Books

TORONTO • NEW YORK • LONDON
AMSTERDAM • PARIS • SYDNEY • HAMBURG
STOCKHOLM • ATHENS • TOKYO • MILAN

Although Venice is real,
the Villa Corelli and the
characters exist only in
the author's imagination

Harlequin Intrigue edition published March 1991

ISBN 0-373-22158-4

UNDER VENICE

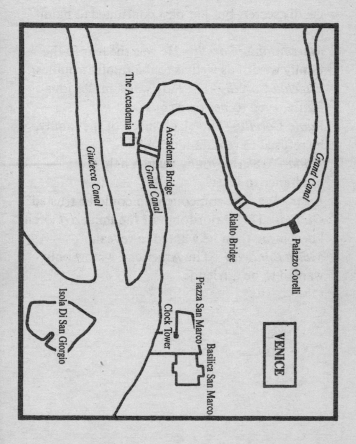

VENICE

The Accademia

Giudecca Canal

Grand Canal

Accademia Bridge

Grand Canal

Rialto Bridge

Palazzo Corelli

Isola Di San Giorgio

Piazza San Marco

Clock Tower

Basilica San Marco

CAST OF CHARACTERS

Clea Beaumont—She fled to Venice to hide a deadly secret, but her past continued to haunt her.

Marcantonio Corelli—He was the heir to the family wealth as well as to the family troubles.

Eugenia Corelli—The lady was a mysterious figure, even to her own sons.

Paolo Corelli—The black sheep of the family, he refused to remain hidden.

Zenia—Was the young maid a help or a hindrance to Clea?

Rosa—Was she someone who could be trusted?

Giorgo—The majordomo of the Palazzo Corelli knew more than he wanted to reveal.

Maria Bonavita—The American widow only wanted to be a friend.

Prologue

I was, unexpectedly, a wealthy woman. I was neither so foolish as to say that I didn't want the money because it was probably tainted, nor so hypocritical as to be sorry that I found myself instantly, if not easily, free. But I had paid a heavy price. My husband was dead, and a piece of my memory was missing. I feared that during those uncounted and unremembered beats of time I had killed him.

For the funeral I bought a widow's hat with a heavy black veil. I didn't want anyone to see the guilt in my eyes. I stood between my twenty-year-old son and my nineteen-year-old daughter and received condolences with the veil over my face. People said "Sorry, sorry," and I said "Thank you, thank you" endlessly, and all the while I tried to remember, to recover the lost time. But I could not.

After the reading of the will, I destroyed the anonymous note. I burned it in a stainless steel bowl and crushed the ashes to powder with the back of a spoon; then I flushed them down the toilet in the half bath off the mudroom. The note had been written in an old-fashioned spidery backhand in blue ink on cheap, thin white paper. It had come to the house, addressed to me in that same spidery hand, no return address, a Boston postmark, enclosed in one of those check-sized white envelopes printed on the inside with blue lines. A kind of envelope you can buy in any drugstore or supermarket. I'd thrown both envelope and note away, but then I had retrieved the sheet of paper with the note and kept it, because its message rang true. I had begun to suspect as much myself, and what I'd discovered when the will was read seemed to confirm it. The anonymous note had said simply, colloquially: "Your husband is a crook."

In the space of five days, I had gone from being a moderately unhappy suburban housewife to being a woman of wealth, and of terrible secrets. A young widow, people called me—perhaps thirty-nine is young for a widow, but I didn't feel young. I didn't feel anything at all.

I hadn't felt anything after the initial jolt, the shock I'd felt at finding out the extent of my dead husband's estate. My husband, Chester Beaumont, was a lawyer. Successful, not particularly prominent, a workaholic. We had none of the trappings of wealth—no huge house, no expensive car, no big vacations. In fact, because Chet worked all the time, we seldom had a real vacation at all; I had never in my life been any place more exotic than New York City. Yet he had left properties I'd never seen and investments I didn't know he'd had, totalling several million dollars. I wondered how he'd come to have so much.

I thought about the note. I recalled seeing it in my hand and realizing that during those moments that were a blank in my mind I must have snatched it back from him. I'd done that before I'd come to my senses and dialed 911 for help, so I must have believed the note told the truth. If only I could remember! But from the first angry reddening of Chet's face, along with his gasp of indrawn breath as he read the note I'd given him, to the sight of his body slumped facedown in a pile of papers on his desk, I remembered nothing. Absolutely nothing.

I didn't know what he'd said or what I'd said or if either of us had said anything at all; didn't know if I'd realized he was having a heart attack and had stood there watching his agony and waiting until he was dead before I came back into conscious awareness. To the rescue squad I'd said, "I don't know, it happened so fast..." And I'd put the note into my pocket. Chet was dead. Now the anonymous note was no more. We had killed him, the writer of that note and I.

In the days that followed, I went about necessary business like a robot. I sent both sets of parents, my husband's and mine, back to their respective homes. I sent my son with his father's parents and my daughter with my mother and father. I said I needed to be alone. My mother kissed me and said when she left, "I know you'll be just fine, Clea. You're managing so well already. You've always been the most practical one in the family."

Oh, yes, practical. That was true. I was so practical that for two years I had been planning to divorce the man who was now dead, but no one knew that. Practical, patient, cautious Clea, that was my style. I had been going to Boston University to finish the college degree I'd abandoned in order to marry Chet Beaumont. I'd planned to be able to support myself before I got the divorce. I hadn't loved my husband for a long time, but I didn't think I'd hated him enough to stand by and watch him die. Had I done such a horrible thing? Was that why I couldn't remember? Had I blanked it out because it was too horrible to recall?

With my unnatural robot-like calm I went to a banker I trusted. Not my husband's banker, but one of my own choice. I gave directions: a trust fund for my son, a trust fund for my daughter, all their college fees to be paid in advance. An account set up to cover the balance of my own college program, which I would finish when I was able. Everything else to be sold, liquidated, and the proceeds deposited in my name. Everything? The banker raised his eyebrows. Yes, I said, everything. He spoke of possible losses, the state of the market; spoke of the wisdom of having so much money invested somehow, used to make more money. Just do it, I said. And he did.

I was not comfortable anywhere. With anyone. The children came back from their grandparents', and as much as I loved them, they were no comfort. I felt strained, there was so much I couldn't tell them. I was relieved when they went on to their summer jobs, my son to Maine and my daughter to Nantucket. I tried sleeping in another bedroom—it didn't help. The coming of the mail was a daily agony: I couldn't wait for it to come, and then I was afraid to go through it. I half expected another note with that spidery blue handwriting, a note which this time would accuse me of profiting from my husband's ill-gotten gains. But none came. I was not myself anymore, I knew that. I went to places I had always loved, the Isabella Stewart Gardner Museum, the Museum of Fine Arts; I had lunch at the Ritz, I shopped at bookstores in Harvard Square. I felt no pleasure. Everything had changed, *I* had changed. I felt like a stranger in my own life.

I decided that I had to get away from my home in suburban Brookline, to leave Boston altogether. Leave the country. Heavy with guilt and secrets, I made an inspired choice: I went to Venice.

Chapter One

My first view of Venice was disturbing. I had a feeling of reality gone slightly askew. My vision played tricks on my mind. Intellectually I knew that the palaces and churches, shops and towers, were built upon the soil of a hundred small islands—but sight said otherwise. I saw Venice as an impossible creation, raised by magicians' hands out of the deep on which she floated, ever unanchored, a magnificent illusion. My boat drew closer and the blue-green waters of the canals became visible. The atmosphere of unreality increased, just when I would have expected the opposite. That was my first encounter with a truth, which is true in other places, but especially so in Venice: To see the reality under the illusion, you must look with more than your eyes.

Now you see it, now you don't—that's Venice. The canals provided my earliest lesson in this peculiarly Venetian form of trickery. From afar they beckoned, they gleamed like semiprecious jewels, turquoise in sunlight and amethyst under shadow. But when my boat entered the Grand Canal and I looked into its jewelled depths, I saw only dirty water. I felt deceived.

I had read that the water was cleaner than it had been a couple of years ago. The government was into tidal management and flood control; Venice was no longer sinking into the sea. It was true, the walls along the canals bore marks of previous higher water. I knew that reclamation and restoration were going on, especially in buildings open to the public. In spite of all this work, and in spite of much surface beauty, decay was everywhere. In places it seemed honest decay, a kind of faded glory. Other places it seemed to be a kind of putrid trick—now you see it, now you don't—a crack in a glorious facade, out of which peeped something dirty and rotten.

The grand old houses along the canal fascinated me. I thought of them as Renaissance courtesans, essentially ageless, the lines of their architecture holding up like good bones, proud and somehow bored with the pettiness of people who would be concerned with a little cracking and peeling. They hid the secrets of centuries behind the shuttered eyes of their windows; they looked not out but in.

I would be living in one of these houses, the Palazzo Corelli. I had rented the second floor through an agent in Boston, not quite sight unseen. He'd had photographs. But just as a thousand pictures could not prepare one for the sight of Venice from the harbor, the agent's photos had scarcely prepared me for the Palazzo Corelli. My boat pulled up to steps that went right down to the water and seemed too narrow for safety or ease. The tall arched doors of the house opened to me, and from that moment all the practical considerations that had led me to the choice of it fell away, no longer important. I tried not to gawk over the shoulder of the servant who opened the doors and introduced himself as Giorgio, but my eyes kept straying while I returned his greeting in my rusty Italian. I entered the palazzo and fell under its spell, I became a part of the grand illusion.

No one lived on this first floor. I knew that in Europe it was called the ground floor, but I continued to think of the floors of the house by my American terminology. I knew from the agent in Boston that the first floor of the Palazzo Corelli was unusable because of past water damage and present damp. Nevertheless, the elegance of its space took my breath away. The floor was tiled, with a mosaic pattern

I could not readily identify. While Giorgio went to the boat for my luggage, I walked across the floor toward a wide center staircase. It zigzagged up and up through the house, which was built in a four-storied square around it. Pale light fell on worn, green-carpeted risers from high above. I was in a kind of reception hall. There were slender columns on both sides of the room, reaching to a ceiling shrouded in gloom. The ceiling was painted; in its vaulted shadows I glimpsed faces and parts of bodies and twisted shapes that might have been vines or snakes. I shivered, from dampness or from strangeness, and then Giorgio returned. He closed the doors behind him and cut off the main source of light. I followed him up the stairs, wondering if the deserted first floor chamber was perpetually dark and gloomy.

Now I'd been in Venice and living at the Palazzo Corelli for a week, and I knew that there were electric torchères built into the balustrade of the stairway at every landing and at the bottom of the stairs. I had not noticed them on that first day, but now I knew where to turn them on and off. I knew that behind and beyond the stairs on the first floor there was a back door that opened into a little brick-paved walled garden where red and white geraniums spilled out of ornately sculpted stone pots. Also in the garden was a small fountain, doubtless very old, with a blackened bronze figure of a pointy-eared Pan playing his pipes out of one corner of a leering mouth while water arched from a disproportionately large male member protruding from between his goat's legs. Some might have found the statue amusing; I thought it obscene.

On the other side of the garden wall was a street, one of the practical reasons I'd chosen the Palazzo Corelli. On the map that street seemed a fairly direct back way through the business section of the Rialto, and eventually to the Piazza San Marco. Of course, like everything else in Venice, the little street was not quite what it seemed. It started out pleasantly enough, but soon narrowed and darkened and crossed back canals on crumbling little bridges. Just when it became unbearable it would open up into a paved square, and for a while it would be pleasant enough again, but not for long. The street frightened me, but I took it, and others, determined to learn my way around on foot. Because, to my own surprise, the canals frightened me more.

I had chosen to escape to Venice because I thought it would be as unlike Brookline and Boston as any place could possibly be, and also because I loved the Italian language and at one time had spoken it well. I expected that ability to return quickly, and it was doing so. And Venice was certainly different. I had been right on both counts. Still, one week into my six-month renewable lease at the Palazzo Corelli, I sat in the favorite of my eight rooms and faced something I had *not* expected: an anxiety so pronounced it could only be called fear. I had been uncomfortable at home, but that was nothing compared to this. Why? There was no danger here. No one knew me in Venice; in fact I could count on my fingers the people who even knew that I was in Venice. I wondered if I should stay. Wondered if I stayed, should I move to another place?

It was easier to deal with the second question first. If I broke the lease I would lose a lot of money. And although the money was all mine now and there was so much of it, years of habit were hard to change. I'd never been one to waste money. I looked around my favorite room and admitted to myself that I liked it very much. The maid, Zenia, called this the Morning Room. It was about twenty feet square, its plaster walls a warm, pale yellow and the rug was a rich, creamy ivory with a gold-and-brown flowered border. The ceiling was easily fourteen feet high; the windows were a good twelve feet tall, rounded at the top, and shuttered. There was a fireplace with a beautifully carved mantel of white marble. I had asked Zenia if she knew how old the mantel was and who had carved it, but she didn't know. The furnishings were few but good: a small oval table and two chairs of fruitwood, two graceful love seats upholstered in lemon-colored brocade opposite each other in front

of the fireplace, a very comfortable reading chair in butter-
scotch velour with a matching ottoman and a good floor
lamp nearby.

The other rooms were equally well-appointed, but not as
much to my taste as this one. The salon, or formal living
room, had a gorgeous parquet floor ruined for me by a collection of slippery little threadbare and probably priceless
oriental rugs. The furniture in the dining room was heavy,
dark and depressing and looked as if it might be as old as the
house itself, which was fourteenth-century. The kitchen was
supposed to be good by European standards, but by American standards it was appalling; Zenia liked it, and since her
services came with my lease and she liked to cook, that was
what mattered. The remaining rooms were three bedrooms
and an enormous bath, which was chilly even on the warm-
est days. The bedrooms all gave me the creeps. I supposed
it had been the fashion for bedrooms to be dark—in a way,
that made sense—but I found their dark wood-paneled walls
oppressive and the heavy curtained beds with their boxtop-
like canopies claustrophobic. Like Goldilocks, I'd tried each
of the beds. Unlike her, I'd found all of them equally un-
pleasant. The only real difference between the bedrooms was
in the colors of their rugs, drapes and spreads, so I called
them the Blue Room, the Gold Room and the Rose Room.
In the end I chose the Rose Room for myself, because I have
always liked the warmth of any shade of pink.

Finally, the clocks. Old clocks, valuable clocks, someone
in the Corelli family must have collected them, because there
was at least one in every room. They made enough noise to
wake the dead and keep them awake. Every night I went
around and stopped those I could stop, the ones with pen-
dulums. Every morning without comment Zenia got them
going again. If I stayed, I would have to do something about
those clocks. I could not get used to their repetitive, me-
chanical noise no matter how I tried; they were driving me
crazy.

The house got on my nerves, that was the truth. I tended to blame the clocks, but it was more than that. I'd never been a fanciful person, but there was something about the Palazzo Corelli that I'd never felt in any house before. I ran mentally through adjectives I'd encountered mostly in books and certainly had never thought might apply to any place I lived: mysterious, disturbing, foreboding, intriguing. All of the above.

I sighed. The strength of my hardheaded, practical nature began to reassert itself. This was an old, old house. Many things had to have happened within these walls. I decided to have a talk with the little maid, Zenia. Even if nothing else came of it, which would probably be the case since Zenia seemed to think that maids were supposed to be neither seen nor heard, I would get a chance to practice my Italian.

I found her in the Blue Room. She had pulled back the drapes and opened the long shutters to let in as much light as possible, and she was diligently polishing the posts of a bed no one slept in.

"Hi," I said from habit as I went through the door, and continued in Italian, "I'd like to talk to you, Zenia." I sat down on the bed and patted a place beside me. "Sit down for a minute."

"Oh!" She looked startled, but she sat down gingerly, obediently. "Yes, *signora*?"

"I've been here for a week, and I haven't yet seen any of the family. One of the reasons I chose to rent this apartment rather than others was because the family lives in the house. Or so I was told. I thought . . . well, it doesn't really matter what I thought." I had thought, obviously in error, that the Corellis would be something like the family of my best friend from childhood, who had been Italian. A warm, openly affectionate family within whose welcoming arms I had learned to speak Italian as my own second language before I was six years old. "Tell me about the Corellis, Zenia. The mama, the papa, the children."

Zenia was tiny, barely five feet tall, and her body still held the round curves of childhood. I doubted she was more than eighteen. She wore her black hair parted in the center and curved, wing-like, back over her ears in a bun on the nape of her neck. Her eyes, too, were black and very bright, they reminded me of onyx. She was shy. She opened and closed her mouth three times before the words came out.

"The mama, the papa—is not right to call them that. The Corelli family, they are old, old grand family of Venezia. The Signora Corelli, she is the Lady. Who you call the papa, is the Old Master, but he is dead for a long time. The Young Master, he is away. Not here. That's all, there is nobody else."

"I see. But the *signora*, whom you call the Lady, she does live here? Upstairs?"

"Oh, yes."

"I'm surprised I haven't seen her."

"The Lady does not go out." Zenia fidgeted. She clearly wanted my questioning to end.

I felt gauche, an awkward American quizzing her, and I smiled to hide my own discomfort. "You must think I have very bad manners to question you like this. It's just that I don't know anyone in Venice, and I thought perhaps, living here, I would get to know the family and that would help me to feel at home. You see, Zenia, I didn't come here as a tourist."

Her eyes widened. "No? You are American, and you are not a tourist?"

I laughed at her amazement. "I'm trying not to be."

"You come looking for your—" she paused while she thought of the word "—your ancestors. That is why you speak such good Italian, no?"

"No." I shook my head. "But I take that as a great compliment. Actually, when I've settled in here, I'll probably be more or less a student. My field is art history. As for my ancestors, as far as I know for at least the last two hundred years they have all come from a part of the United States called New England. Have you heard of it?"

Zenia bowed her head. Her shoulders sagged a little. "No, *signora*. I did not have much school, though I would liked to have more. My sister Rosa and I have worked for the Lady since Rosa was twelve and I, eleven." She straightened up. "We have learned the old ways. It is an honor to be in service to one of the oldest families!"

"I'm sure it is," I said to encourage her. Privately I thought it a crime to take a girl so obviously bright as Zenia out of school and train her to Old World subservience. "And I'm sure that one of the things you were taught was not to talk about the family. Am I right?"

She looked at me from the corner of her eye and ventured a shy smile. "Yes, *signora*."

"Well, you must please forgive me. We Americans have a word for what I've just done. It's called being nosy."

"Nosy?" She wrinkled her own nose and she laughed, a brief but rich and surprisingly low sound. "Americans are very funny!"

I grinned. I hadn't learned much about the Corellis, but I felt that I had broken the ice with Zenia and that she would not be quite so shy in the future. That was an accomplishment. "Just a moment more, Zenia, and I'll let you get back to your work. I've met Giorgio, though I haven't seen him since he brought my bags up the first day. Is there anyone else in the house besides you, me, your sister Rosa, Giorgio and Mrs. Corelli, uh, the Lady?"

Zenia looked at me. An expression I couldn't read passed through her dark eyes, and was gone. "Giorgio, he is majordomo. Giorgio's wife, she is the cook, her name is Anna. You have, ah, seen someone else?"

"No," I assured her, "quite the opposite. I've seen no one at all except you since the day I arrived. I thought it a little odd. I guess even if the house is very large, like this one, I still like to know who else is in it with me. Now I understand. Thank you, Zenia."

I LEFT ZENIA AND WENT for a walk, determined to think things through. The conversation had helped. The fear was still there, I knew, but it was quiescent. Perhaps I could, by being completely rational, eliminate it altogether. I walked to the nearest square, or *campo*, which was next to a church with a tower I could see above the red-tiled roofs of the houses. I had already learned that just because you could see some landmark ahead of you didn't mean you should take the street that looked to be in line with where you were going. That was more of the deceptiveness of Venice, more of the "now you see it, now you don't" trick. Because of the way the streets twisted, turned, closed in and suddenly opened up, you could seldom really see where you were going. Nor was a map much help, all those intricate turnings were not on it. You had either to know the way or to have an unerring sense of direction, or else you had to ask. I had done a lot of asking. My sense of direction had always been pretty good, and old parts of Boston were rather like this, but still I felt anxious enough to hurry along through the dark, narrow bit. I let out a breath of relief when I reached the little square, my destination. I sat on the edge of the fountain in its center and thought about my situation.

What, really, had I learned from my talk with Zenia? Mainly that my dream of being included in a warm Italian family, of being brought out of my rented rooms and into their bosom so to speak, wasn't going to happen. The mother, whom Zenia for some reason called the Lady, must be a recluse if she never went out. Or perhaps she was ill, chronically ill—but if that were so, Zenia could have said. The "Young Master" had to be a boy away at school. Where else would a young master be? I wondered how old he was, if he might be as old as my own son. I wondered how the "Old Master" had died . . . and I shuddered. That thought came too close to home, too close to my own secret.

I understood then, or thought I did, where my fear came from. It was my own inner fear, fear of an unknown contained in my lost moments out of time, which I had externalized and projected outward onto Venice. Onto the Palazzo Corelli.

I sat in the *campo* and told myself there was no reason to fear. I took a deep breath and called out every ounce of stubbornness I possessed, every rational, practical shred I could find in my mind. I hadn't killed my husband, not really; nor had I ever wished him dead. I had wanted out of the marriage, yes. And I had known when I went to give him the anonymous note that day that I might end by telling him so, even if I hadn't finished my degree and didn't yet have a job. I couldn't stay with a criminal, that was one thing too many and worse than the other things I'd learned about him over the years. But Chet had had a heart attack before I could tell him any of that. A massive heart attack, the doctor had said, no chance of saving him. *No chance of saving him!* I had spent so much time trying to fill in the blank space in my memory that I hadn't allowed the doctor's words to sink in. I repeated them silently to myself, several times, and I felt my guilt ease. I hadn't, hadn't, *hadn't* wanted Chet to die. But I still wished I could remember.

Another source of fear niggled at me: the anonymous note. I had waited weeks for another to come, and none had. If one did come even now, it would be forwarded to me, I would eventually get it. I already knew what I would do if I learned that my husband had had dishonest dealings: I would make restitution. That was why I had liquidated everything and kept the money in the bank, so that I could pay if I had to, whomever I had to. If, as the note said, Chet had been a "crook," I would gladly use the money he left to right his wrongs. So I really had nothing to fear from that anonymous note.

I did not know, on that late-summer afternoon at the end of my first week in Venice, that when my husband died I had brushed up against the dark underside of reality, and I would be sensitive to it ever after. I did not realize how much of my life up to that point had been spent only on the surface of things, where all seems light and *C* always follows on the heels of *A* and *B*. I certainly did not know that Venice, where I sought to escape what had become uncomfortable and ugly in my world, would provide no escape at all. Venice long ago acknowledged and embraced her underside. I came to seek solace in the beauty of Venice, and that beauty is real enough. But it is only a mask, and underneath Venice throbs with darkness.

These things I did not know that day, and I was able to summon up enough of my old self that I could deny the warning fear. I had called up a ghost, my own ghost—my old self was dead, she had died with her husband—but I didn't know that yet.

Chapter Two

"You are going out, Signora Beaumont?" asked Zenia. "Would you like me to brush your hair for you?"

I started to refuse, then checked myself. I was so often refusing her offers of help that I was afraid she might feel unappreciated. So I said, "Yes, that would be very nice," and handed her the brush.

My hair in its natural state looks like it belongs on one of the Muppets. It's too thick, and mats and tangles because of a too-fine texture. And it's multicolored, various shades of brown from lightest to darkest to reddest. All my life I've been kidded about wearing a wild animal on my head. It's no wonder that I'd hated my hair until recent years, when I'd made the interesting discovery that incoming gray hairs only made highlights in the varicolored mass.

Zenia brushed competently and began to discipline the ends under, the way I always wore it. I laced my fingers together in my lap, to quell an instinct that told me it was all wrong to let her do for me things I could perfectly well do myself. I tried to think about something else. About the appointment I had shortly with a Professor Tedesco at the Accademia, and the letter of introduction I'd brought from my adviser at Boston University.

Zenia interrupted my thoughts. "The *signora* uses pins behind the ears?"

"Combs." I handed them to her. Then, on a sudden impulse, I said, "Zenia. I want you to do something for me."

"Oh, of course, *Signora* Beaumont." She smiled. When she smiled she was pretty, blooming with youth.

I smiled, too, and turned to face her. "This is what I want you to do, I want you to call me by my name, Clea. No more Signora Beaumont."

Her smile turned to shock, her mouth made a perfect O. "Oh, I could not do that. Oh, no!"

"Why not?"

"The Lady would not like it. The Lady would never permit such a thing!"

"The Lady does not have to know."

The shock passed, and now Zenia was intrigued, her quick mind dealing with a new idea. "Is that what is done in the great houses of your country?"

I laughed. "I don't know what is done in great houses. It's what I do in my house. I treat people as equals, or at least I hope I do. This master/servant stuff just isn't for me—it makes me very uncomfortable. You and I are going to be seeing each other every day for months to come, and I will feel much better if you call me Clea, as I call you Zenia."

"Clea," she said thoughtfully, as if she were tasting the name. I could tell she wasn't sure yet, she was thinking about it. "I don't understand. I am a servant. You and I are not equals."

I groped for the right words in Italian to tell her my philosophy, a philosophy my now-dead husband had once told me was only a rationalization. It was hard to find the words, so I tried the easy way out. "How about if you just do it, and think of me as an eccentric old lady?"

Zenia giggled. "You are not old. You are—you are beautiful! And you are not eccentric. The Lady, she is eccentric!"

How interesting! I longed to know more, but could not take us down that side path at the moment, not if I was to be on time for my appointment. I said, "Thank you for the compliment. However, the important thing is that I don't like either the word or the concept of 'servant.' You have your work to do, and I have mine. Your responsibility is to keep the apartment so that I am free to do other things. My responsibility is to pay you a salary and see that you have the right supplies and equipment to work with, and that your working conditions are good for you. We have a kind of partnership, we are in that way equals. You are just as important to me as I am to you, even though we each do different things. Now do you understand?"

She backed up against the blanket chest at the foot of the bed and sat down, thinking. She did not reply. I decided to go on.

"You don't have to wear a uniform anymore, unless you want to. I want you to always feel free to ask questions, and to say what you think. That's in addition to calling me Clea. Okay?"

"Really?"

"Yes, really. Of course, like the Lady, I do have certain standards I want kept in my house. They are the same for everyone. As my children and their friends would tell you, I expect honesty and kindness. Always tell the truth, and treat others with the consideration you deserve yourself." I heard my own words lingering in my ears, honesty and kindness, the same for everyone. I wondered, as I often had, when my husband had decided he was exempt. Certainly the unkindness had gone on for a long time. And how dishonest had he been?

"Your rules are like the nuns taught us when we were children," Zenia smiled. "It is not the way of the world, *signora*."

"So I've been told." By my dead husband, among others. I bit my lip to keep from saying more.

"I want to try to think as you do," Zenia said hesitantly, "but there is something which bothers me."

I raised an eyebrow. "Yes?"

"I do not really work for you, *Signora* Clea. I work for the Lady. For her I serve those who live in these rooms. It is the Lady Corelli who pays me, not you, and her rules are very different!"

"The Lady, as you call her, pays you with money I've given her for this apartment, and my lease says that I will have a maid. So long as I'm here, I think we can therefore consider that you work for me. I'm not one for the old ways, Zenia. Will you try my way?"

"Since that is so, that you pay her and then she pays me... Yes!" She bounced up. "Clea, it will be very interesting to learn new ways!"

I felt I'd won a great victory. Zenia was so charming I wanted to hug her. Perhaps six months from now I could do that without embarrassing her, but today I just grinned and sent her off so that I could finish getting ready to go out.

I DIDN'T SEE THE MAN until I was almost at the bottom of the stairs. I might have screamed, or perhaps I only felt like screaming. I knew immediately that the figure in the gloom was not Giorgio, and without any conscious process of thought I heard my voice challenge in perfect Italian:

"You, there! What is your business in this house? You should ring, and wait outside the door for the *signora*'s man to come!" And how the heck did he get in, anyway? I seldom used the front door and had assumed it was kept locked.

I heard the sound of his footsteps, the dark bulk of the man moved forward, and still I could not see his features. I gripped the stair railing and cursed myself for not turning on the stairway lights.

"Oh? Is that so?" The voice was deep, and managed to inject contempt into the few words.

I wanted to turn and run, but I could not. For days I'd been washed back and forth on waves of fear when there was nothing tangible to be afraid of, but I thought I'd gotten that under control. Now here was a direct threat, a stranger in the house. My heart pounded and my body turned cold, and I couldn't move. It took all my will to say, "Yes, it is so."

Step by step he came across the faded and cracked mosaics of the floor. At last he stopped, at the foot of the stairs.

I drew in a shuddering breath. In the thin gray light the man looked as if he had stepped out of a Renaissance portrait, the sort where the face is dominant and the clothing, dark, is lost in shadow. He had a classic Italian face: a high forehead framed by thick, waving black hair, a straight, pure line of nose, a sensual mouth curved within a perfectly trimmed black beard. And his eyes! They were huge, heavy-lidded and darkly lashed, under dark brows, and shockingly light in color. He pierced me with those eyes. I lifted my chin and glared back at him. This had turned into a personal confrontation and, strangely, my fear disappeared.

He broke the eye contact first. He put his hands casually into the pockets of his dark suit and slowly looked around, revealing a profile straight out of an El Greco. "As I thought," he said, his inspection completed, "this *is* the Palazzo Corelli."

"So?" I snapped.

His mouth twitched, as if he'd started to smile and thought better of it. "So. I will ask the question you asked me. What are *you* doing here?"

I felt a sudden, hot rush, a blind atavistic heat I couldn't control. It came out as anger, and my voice was harsh, almost guttural. "I don't see what business that is of yours, or why I should answer your questions when you do not answer mine!"

The pale eyes flashed. In the tone of one accustomed to being obeyed, he commanded, "Come down here so that I can see you properly."

I went down one step, stopped, and said, "No." But softly. I recognized that heat now. It was the quick, hot warmth of instant physical attraction, something I had not felt in many years.

"Well, then, we will compromise. I will come up to you." He did, and when he stood on my step I had to look up at him. He subjected me to a thorough scrutiny. His fine nostrils flared. His eyes softened. They were the color of aquamarines, and I saw them go from ice to liquid warmth in the space of a heartbeat.

"I have just realized who you must be," he said, "and I owe you an apology. You're surely the new tenant, and I'm sorry to say I've forgotten your name."

"Clea Beaumont. And who, may I ask, are you?" My head swam in confusion. Who could he be? A cousin? A close friend of the family?

He ignored my question, preferring his own train of thought. "Surely you can understand my mistake. I was told the Beaumont woman was a widow, and an American. I thought of someone—" his glance took in my face, my whole body, like a caress "—older. And you can't be an American, you speak our language too well. You don't even look like a tourist!" He leaned toward me and his hand reached for my hair, but he recovered himself and drew it back.

"Thank you. I didn't come here as a tourist. I came to study and just to—to live. Are you, perhaps, a younger brother of *Signora* Corelli?"

He laughed, white, even teeth flashing in contrast to the very black beard. "You really don't know, do you? You are very brave, if you thought me an intruder. This is my mother's house, and mine. I am Marcantonio Corelli."

"Oh!" I couldn't have been more astounded. "The son! I thought you were practically a child, away at school!"

"I assure you I haven't been a child in a very long time. And I have been away on business. I thought surely my mother... But I see she didn't. I'm sorry. She becomes more and more a recluse, I'm afraid. So I was away, and you moved in without the slightest welcome."

"I, I didn't really expect anything. The apartment is—is lovely, and Zenia has made me . . . feel . . . quite at home," I stammered. His smile was all the welcome I would ever need, anywhere. My heart hammered, I burned inside. I didn't understand and couldn't control the feelings this man invoked in me.

He took my hand and folded it inside his. "Welcome to the Palazzo Corelli, Clea Beaumont."

"Thank you, *Signor* Corelli." My hand throbbed to his touch. "I really must go. I have an appointment, I'll be late."

"Marc. Everyone calls me Marc, except my mother who insists on the whole mouthful of Marcantonio. Now that I'm home, I know she will want to meet you. Soon. Perhaps tonight, if you have no plans? If your appointment is for the afternoon only?"

"I have no plans," I murmured.

"Then, I will come for you. I'll let your maid know what time, when I've spoken to the Lady."

He let me go. My hand throbbed for a long time after. And I wondered why a grown man, a powerful man, would call his own mother "the Lady."

VENETIANS DINE LATE, and I don't think they have ever heard of tea. I was invited for sherry at the time I usually eat, so I sent Zenia off and made myself a sandwich in the kitchen. I didn't want to drink even a small amount of alcohol on an empty stomach, particularly not when I was so nervous. I felt I'd come too close to making a fool of myself on the stairs, and I wanted to be on my best behavior. I was as nervous as if I had an audience with the Queen—not to mention the Queen's son, the Handsome Prince.

At the last minute I realized that the Corelli household was likely to be quite formal in the evening, and I wished I'd asked Zenia what I should wear. I'd brought nothing even vaguely formal with me, but I didn't think the linen dress I'd worn to the Accademia would do. I tugged it off and dropped it on the bed. Why hadn't it occurred to me earlier that I should change my clothes? I pawed through the few dresses I'd brought with me—there was nothing, nothing suitable. Nothing except the black silk, staple of business dinners and cocktail parties, my one really "good" dress. I almost hadn't brought it to Venice because the color reminded me of the inadequacy of my mourning, but now I was glad to have it. Hurrying, I stripped to the skin and rummaged in the chest of drawers for my black underwear to go with the dress. I had just finished tying its cummerbund-style sash at my waist when I heard Marc's knock. He knocked again while I shoved my feet into plain black high-heeled pumps, and then I went to let him in through the salon door.

I had to struggle with the door. All the doors in the palazzo had a very old sort of latch at shoulder height, nothing so simple as a doorknob, and I was still unfamiliar and awkward with them. I pushed when I should have pulled, and greeted the man with a string of apologies. "I'm sorry to be so clumsy, I'm not used to the doors yet, I'm not quite ready, sorry to make you wait...."

Marcantonio Corelli was amused, especially when I grabbed a handful of my wild hair and explained that the humidity made it more of a bush than it usually was and I needed about five minutes to brush it, please.

"I think," he said, "that some women pay a lot of money to get their hair to look like that. But by all means, take as much time as you like. Do you mind if I wander around? I haven't been in these rooms recently."

"Of course, whatever you want." I fled, my cheeks flaming, and just missed turning an ankle on one of those little oriental rugs. What was wrong with me? I'd wanted to be so cool and charming, and instead I was as flustered as a girl on a first date!

I paused in the familiar act of tugging a brush through my hair. The edges of the mirror blurred as I stared at the face. My face. The same amber eyes, same tilted nose, same squarish jaw and chin with its shallow cleft in the center. My lips, bowed and faintly pink, were parted and they trembled. It was like looking at someone else, the woman in the mirror looked like a child in a woman's body. No, that was how I felt . . . uncertain, insecure. Not myself, at all.

My inner universe tipped, my breath stopped, my stomach rose up into my mouth, I was completely disoriented as a horrible thought thundered through my head: I don't know who I am anymore! I dropped the hairbrush. It clattered on the dressing table and fell to the floor as I wrapped my arms around my middle and bent over. The moment passed. I retrieved the brush and began to work again on my hair. When I next looked up, Marc was half into the room, leaning against the door frame.

"This is my bedroom," I growled. Inwardly, I winced. Where was the cool, the charm? But damn it, he was invading a private place!

He strolled in. "I know, but you're dressed." He looked around with interest, as if he'd never seen the room before. Then he flashed a mischievous grin. "And my intentions are honorable. At least, so far!"

I turned to confront this arrogance, and whatever words I might have had died on my tongue. He was so darkly handsome, so very different-looking, almost exotic. I was sure I'd never seen such a sensual mouth; perhaps it was that the beard made it so. I swallowed hard and turned back to the mirror. I was really having trouble with my hair, and having him watch was no help.

"I wanted to see which of the bedrooms you've chosen for yourself," said Marc.

I tugged out a painful tangle and said through clenched teeth, "You could have told that by process of elimination. I'm not in the others."

My afternoon's dress and my underthings were strewn across the bed where I'd thrown them off. Marc chuckled at my remark, and his roving eye roved over the bed and lingered on every untidy, intimate article of clothing. He asked, "Why this room?"

I had by this time given up on my usual hairstyle and resorted to the one reserved for emergencies. I mentally ran through possible answers to his question while I pulled the whole unmanageable mass of my hair back from my face and secured it with a rubber band. Then I looked in the dresser drawer for the thin gold net which would hold the hair in a bun on the nape of my neck. Finally I found it, and an answer. The simplest answer, the truth. "I chose this room because of the color. I like warm colors."

"Um-hm. And the other rooms of your apartment, what do you think of them?"

I clasped on gold earrings and was ready. I turned around and was surprised by the seriousness of his expression. He looked as if he really wanted to know. So I said honestly, "I prefer the yellow room, the one Zenia calls the Morning Room, and I spend most of my time there."

"Why do you prefer it?"

"Because of the light. And because the simplicity of the decor points up the best architectural features—the windows and the fireplace."

"I'm interested to know what you think about the other rooms, the ones you do not prefer."

"Why should you care what I think? I'm just some American woman who will be here a few months. For all you know, I could be as tasteless as those female tourists who wear polyester pants too tight in the behind."

"No." His face was grave. "I look at you and I know that you are different and that I do care what you think. I don't know why, but I do. Please?"

I was puzzled, but I told him. I kept it brief, terribly aware that we were in my bedroom, that the untidy bed seemed both an embarrassment and a beacon, and that his mysterious mother waited upstairs. When I had done, Marc said "Thank you" and inclined his head in an acknowledgment that was almost a bow. What a surprising man this was, arrogant and courteous by turns. He came across the room and offered me his arm.

As I took it, I remarked, "You take your house very seriously."

"Yes, I do." He explained as we went through my rooms and toward the stairs. "The palazzo was originally built in the fourteenth century, restored and improved—this stairway added, among other things—in the sixteenth. My grandfather put in plumbing and electricity, but now I am attempting the first major restoration in four hundred years. I began in the rooms where you live. Frankly, I did not have much money to work with, and at that time we badly needed the rental income. I could not do all I would have liked." We mounted the stairs and he continued, "I would like to show you the rest of the house some day. Then you will have an idea of the size of the task I've undertaken."

"I'd like that," I said. We had reached the third floor. The walls of the open corridor around the stairway were hung with portraits. I looked at Marc Corelli, certain that his face, with and without the beard, would appear again and again in those gilded frames. I thought how many centuries of Venetian women must have warmed to those features, as I did, and I smiled at him.

He returned the smile, and squeezed my hand. "Now we go to meet the Lady. Don't be too surprised by anything she says, please. My mother is . . . unpredictable."

I nodded. I was nervous again, there was a cold lump in the middle of my chest.

Marc paused outside a double door with the usual shoulder-high latch. "This room is called the Grand Salon." He opened both doors, and I walked in.

It looked, to my overwhelmed eyes, as if the history of Venice had been crammed into this one enormous room. We walked across a Persian rug, all medallions and curlicues, about the size of a football field. I couldn't allow myself to stop and take it all in, for Marc propelled me steadily ahead with his hand at the small of my back. I bit my lip to keep from gaping like a child at the circus. I focused through the opulence and profusion of shapes and colors on a figure seated at the far end of the room. I recognized Giorgio hovering in the background. The seated figure had to be Marc's mother.

Chairs were grouped in front of a huge fireplace. Its mantel of carved stone was shaped like a hood and rose to the ceiling. I thought that a small house could fit in that fireplace. I felt cowed, inadequate. I faltered, but Marc urged me on, his fingertips on my spine insisting I move forward. The closer we came, the more formidable she seemed. Finally we stopped.

"Mother," Marc addressed her, "I present Clea Beaumont. Clea, this is *Signora* Eugenia Corelli, my mother, the Lady."

By which of those titles was I supposed to call her? I didn't know what to say, didn't know what to do, because I felt stupidly that I should curtsy and I'd never done that in my life.

The Lady solved part of my problem by extending her hand. I opted for no titles, and said simply, "I am very pleased to meet you." I swallowed hard. The feel of her hand was appalling, like a lump of biscuit dough—cool, damp, sticky, puffy. Marc's mother, the Lady, Eugenia Corelli, was very, very fat. I was unprepared for that. Her size had not been immediately apparent as we approached; she was, in a sense, in scale with the enormous room.

"Welcome to my home," she said. Her voice was surprisingly pleasant, even beautiful.

A few blessed moments were taken up with the mechanics of seating me at right angles to her, getting the sherry served in small stemmed glasses of exquisite, shimmering crystal. Venetian glass, I thought. Giorgio brought a little round table and set it with a plate of antipasto, which looked too perfect to touch much less to eat, and small glass plates.

I glanced obliquely at Mrs. Corelli, which was how I had decided to think of her. I remembered Zenia saying that to call this woman "Mama" was not right, and I had to agree. She was a colossus, an Italian Valkyrie. Her chair was throne-like and did not dwarf her. She wore a kind of caftan of deep purple brocade, embroidered down the front and on the sleeve edges with gold. Probably the neckline was also embroidered in gold, but I would never know as it was entirely concealed under her several chins. I sipped sherry for courage and looked at her face. Her attention was diverted from me as she said something to Marc in that low, almost musical voice.

In spite of the extra flesh, Mrs. Corelli was a commanding woman. She had masses of hair, still black whether by nature or artifice. It was beautifully arranged, swept back off her face and wound about her head in loops and braids. I thought how skillfully Zenia had brushed my hair, and imagined her learning to do the hair of the Lady. Mrs. Corelli had the black eyebrows and large eyes of her son, but her eyes were darker, more brown than green, I supposed one would call them hazel-green. Her eyelids looked padded. There was a suggestion of strong cheekbones, now covered by pudgy cheeks. Her mouth was ruby-red with lipstick, and her skin had the color and texture of white mushrooms. This woman's skin had not seen sunlight for a long, long time. She turned from her son to me, and spoke in her musical voice, and the evening began.

I went on a sort of automatic pilot, letting well-learned social graces take over, and was glad the expected phrases came out as automatically in Italian as in English. I was having a terrible problem: Mrs. Corelli revolted me. It was not that she was fat. I think in general our society makes too much of thinness, and I am not over-thin myself. As I responded to her questions and Marc's, I searched within myself for the compassion I knew should be there, for to be as grossly overweight as Mrs. Corelli surely meant that she had a physical problem, or an emotional one, or both. Yet I could find no compassion. I could find no appreciation for her graciousness, though I could not have wished for a better hostess.

Marc looked relaxed, he was smiling and approving. I wondered what else he had expected, why he'd warned me not to be surprised at anything she said. She was unpredictable. Was this, then, her best behavior? Probably. A chilling thought! If his mother on her best behavior revolted me, what would I feel when she acted in another mode?

I drank more than I should have. Perhaps it was the wine, perhaps it was an undeniable attraction to Marc, perhaps it was just that the spell of the palazzo and the spell of Venice herself got to me. Whatever it was, the Lady gradually charmed me. It was like snake-charming in reverse. The Lady Corelli was the snake, huge, glittering, purple; and she charmed me. I swayed to her lovely voice, I reveled in the colors and the richness of the room, I drowned in the aquamarine seas of Marc's eyes. I told them of my interest in art history and of the independent-study course I planned with Professor Tedesco, and the Lady Corelli said things I wanted to hear. We must introduce Clea to so-and-so-and-so; Marc, you must take Clea here, and here, and there. I said Yes, oh yes. Please, yes.

Fortunately that social automatic pilot was working and I heard its warning bell loud and clear. If this had been a dinner party, the bell would have meant that I must drink no more until I'd eaten. But it was not a dinner party, and the bell meant it was time for me to leave. Time to take my muzzy head and my feelings of false warmth and go home, downstairs to my apartment. I began to make the noises and the motions preparatory to doing just that. I'd caught Marc's eye and was inching onto the edge of my chair, when suddenly there was a sound of female screeching followed by several thuds. Giorgio was quickly halfway across the vast Persian rug, when the double doors exploded a huge man into the room.

Marc leaped up, fists clenched, but he stayed where he was. Giorgio stopped in his tracks. The man strode toward us without stopping. He was blond, and had the height and breadth of a professional wrestler. In his wake came a little black-and-white-clad figure, for all the world like a harrying terrier. From her resemblance to Zenia, I knew this must be the sister Rosa. She wailed in a high soprano, "Oh Lady, oh Lady, oh *Signor* Marc, I couldn't stop him! I couldn't!"

I looked at the Lady Corelli. She hadn't moved a muscle, but she was smiling.

The blond man was muscular, tanned and blue-eyed, and he wore a white suit with a blue shirt open at the neck. Gold glittered on the thick column of his throat.

"It's all right, Rosa. You may go," said Marc. "You, too, Giorgio. I will deal with my brother."

Brother? No two brothers had ever looked less alike. Clearly there was no love lost between these two, either. Rosa and Giorgio left and closed the doors behind them.

"You know you are not allowed in this house." Marc's voice was deep and hard. "What are you doing here, Paolo?"

The newcomer's eyes strayed to me, snapped back to his brother. "I didn't expect a welcome from you, Marc. Actually, I thought you were away. However, I must speak to our mother on a matter of importance. Now."

The Lady Corelli rose from her chair majestically and I saw for the first time how tall she was, easily six feet, almost as tall as Marc. She swept past me and her robe brushed my knees. She extended her arms, crying, "Paolo, Paolo! My son, my baby!" She embraced him. They were exactly the same size, though the man was all muscle; though their coloring was different, the resemblance was strong. Mother and son. Other son. She stroked his head and cooed endearments.

I glanced at Marc, and his controlled fury convinced me it was definitely time to leave. For whatever reason this other son was denied the house and whatever had led him to violate the ban, it was an explosive family situation. I had no wish to be involved. I got my feet under me, stood up, and politely cleared my throat.

"Ah, Lady Corelli . . ."

"Oh, my dear girl!" She released her son and turned to me, beaming. The effect of such an expression on her face was grotesque. "You really must call me Eugenia. How fortunate you are to be here tonight, so that you can meet my other dear son, my baby, Paolo Corelli."

"How do you do, Paolo," I said. Up close he looked harmless enough. In fact, with his closely cropped light hair and blue eyes he looked like an American jock. He inclined his head and smiled engagingly. I couldn't let myself be diverted. "I'm pleased to meet your son, Eugenia," I said to her, "but I really must go now. Thank you for a lovely evening."

Marc came around to me. "I'll walk you to your door."

"It's not necessary. I'm sure you want to stay with your family."

He put his hand on my arm just above the elbow, and his fingers were tight enough to hurt. "On the contrary, I have just remembered an important business engagement. I can't stay. Mother, I will see you later. Paolo, I trust that you will not be here when I return. Good night." He set off down the rug without waiting for a reply, pulling me along with him.

"Good night," I said over my shoulder. I had to hurry to keep up with Marc's long strides. I was dying with curiosity as he dragged me along, but I sensed questions would not be welcome. Besides, as I found out without a doubt when we reached the stairs, I really had had too much to drink. I was dizzy.

"Slow down, Marc, please," I begged.

"What?" He looked at me as if he'd forgotten he held me by the arm. "Oh, I'm sorry. Say, are you all right?"

"Yes. It's just . . . well, I hate to admit it, but apparently I lost track of how much sherry I was drinking. I don't usually drink very much."

Marc gave up his grip on my arm and slid his own arm around my waist. He tucked me securely against his side. We descended the rest of the stairs at a sedate pace. "It's not your fault," he said. "The Lady often has that effect on people, especially the first time."

"She's, ah, overwhelming."

Marc raised a heavy eyebrow. "Not a bad choice of words."

"And speaking of overwhelming, there's your Grand Salon. I'd give my eyeteeth to be loose in there on my own for about a year!"

Marc laughed. "I'll see what can be arranged."

At my door he released me, and I was sorry. I'd quickly gotten used to the feel of his arm around me. I'd felt safe and secure and warm and loved—all of which I knew was due to the alcohol I'd consumed. I took the door key out of my pocket and handed it to him. "You open it, please. I don't feel like fighting with the door tonight. For your information, landlord, I have a lot of trouble with your doors."

"Really?" He gave the door an effortless push and it swung inward. "I don't think there's anything wrong with the door. I guess you'll just have to practice." He stood with his arm across the doorway, blocking my entrance.

"Thank you for escorting me home," I said. I took a step toward the door.

He didn't budge. "You're welcome. Do you have any American coffee?"

I blinked. "No. But I have African."

"African coffee?"

"It's Ethiopian, actually. Zenia found it in the market, and it's really very good. Are you trying to suggest that coffee might sober me up?"

Marc smiled, a lazy, caressing sort of smile. "Not exactly. I'm trying to get you to invite me in for coffee. I have a passion for the American variety, and if you like this Ethiopian stuff I'm sure it must be good."

I frowned. "I thought you had a business engagement."

"A benevolent prevarication."

"Oh? You mean you lied."

"Yes, for good reason. I had to get out and leave Mother and Paolo to do whatever they have to do. I can't stand to be around him. The Lady knows she should send him away, but she won't. As you saw, she's partial to him. Now, will you invite me in, or must I go out and prowl the streets of Venice alone?"

"I have a feeling you wouldn't prowl alone for very long. But all right, come in. I think I can stay on my feet long enough to make coffee."

I kicked off my shoes in the kitchen, the better to stay on my feet, and Marc shed his jacket and loosened his tie. Once I got going I realized that I was hungry again, and Marc hadn't eaten, so I made a big Western omelet and lots of buttered toast while Marc hung around and watched. Strangely enough, he didn't seem uncomfortable or out of place kibitzing in the kitchen.

We took the food to the little table in the Morning Room and ate in companionable silence. We lingered over second and third cups of the coffee, which Marc proclaimed as good as I'd said it was. I felt more relaxed than I had in months, maybe years. I took off the gold hair net and shook out my hair. Marc smiled at me.

"You have the most amazing hair, Clea," he said.

"That's not how most people put it! But thanks, anyway."

He moved his empty cup aside and leaned with his elbows on the table. "You know, you made a remarkable impression on my mother."

"Well, then, we're even. She made quite an impression on me."

Marc chuckled. "How could she not? Seriously, you have no idea how rare it is for her to ask anyone to call her Eugenia."

I was silent, thinking about what had happened upstairs. Finally I said, "I don't know how she did it. At first I would have bet any amount that I could never even think of her as that, as Eugenia. I didn't want to call her the Lady, either. But she drew me in, Marc." I felt a chill down my spine and folded my arms across my breasts against a shiver. "I mean no disrespect, but the truth is that I started out feeling rather, uh, put off by her. And I ended by wanting her to like me. Wanting her approval. With the arrival of your brother, and all, I didn't realize her invitation for me to use her given name had that much significance."

But of course it did. I of all people should have realized that. My earlier conversation with Zenia on the subject of names came to mind. I muttered, "I wonder why she did that? I'm not sure I like it."

"You've lost me."

Startled, I looked up at Marc. His clear, pale blue-green eyes studied me intently, and I knew what I'd done. I'd fallen into my unfortunate habit of saying parts of my thoughts out loud. I wished I hadn't, because he was Eugenia Corelli's son, and I couldn't tell him what else I was thinking: that she had, in a way, seduced me. That the whole episode had been so far out of my usual experience that I needed time to consider, and when I had considered, I might very well not want to be on a first-name basis with his mother. I might not want to know her that well—or want her to know me that well. I shrugged. "Just talking to myself. If you're done, let's sit where it's more comfortable."

We moved to the love seats, he on one, I on the other. I tucked my stockinged feet up under me. Marc stretched his long legs out in front of him, slouching comfortably. He looked as if he were settling in for the night, and suddenly, irrationally, I wanted him to leave.

"I have no illusions about my family," he said. "That's why I've never married. One reason, anyway."

"Oh?"

"You've asked me no questions about what went on up-stairs, and yet you must be curious. You're too intelligent not to be."

I had been curious earlier, yes, but now I had the uneasy feeling that if I asked questions I might find out things I'd rather not know. Right now I was well enough occupied with the fact that he'd told me, unasked, that he was not and had never been married. And that he thought me intelligent. A warmth spread through me, and I no longer wanted him to leave. I said, "I've only just met you. I think I can restrain my curiosity for a while longer."

"Mmm. I shall have to remind myself that, in fact, we do not as yet know one another. And yet," he sat up straighter, and searched my face, "it's odd, I feel that I have perhaps met you, known you somewhere before. But I am too bold. You must think that I take for granted my right to be here with you so informally because this is my house."

He seemed to be struggling, and I was sure Marcantonio Corelli could not be a man who often struggled for words. I said softly, "I'm comfortable with you, too. And I know you respect the privacy of your tenants. You said before that you haven't been in these rooms in a long time."

Marc hung his head and rubbed his left hand hard on the back of his neck. When he looked up again his face seemed naked, open, like a boy's. The presence of his beard made the open look all the more astonishing and appealing. It took a while to place that look, to give it a name: vulnerable. Marc looked vulnerable.

He spoke, his voice husky with emotion. "It's very strange, but I feel that I already know you. Intimately."

I could have said, I know, I feel the same. For a moment, I did; I knew just exactly what he meant. But the border between what appeals and what appalls is razor-thin, and he had crossed it. The land of intimacy had been a hostile one to me, and at the mention of the word all my defenses flew up around me for protection. I heard myself say nastily, "That line may work on Italian women, but it doesn't have the desired effect on me!"

His face paled, his eyes hardened, his stare was like a dagger of blue-green ice. The corners of his mouth turned downward with aristocratic disdain. He said coldly, "I assure you, I have never said those words before to any woman. Never in my life!"

The change in him stung me, as my cruel words had stung him. "I'm sorry..." I began, but I fell silent. I had hurt both him and myself, and I didn't know how to make it right. I sat with tears pricking at my eyes, blinking, helpless. Silence grew around us.

In the silence I heard the ticking of the clocks, and I did something I had never, ever done before: I vented my complex emotions on those inanimate objects, I exploded.

"Listen to that! Listen to all that ticking! I hate those clocks! They destroy my peace, they keep me awake at night, I swear sometimes I think they will drive me insane!"

"Are you serious? They bother you that much?"

Still panting from my outburst, I nodded. I felt awkward, but I answered him honestly. "Yes. They do. I'm sorry, I know someone in your family must have collected the clocks, but they do."

"My late father was the collector. Let's remove them. He wouldn't mind."

"Right now?"

"Now." Marc stood decisively. "If you are up to several trips up and down stairs, you can help. Otherwise, I'll do it alone."

I jumped up. "I'd climb Mount Everest to get rid of the things."

Marc grinned, and I knew he had forgiven me, all was well between us again. He said, "You can carry the smaller ones, but I suggest you change out of that elegant dress. We'll take them to a storage room on the top floor, and it's dusty up there."

The removal of the clocks became an adventure. Marc went ahead with the biggest one, a rococo gilded thing from the salon, which was more statuary than timepiece, while I changed my dress for jeans and a pink shirt and sneakers. He had alerted Giorgio to what we were doing, so as not to raise an alarm. Then up and down we went with our arms full of ticking clocks. The torchères lit the stairway and cast our shadows, distorted and wavering, against the walls. I giggled and whispered and felt like a child playing at hide-and-seek in an old house full of ghosts. I was not scared only because Marc was with me. He had grown up here; he knew what was concealed behind the tall, closed doors, knew that nothing lurked in the dark reaches of the corridors or hung in the high gloom of the ceilings. Myself, I was not so sure. The Palazzo Corelli at night was a spooky place.

In my apartment we were ready for the last of three trips. Marc removed the pendulum from a brass-and-glass wall clock and gave it to me to carry. In my other hand I had a small cloisonné clock with a very loud tick.

"Heavy," he said, as he lifted the large clock down. "You'll have to get the doors."

"Okay."

Up and up we went for the last time. I was in the lead, and I played a game with myself: I would be brave, I would not be afraid of the shadows or of the vast house itself; I would not look to Marc for reassurance. I pretended I was all alone as I trooped up the stairs, past the third floor with its staring portraits and somewhere, perhaps sleeping, the Lady. Up, up to the fourth floor, my blood pounding from the climb. The servants stayed up here, on the other side from the abandoned rooms used only for storage. It was so gloomy. The plaster was cracked, the cracks seemed to move, the walls seemed to sigh. The corridor where we must go gaped like a black hole.

That was all wrong! We had left a light burning in that corridor!

"Marc," I gasped, and whirled around, "the light! It's gone!"

He moved slowly because of the weight of the clock, and I had to wait for him to gain the top step. He peered over my shoulder. "Probably the bulb just burned out. It's okay, I know this place like the back of my hand. Follow me."

I followed him, and I told myself there was nothing to fear. But my silly game was over. I was truly frightened. Never mind that I hadn't been afraid of the dark since childhood—I hadn't ever been in the dark in a place like this ancient house. Darkness was total in the narrow side corridor where we went. I couldn't see anything at all.

"Stop where you are, Clea," said Marc. I could hear him moving away from me. "Stay there."

I obeyed him. I was now so terrified I couldn't even reason with myself anymore. The hated ticking of the clock in my hand grew to a din in my ears, it filled my whole black universe.

"Clea?"

I opened my eyes. I hadn't known I'd closed them. A dim light shone from behind Marc. He no longer carried the clock, and he had a lighted candle in his hand.

"My God, Clea," he said, "you look scared to death. Why didn't you tell me you're afraid of the dark?"

"Be-because I'm not," I gulped, I had trouble getting my breath. "At least, I never was before. It's just something about your house being so old."

"And about you having a big imagination, I'll bet." Marc touched my cheek gently. "Come on, it's all right. I turned on a light in the next room down. We'll put these clocks in this room with the others, and then we're done."

I nodded. The room where we were putting the clocks looked menacing with only Marc's candle for illumination. Filled with humped shapes of discarded things, alive with the clocks that would continue to tick until they ran down, one by one.

"Are you okay now?"

I nodded again, though I trembled inside.

He set the candle on top of a dust-covered chest. "I left the glass-case clock in the next room, when I turned the light on in there. I'll get it."

"All right." I stood and waited while he was gone, listening to my heart bump and thump. When he returned I said, "I feel so foolish. About the clocks, about getting scared."

"Don't. There's no need." He settled the heavy clock on the seat of an upholstered chair. Dust rose in a cloud, as he eased it into place. He turned and took its pendulum from me.

"I can't help it," I insisted. "I feel about three years old. It's so silly. What are you doing?"

"Trying to get you to loose your death grip on this fancy little clock," Marc grinned. He was loosening my fingers one by one. I had forgotten the cloisonné clock, ticking, and all—I'd been that afraid.

"Oh." I let go. My fingers were stiff.

Marc placed the little clock on the chest next to the candle. "There. Now you will have peace and quiet all through the night." He smiled at me.

I tried to smile back, but my face, like my fingers, was stiff. I looked away, and wished for an incredible moment that it was dark again so that I could pinpoint something. It hadn't been merely the dark I feared, but something more, something so bad I had pushed it away until I could deal with it. A presence, almost palpable. Had I heard breathing? I listened now in the dim light. Heard only tick, tick.

"Clea? Look at me."

I raised my eyes to his, which were filled with concern. I tossed my head. "Thank you, Marc, for all this. I hope you don't think I'm crazy." I didn't yet sound like myself. My voice was tiny, like the three-year-old I'd felt.

"I think only that I must remember never to give you a clock for a birthday present. Or," his voice dropped to a low murmur, "an anniversary present." He smiled but the smile faded, was replaced by a stronger emotion. He took a step toward me; he stood only a hand-span away.

I was caught between a cacophony of ticking, which made me want to run, and the intense desire that burned on Marc's face and held me.

"Clea," he said hoarsely, "let me, I have to . . . do this." He buried one hand in my hair; his other hand, under my chin, lifted my face to him.

There, among the menacing shadows, amid the noise of the clocks, Marc kissed me for the first time. A tender first taste, delicate, thrilling. I forgot the shadows, no longer heard the clocks. I yielded into the kiss, went deeper and deeper. His wonderful mouth, the strange silkiness of his beard, his warmth, incredible warmth and softness enveloped me. I was not inexperienced, and yet I felt that I had never before known what a simple kiss could be: exquisitely tender, deeply arousing. Both, at the same time.

When his lips left mine he folded me into his arms and held me against his chest. "Incredible," he breathed into my hair.

Incredible!

Chapter Three

The workings of the subconscious mind are perverse. At last I had slept without waking, but I had nightmares. When Zenia tapped on my bedroom door to announce a new day, I broke out of my dream with a gasp and a start. For a horrible moment, I didn't know where I was. Then I called out, "I'm awake!" and sat up in the canopied bed, hugging myself for comfort.

The bad dreams had been in color. I couldn't remember specific content, but the colors stayed with me, too-rich jewel colors like bits of Venetian glass. And a feeling of threat, of danger to me. Sounds, too—the tick, tick, tick, tick of clocks.

I shook my head and got slowly out of bed. I must be getting reality mixed up in my nightmares. The clocks were real. Marc and I had taken them all up to the fourth floor. Even now they were up there, still ticking away in that dusty room. Tick, tick. Ticking away with the accompaniment of that other sound I'd heard, or imagined, someone's breathing. Nonsense! I shuddered once and got up.

I went to the window and opened the shutters. Pale streamers of mist hung in golden air. A cool breeze touched my face and brought with it a hint of soon-to-come autumn. Row upon row of tall houses were already clothed in fall colors—terra-cotta, buff, burnt sienna. I breathed deeply and appreciated the glowing quiet of the morning.

No city in all the world is as quiet as Venice, because here there are no cars and trucks, no noises of traffic.

My ears caught the soft plash of falling water and I looked down into the walled garden. There stood the fountain, eternally recirculating its stream of water through the swollen phallus of that wicked little Pan. Such blatant sexuality! A hot, liquid feeling flooded me, a long-dormant feeling now very much alive. One kiss had done this to me. Only one. I had been sexually reawakened by Marc Corelli. And I was not ready for it, not at all.

After breakfast I walked to the Rialto Bridge and from there took a vaporetto through the Grand Canal and around to the Fondamenta Nuove on the north side of the city. The vaporetti are the water-borne buses of Venice, crowded and not glamourous, but they get you quickly where you want to go. I was in no mood to be lost in the streets today, and from the Fondamenta Nuove I intended to take a boat to the island of Torcello. I caught the boat with no problem and as we moved out into the lagoon on the fifty-minute trip, I found that I breathed more easily. Odd, I thought, that my anxiety about water travel seemed limited to the canals. Perhaps it was a kind of claustrophobia; on the wide waters of the lagoon I felt no fear.

I had made a snap decision to spend the day on Torcello. Ostensibly, it was a good place to begin the independent study I'd proposed to the professor at the Accademia. He had given me a free hand to structure my own course, which would later apply toward my art-history degree. I hadn't yet decided what my focus would be, but I knew that the Cathedral of Santa Maria Assunta on Torcello was the oldest building on any of the Venetian islands. It was a logical place to start. However, the real, compelling reason for the trip had been my need to put distance between myself and Marc and Eugenia Corelli.

From the deck of the boat I looked back at Venice. Receding, wavering in a haze under a violet sky on this slightly overcast day, she seemed as much an illusion as when I had first seen her from another direction, and in full, blazing sunlight. For centuries Venice had been called *La Serenissima*, the Most Serene Republic. Venice, serene? I thought not. Beautiful, yes; sumptuous, sensual, complex, mysterious, disturbing... never serene. But the paradox of that title, *La Serenissima*, struck me. Already I was convinced that Venice was not what on the surface she appeared to be. The blatant irony of it pleased me, in a perverse sort of way.

What was left of the town on Torcello was spare, monochromatic as a sepia-toned print and very, very old. The cathedral had first been built in 639 and parts of that original building still remained. The "newer" church of Santa Fosca, in front of the cathedral, dated to the eleventh century. There were no tour groups to distract me, just a few solitary wanderers like myself, and I gave myself over to the quiet. The austere, Byzantine features of the Virgin and the Apostles in the cathedral's mosaics seemed to accept me without question. Gradually I grew as still inside as the place itself. There was something humbling, perspective-making, about a place of worship thirteen centuries old. I listened to the resonance of its ancient silence. L'Assunta felt like a good place, a blessed place.

But even in that blessed place I could not let my thoughts run free. There were too many things I didn't want to remember; and new things I didn't want to think about. I needed the old order, the old control I used to have. Slowly, and then more confidently, I began to make notes about the cathedral. That was a familiar activity, reassuring. My desire to know the Corelli family had been a mistake. I would not allow myself to be seduced into that path, by mother or son. No, I would concentrate on my work. I would study the history of Venice through her art and architecture, that's what art historians do and I had been in the process of becoming a legitimate art historian for a lot of years. A good, solid independent study would both heal my troubled spirit and give me a boost toward that goal.

I formulated my project: starting from a near-zero knowledge base, I would put in six months of concentrated work to achieve a broad overview. I needed no narrower focus. If any one particular area caught my interest, I could explore it in an additional six months—or I could return sometime in the future. I would study, period. I had always been good at keeping to my own company, and my own counsel—it was a survival technique I'd learned in my marriage. I could call on that ability here, in Venice. I would go my own way undistracted by Marc Corelli, or his strange mother, or his wholesome-looking giant of a brother. The Virgin of the Assumption looked at me out of her long, sad eyes. I thought she approved of my decision.

On the return boat trip I felt in control for the first time in a very long while. I felt as if the wind, which scoured the bare earthen *campo* before Torcello's cathedral, had also swept through me and cleansed me. I knew I could return to Torcello whenever I needed to get my head straight. My day had been so successful that I went from the boat to a waiting vaporetto without a qualm, all the way back to the Rialto Bridge where I had started.

I returned late to my apartment. I had decided to reward myself for making so many good decisions, and I did it by shopping in the Rialto. I bought a wonderful pair of knee-high flat-heeled boots, in smooth russet-colored leather. Deep purple twilight had set in by the time I hurried through the walled garden and let myself into the palazzo by the back door. The torchères on the stairway were lit, and Zenia waited in the apartment for me.

"Did you have a good day, *signora*? I mean, Clea?" she asked. "You've never been so late before, I didn't know what to think."

"I had a lovely day, the best yet, and I did some shopping on my way home. That's why—oh, my goodness!" Halfway across the salon I stopped. Where the rococo clock had been there was now a huge bouquet of yellow roses. "Where did we get the flowers, Zenia?"

She giggled. "*Signor* Marc brought them. To make up for the clocks, he said. There are so many more, he put them around himself. Wait until you see, Clea! And he asked that I tell him when you had returned."

"I see." I walked through my rooms with Zenia following. There were yellow roses in every room. After the austerity of Torcello, the spare, clean order I'd made in my mind, the profusion of flowers jarred me. I should have been flattered or pleased, I knew that, but I was not. There was a too-muchness about it. And a coincidence that made me uneasy: Marc had chosen yellow roses, and my favorite of all flowers is the Talisman rose, which is yellow with a deep pink center.

In my bedroom, I threw my notebook and purse and the box that contained my new boots on the bed. From the corner of my eye I saw that for this room only, Marc had provided different flowers. Tiny, pink sweetheart roses. I wondered why.

Zenia hung back in the doorway. I turned to her. "Zenia, please go upstairs and tell *Signor* Corelli that I am grateful for the flowers, but I am tired from a long day and I will thank him myself another time. I cannot see him this evening. And you may go on, then. I'll get my own supper."

"I prepared your dinner, Clea. There is a casserole that needs only to be heated in the oven." She looked terribly letdown. No doubt she had expected a different reaction from me over the roses. Well, I couldn't help that.

"Thank you," I said. "I didn't mean for you to have to stay late. In the future, if I'm not back by, say, five-thirty, you can assume I'm going to eat out and you may leave. Okay?"

Zenia nodded. "Okay." She turned to leave, then turned back just as I was about to wish her good-night. "Clea?"

"Yes?"

"You said, the other day, you said that I could ask questions."

"Sure. Go ahead."

"Why didn't you tell me you did not like the clocks? I would have taken them out for you!"

I shrugged. "I intended to tell you, I just hadn't gotten around to it. And I was trying to teach myself to at least tolerate the things. But now I wish I'd told you instead of Marc Corelli. Then I wouldn't have to be embarrassed by all these flowers!"

Zenia smiled and ducked her head in a shy gesture. I would have liked very much to know what she was thinking. All she said was, "I will give the Young Master your message."

THERE WAS NO GRACEFUL WAY around it, I did have to thank Marc myself. The next day was Saturday, and I thought perhaps he wouldn't be working. After breakfast I sent Zenia to ask if he would meet me in the garden at eleven o'clock, and I told her after doing that to take the rest of the day off. She said the Lady wouldn't like it, and I said in my house nobody worked more than five days a week. I got the impression Zenia thought she would never get used to my odd ways, but she went.

It was the kind of hot, soggy late-September day that in the U.S. we call Indian summer. Not my favorite weather in any country. I thought wistfully of more typical late-September weather in New England—cool, crisp days and cooler nights, sweater weather, falling leaves and football games. Then I remembered Chet's behavior at our last Harvard game and my nostalgia vanished—poof! As if it had never been. After that I was content to put on a summer float dress, thin cotton with lace at the neck and sleeves. The dress was turquoise, the color of the canals on bright, sunny days like this one. I brushed my hair into shape, not that it would stay long in the humidity. At five minutes before eleven I went down the stairs and waited in the garden. Shadowed by the height of the surrounding houses, it was cool, and the pure, crystal notes of water falling from the fountain added a welcome freshness. I closed my eyes and drew in a deep, relaxing breath. The moist air was spiced with the tangy, slightly bitter scent of geraniums.

"Ah, Clea! Good morning."

My eyes flew open and focused on Marc at the sound of his voice. I swallowed hard to get hold of myself. My breath quickened, and my heart beat too fast. In casual clothes, tightly fitted dark pants and a knit shirt, which showed the beginning of dark hair on his chest, he was even more attractive than before. My body desired him, even if I was determined in mind and will to have no more to do with him. I managed to say, "Good morning."

"How beautiful you are in my garden, in that dress!" He came straight to me and sat beside me on the stone bench, which was just big enough for two. He took my hand out of my lap and brushed his lips across the knuckles. A perfectly acceptable continental form of greeting, of no great importance, but at the touch of his lips on my skin I burned inside. He excited me, and for a thousand reasons I feared the feeling.

"Thank you," I said.

Marc's eyes sparkled, crystalline-pale. "You liked the roses, yes?"

"I liked the roses. Yes." I pulled my hand away and half sat on it so that he could not reclaim it from beneath my skirts. How could I say what I had to say to this man, when he had such a profound physical effect on me? I steeled myself, and began. "Yes, and . . . No."

"No? How, no? I chose the wrong color? But the yellow rose seemed so right for you. I was so sure . . . !"

I felt like the world's most ungrateful woman. "I do thank you, Marc. It's not the color. I love yellow roses."

"Except for your bedroom," he broke in. "The yellow was too sunny for the room where you sleep, so I thought the pink ones, tiny, perfect. The name is also perfect. They are called sweetheart roses, did you know that?"

"Yes," I said miserably, "I know. We call them the same at home. The problem isn't the flowers, it's—it's your intention behind the flowers. There was no reason for you to give them to me in the first place, especially in such large numbers! That kind of extravagance makes me uncomfortable."

I couldn't stay on the bench beside him any longer. I walked across the garden and stood by a waist-high pot of geraniums.

Marc followed. He stood right behind me and said with soft intensity, "I meant the roses to show how I feel about you. If I could have obtained the moon, and if it would fit in your rooms, I would have given you the moon, Clea. If that is extravagance, it's because my feelings for you are out of all proportion to anything I've felt before, for anyone. It has never happened like this for me before."

I choked down a lump in my throat. I'd rehearsed what I meant to say, but Marc wasn't playing fair. He was saying incredible things in a sincere way that baffled and weakened me. I didn't dare turn and look at him or I knew I'd be lost altogether. I clenched my fists and went on. "It's no good, Marc. Whatever you think you feel, nothing is going to happen between us. I'm afraid you spent a lot of money on those flowers for nothing."

"Clea, something has already happened between us." He placed his hands on my shoulders. "You can't deny it. From the first, when I stood with you on the stairs, I've known. And so do you. I felt it, felt it with you, when I kissed you."

I hung my head, shook it back and forth. "That kiss was a...an aberration. I'd had too much to drink, the whole evening was so strange—your mother, the clocks, the darkness, it was like a nightmare. I didn't know what I was doing."

"An aberration?" His hands were snatched from my shoulders and I felt him back away. "My God. A nightmare."

The scenario in my head, when I'd rehearsed what I would say, did not play like this. I'd managed, mostly, to stick to my lines, but Marc wouldn't say the words I'd imagined for him. I'd expected him to be cold, proud, perhaps disdainful. He was supposed to say something like Okay, But You Don't Know What You'll Be Missing. I hadn't expected him to display any emotion, but if he did, I'd thought it would be anger. None of that was happening. I turned my head, cautiously, and looked.

Marc had backed up to the bench and now he sat down, heavily. He stared at nothing, a kind of puzzled sadness on his face and in his voice. "How could I have been so wrong? For me, it was the most wonderful, hopeful night in the—I don't know—years."

His eyes searched the air and found me. "But for you it was a nightmare." He put his elbows on his knees and his head in his hands. Again he asked his question. "How could I have been so wrong?"

He had said a word that tore at my heart: hopeful. I understood that, the need for hope; I needed it, too. I went back to the bench and tossed my mental script away. So much for single-minded study, for going my own way undistracted. So much for promises made under the influence of the long-eyed saints of Torcello.

"Marc." This time it was I who put a hand on his shoulder. He raised his head. The little boy look was on his face. "You weren't wrong, not entirely. I did feel some of what you felt. But—" I couldn't finish. Nor could I turn away from him, not again. So I closed my eyes. The tears I'd felt coming leaked out beneath my eyelids.

"Clea?" He pulled me down next to him and put his arm around me. *"Carissima,"* he said. He stroked my hair and suddenly, inexplicably, all my control was gone. That outward calm that had clothed me for months vanished. The trickle of my tears became a stream and the stream became a flood. In the haven of Marc's arm, my face pressed into his shoulder, I cried and cried.

Eventually he said, in English, "Do you want to tell me why you are crying?"

I burrowed my head into his shoulder. My tears were subsiding. I noticed that I felt warm, safe, protected in the curve of his arm. Loved. And this time I knew the feeling did not come from alcohol. Slowly I began to speak. "I'm not quite sure. I haven't cried like that since—since my husband died."

"Ah. Now I understand. You loved him very much."

"No. No, you don't understand. I didn't . . . didn't love him." I shuddered and Marc's arm tightened around me. "But I didn't want him to die."

"Of course not. How long has it been?"

"Three, no, four months." Suddenly I realized we were both speaking English. I straightened up and blinked at him in surprise. "What are we doing talking in English? You sound just like the BBC!"

"*I* am speaking English," Marc grinned. "*You* are speaking American. Since you were so upset, I thought it might be easier for you if we spoke your language."

"Perhaps. But where did you learn, I mean, with that beautiful accent?"

"I was at Oxford for three years, and English is a common language for business all over Europe. I use it all the time. Do you feel better now?"

"Yes. I do. But I'm afraid nothing has changed. I can't do what you want. I can't have an affair with you, Marc. I just can't handle it, that's all."

"That's what you think I want, an affair? A sexual relationship? You think I gave you all those roses so that you would go to bed with me?"

"Of course. What else? I may not think of myself as a tourist, but that's what I must be, to you. A single woman who lives in your house for a few months and then is gone. A perfect situation for an affair. There is an attraction between us, I grant you that. It's just that you're normal and, well, I'm afraid I'm not. I can't have an affair with you, and that's all there is to that."

"Let me see if I've got this straight." Marc regarded me seriously and stroked his beard. "You admit you are attracted to me, as I am to you. Physically attracted."

I nodded.

"But you say you are not normal. You also said earlier that you did not love your husband, even though you did not wish him dead. Are you a . . . damn, what is the word in English . . . Oh. Are you a lesbian?"

"No!" I protested. I caught a hint of a smile curving Marc's lips. Exasperated, I said, "Oh, what's the use! We're starting to have the very discussion I wanted to avoid. I can't do it. I don't have to tell you why."

I got up briskly and started to leave. Marc's hand closed around my wrist as I passed him.

"Clea, you misunderstand. An affair is not what I want. Look at me, please."

Impatiently, anxiously, I looked down at him.

He said, "I believe I am falling in love with you."

A tremor, a current, a shock of energy started where his fingers circled my wrist and traveled all through me. "You can't!" I whispered.

"Oh, yes, I can." Slowly he stood and took both my hands in his, as solemnly as if we were about to begin a ritual dance. Which, in a way, we were. He looked at me as if he would see into my soul. "You do not have to tell me anything you do not want to, Clea. Not now, not ever. You have secrets. I see this in your eyes. And I see pain. He must have hurt you, that husband of yours. You are a little bit afraid, no? You do not trust. Four months is not a very long time. You will heal. I won't rush you. I can wait."

"Marc, I—"

"Shh, don't say anything. Not now." He bent his head and kissed my temple. So gently. "I can wait, because if, as I believe, I am falling in love with you, then the longer I wait the stronger that love will be. In the meantime, I will be your friend. You will learn to trust me, and then our love can grow.'' He dropped my hands and strode away swiftly, into his house.

I followed with my eyes, but he did not look back.

I WASN'T SURE how long I'd stood rooted to my spot in the garden, but gradually I realized I was not alone. I could feel someone looking at me. I scanned the garden, thought for a moment it was only the wicked little statue in the fountain whose gaze I felt, but no. A pair of eyes stared over the gate. Up, down, they appeared and disappeared. I shook my head to clear it, and smiled. It was a little old woman, stretching up on tiptoe to look into the garden.

The eyes came up again and with them a thin, pleading voice. ''I wonder if you could help me? I seem to be lost!''

She spoke Italian but very badly, with a definite American accent. I went rapidly to the rescue. I floated across the garden, my steps, my whole body lighter than I had felt in months. I tugged the gate open, laughing. ''I spend a lot of my time in Venice being lost, too,'' I assured her, in what I was certain was her native language. ''But perhaps I can help.''

''Oh, thank goodness. You speak English. How do you do?'' She extended a tiny hand. She was a short, plump woman with white hair, a round face, myopic blue eyes, and small hands and feet. ''I'm Maria Bonavita, but my name only sounds Italian. I don't speak it very well, at all. Venice is lovely, isn't it? But so confusing!''

''Yes, it is both those things.'' I smiled down at her. ''Where is it you want to go?''

''Well, now, let's see.'' She pushed her fingers distractedly through her white curls, which snapped back into place as if they were on springs. ''I was shopping in the Rialto, and I thought instead of going back to my hotel on one of those water buses I'd just walk back, and I got on this street. But now I'm so turned around I don't even remember which way I came from!''

"If you came from the Rialto, it's that way." I pointed to my right. "And where is your hotel?"

"It's on the Grand Canal."

That wasn't very helpful. The Palazzo Corelli and just about half of Venice was also on the Grand Canal. I tried again. "Yes, but in which direction?"

Her face puckered. "Well, dear, if I knew that I wouldn't be lost, would I?"

She was a trial, but it's hard to be too put out with someone who looks like everybody's grandmother. I said patiently, "Is it above or below the Rialto Bridge?"

"That depends on what you call 'above' and 'below.' I really don't know, dear."

I tried yet again. "Well, then, what is the name of your hotel?"

Maria Bonavita wrinkled her already wrinkled brow. "Oh, dear, I've forgotten the name. I only got here yesterday, you see. By way of Milan. I came on the train. But it's one of those palaces, a big pink one, with white gewgaws and gimcracks all over the windows. Looks like a big birthday cake."

"Ah!" Fortunately I recognized her description, gewgaws, gimcracks, and all. And I knew the hotel was an expensive one. The lady might be a little vague, but she had money. "You just went in the wrong direction when you left the Rialto. Come, I'll walk with you. It's a good day for a walk, and this street can be deceptive the first time."

"That's very nice of you, my dear, if you're sure you can spare the time. What did you say your name was?"

"I didn't. But it's Clea. Clea Beaumont."

By the time we got to her hotel, Maria and I were chatting like old friends. Our stories were, on the surface, similar. She was a widow, traveling alone for the first time. Her home was in New Jersey, and her husband had been a manufacturer of heavy equipment— "Bulldozers and such-like things," she said. When I mentioned that I thought I detected a little Boston in her voice, she smiled and said Yes,

indeed, she had lived in Boston until she married Mr. Bonavita, rest his soul, but that had been so many years ago. We
talked about Boston; I told her the city had changed and yet
not changed.

As we parted, Maria said she intended to stay in Venice
for a while because she was tired out from all her traveling.
She seemed delighted to learn that I too would be here. We
made no definite plans to meet, but I was sure I would see
her again. I walked back to the palazzo feeling that I now
had a surrogate grandmother in Venice, at least for as long
as Maria Bonavita stayed. It was easier, much less disturbing, to think about her than to think about the things Marc
had said.

I reached the garden of the Palazzo Corelli and looked
over the gate, as Maria had done. Was there a bit of a snoop
in the little old lady? She must have had quite a stretch to see
over the top—I could barely see over it myself and I was at
least a head taller than she. I thought of all the times I'd
needed directions. I would never have had the audacity to
look into someone's garden, it would have felt too much like
an invasion of privacy. And besides, there was always
someone in the street to ask.

I went through the gate, closed it, and looked back, recalling those little blue eyes bobbing up and down. Perhaps
Maria Bonavita was audacious for an elderly lady, but that
was all right. Otherwise I'd never have met her, and it was
good to have an old-fashioned grandmother-type friend in
Venice.

Chapter Four

I was rather frivolous the following week. I wanted a new image. Maybe I didn't exactly know who I was these days, but I did know how I wanted to look. Different. A bit European, a bit like the art student I was, even if a middle-aged one. Anyway I had intended to buy new clothes once I got here, which was why I had brought very few with me. I don't usually like to shop for clothes, so having only a few along was a way to force myself. Besides, the season was changing and new things were necessary.

In the midst of a flurry of shopping, I decided to have my hair cut. I asked a chic-looking woman, a fellow shopper, where I might go. She recommended her own hairdresser, and got me an appointment. He loved my hair. He clucked and fussed and plunged into it as if my head were a playground. "Make it simple," I said, "I want to be able to do it myself and I don't want to fight with it anymore." He called me a splendid challenge and set to work. I closed my eyes, bit my tongue and endured.

"Open your eyes, *signora*," the hairdresser said.

I did, and was amazed. For twenty years I had worn my hair shoulder-length or longer, because my husband had detested short hair and I hadn't cared much one way or another. Now my hair was cut to a uniform two inches all over my head. Freed of its length and corresponding weight, it curled and did not frizz. I laughed, I thought I looked like a little kid. I tossed my head, the curls bounced and didn't lose their shape. The lighter strands of hair gleamed. I felt as if I had acquired a curly halo. I laughed again. "I love it!" I declared. The hairdresser showed me how to bring a few of the curls forward on my forehead and at my cheek-bones, and he gave me a tortoise-shell headband I could use to hold the curls back for an opposite effect. I was so pleased that I gave him an enormous tip, which pleased him. Then I went out and bought more clothes.

The Italians make wonderful knits, and no one except the Spanish can equal them in the handling of leather. I bought plenty of both, in casual, comfortable styles suited to the hours I would be sitting and standing in museums and churches. I thumbed my nose at anything that looked even vaguely like a Junior League lunch or a husband's business dinner. My most prized purchase was also one of the least expensive: a long, fringed cape, so long it reached almost to my ankles, of luxuriously soft wool. The cape was hand-woven and the color of a Venetian sunrise, or of my favorite Talisman rose—golden yellow shot through with peachy pink. I bought it from the woman who made it, a tiny, bent, dark woman who looked like a little old witch, but who obviously had magic in her fingers. She sold her things in a shop on a street so narrow and dark it was more of a tunnel. A sinister-looking place, it was a wonder I had gone in there, but I was very glad I did. How like Venice, I thought as I went home with my prize, to hide the beautiful under the ugly. Although, now I thought about it, it was more likely to be the other way around.

I saw Marc only once, by accident, on the stairs. He appeared distracted. I thought he might notice my new hair-style, but he didn't. He acted like any businessman on his way to an important meeting, a mode of behavior with which I was all too familiar. I wondered what was the Corelli family business, if Marc did what his ancestors had done before him. Probably someday he would tell me. For now I was content, even relieved, with the distance between us.

By the end of the week I had put frivolity aside and was spending my days in the library of the Accademia, where I put together an outline and a timetable for my independent-study course. At home on Saturday I lugged a square game table from the salon into the Morning Room. It was heavier, and probably also more valuable, than it looked, but it was the right size to become a worktable for me. I set it up near the windows and put my typewriter on it, and my notebooks and a couple of reference books and a new box of typing paper. With a satisfying feeling that I was once again doing something I understood and was good at, I sat down and rolled a piece of paper into the typewriter.

I was typing the last page of my outline when I heard a knock, not on the salon door but on the door from the Morning Room to the corridor around the stairway. Actually I had no front door, though I always used the one into the salon for that purpose. All my rooms opened out onto that corridor, and into one another. There was another knock, definitely on the Morning Room door. I went and clicked off the bolt. I felt a little breathless and had a lump in my chest. It had to be Marc, no one else would think to knock on this particular door. I worked the latch, but the heavy door didn't budge.

"It's stuck," I called out, "you'll have to push from your side."

Marc pushed, and I waited . . . and there he was, with his aquamarine eyes and his black hair and beard and in casual clothes again, with the dark hair of his chest showing through. He looked wonderful. I would have had to be blind not to observe that.

"I knocked on the other door," he said, "but you didn't hear me. I thought you might be in here. I'm glad I was right." His eyes roamed my face, my body; he smiled, and the lump in my chest dissolved into a warmth that spread from my torso through my stomach to parts unnamed, down my legs and out my toes.

"I was typing." I waved an arm behind me, in the direction of my worktable near the windows. "Would you like to come in? Have a glass of lemonade with me?"

"I'm interrupting your work," he said, but he came in anyway. He closed the door by its ornery, shoulder-high latch.

"I can stop for a while. Do you want that lemonade?"

"Yes, please."

When I returned from the kitchen Marc was leaning over the worktable and reading my outline. He said, "This is interesting. If you do all this, you may end up knowing more about Venice than I do!" He accepted the glass I held out to him and we moved to the love seats.

"I doubt that. It's nice of you to take an interest, but the truth is that what I'm doing is pretty elementary."

Marc stroked his beard thoughtfully. "Are you just naturally modest, or do you have a habit of putting yourself down?"

"I—I..." I stammered, embarrassed. No one had ever suggested such a thing to me before. I had to think about the answer. "I guess I'm just not in the habit of talking about my work, except in class or in a museum with my fellow students. In that setting, I think I'm realistic about my ability. But at home, no one was ever interested."

"Mmm-hmm. So you have developed a habit of deprecating these particular abilities at home."

I felt my face flush. "I'm afraid you're right."

"Well, that has to change. Your apartment is home now, at least for a while, and I am interested, Clea. I am interested in everything you do. And I'm not flattering you. I know a good bit about history, but the only thing I know about art is that it's a better investment now than, for example, property around here."

"Investment?" I seized the opportunity to get the subject off me and my interests. "Are you a broker, then?"

"Sometimes." Marc's smile flashed. "Turn your head to the side. Yes. You've cut your hair, I thought so, but one has to be careful what one says to a woman about her hair. I like it."

"Thank you. I like it, too. Would you think me very nosy if I ask what kind of business you're in?"

"No." He drained his glass and put it on the floor. "Basically, I'm a banker. I handle other people's money. Venice isn't the banking capital of the world anymore, so I travel a lot. Now it's my turn to ask you something I've wondered about for some time. You told me and the Lady that you've never been to Italy before, and that you have no Italian blood. And yet, you speak Italian with a perfect Venetian accent. Our accent is quite distinctive, it's certainly not taught in schools, and yet you speak it as if you had been born here. How is that?"

"Simple. My best friend when I was a child was Italian, her parents had come over from Italy just before the Second World War. They must have been from somewhere around here, though of course I didn't know that. I learned from them, before I was six years old. We always spoke Italian at their house, and I've loved the sound of the words ever since I can remember. When I was just a little girl I loved the way the words kind of roll around in your mouth. It was almost like tasting the syllables with my tongue." I hugged my arms to myself, holding the memories close. I wasn't talking to Marc anymore, I was saying my thoughts aloud. "They were such a wonderful family. So warm and loving, always kissing, always touching...."

"That's us Italians," grinned Marc, "great kissers, great touchers."

I heard him, came out of my reverie into his grin, and smiled back. "I guess I walked right into that."

"Mmm-hmm, you did. Which, in a backward sort of way, brings me to why I'm here. There's something I thought you might like to see, if I promise to, er, not indulge my natural tendency for kissing and touching. We'd be alone, way out in the country, it won't be easy for me, but I'll try." He winked. "I know it's the kind of situation you'd prefer to avoid, but there won't be another opportunity after today. Or tomorrow.''

Alarm bells went off in my head, but I was intrigued. "Okay, I'll bite. Opportunity for what?''

"Last chance to see the family villa. I've sold it, sold it before you came here, in fact, and the deal is to close next week. It occurred to me that because of your interest in art and architecture, you might like to see it before it's too late. The villa is seventeenth-century, was designed by a student of Andrea Palladio, and it's still in pretty good shape, all things considered.''

These villas were rare, I hadn't dreamed the Corellis would own one. I'd read about them when I was preparing my outline, how the wealthy Venetians of the sixteenth through eighteenth centuries had built themselves summer homes on terra firma; how Palladio had invented the neoclassical style for these villas, and from this part of the Italian coast the Palladian craze had spread to the rest of Europe, to England, and even to America where Thomas Jefferson was the chief proponent. This was certainly an opportunity not to be missed!

"Of course I want to see it!" I exclaimed. "How soon can we start?''

WE TOOK THE CORELLI family motorboat from the front steps of the palazzo, where once the family's gondola would have been moored, to a boat yard on the land end of the causeway. It looked for all the world like a parking lot for boats. Next to it was a multistoried garage, where Marc kept his car. I wished I knew him better, I would have teased him about that car—it was so extremely proper, so sedate. A black Jaguar sedan. He drove it as well as he had handled the boat, neither too fast nor too slow. I soon relaxed and enjoyed the ride, glad he didn't make idle conversation.

It was comfortable to be with someone who felt no need to talk unless there was something interesting to say, because I prefer to be that way myself. He pointed out landmarks, that was all. We passed the town of Stra along the Brenta Canal, and a few miles farther Marc turned off into a private road. The countryside was rather flat and the road was straight, so that I could see the villa and its few surrounding trees and dark lines of low hedges, long before we were anywhere close.

"It looks so bare," I commented, "so open. I'd have thought there would be more landscaping, more trees."

Marc glanced my way and chuckled. "That remark comes straight out of your genes, my dear, out of your English heritage. Subconsciously you expect an English country house, a curving drive, lots of trees, the famous park-like setting. I, on the other hand, when I was in England and visited those houses, which of course were modeled after our Italian villas, wondered why they felt they had to clutter up fine architecture with so much greenery! I think the native Venetian has a basic mistrust of trees in large numbers. We're just not used to them."

"That's interesting," I said. "You know, it makes sense, psychologically. The people who built these villas were enormously wealthy—"

"Would that it still were so!" interjected Marc.

"Well, anyway, they were. The point is that they could build anything, absolutely anything they wanted. And they wanted, it seems, long, low houses, spread out to hug the ground. Not exactly Frank Lloyd Wright, of course, but the late-Renaissance equivalent. And they wanted their houses surrounded by lots of open space. Think about it, Marc. In Venice by the end of the fifteenth century every available inch of dry land had some sort of structure on it. A 'great house' was great vertically, it spread its rooms up, not out. So you see, it makes sense that a luxurious change, for them, would be miles of bare ground and a house with horizontal rather than vertical lines."

"You're right. I never thought of it that way. Well, here we are. The Villa Corelli-Leone-Polcari. The Leones and the Polcaris were related through marriage and have long since died out. Now the Corellis, too, will be gone." He stopped the car with the motor idling, about a hundred yards from the villa. "You can get a better view from back here. It's too big to take in from the top of the drive."

"Ooh! I—I can't....There are no words, Marc." My mind boggled. I simply could not deal with the fact that the magnificent building right before my eyes was not a library, not a public monument, but a house. Not even a year-round house, but a summer home; and it belonged to the family of the man sitting next to me. Belonged to that man himself. No matter that he had had to sell it, it was still his, still the Villa Corelli-Etc. My egalitarian little mind rebelled and I thought it was too much, too much for one family of flesh-and-blood people to own a place like this; but then I succumbed. Oh, it was magnificent! If I had been a Corelli of a previous time, I would have gloried in this villa.

The central section of the villa was two stories, and had four columns rising to a pedimented roof. The famous Palladian windows were balanced in rows on both levels of the facade. Above the pedimented door, which precisely echoed the line of the roof, was a small balcony. Arched colonnades spread out at one-story height on either side and led to two smaller buildings, which looked like scale models of the main, center structure. All was done in stucco and marble, and though on closer inspection the stucco needed painting and patching and the marble needed blasting, the Villa Corelli-Etc. was still absolutely grand.

"Ready to see the inside?" Marc asked. He had brought the car slowly up the driveway as I made my inspection, and now he stopped and turned off the motor.

"Yes, please." I opened the car door and jumped out. I was on the steps before him. I felt as if my eyes were as big as saucers and probably looked it, too, but I didn't care. "How awful to have to sell this magnificent place! And who bought it?"

"A man from Amsterdam, with a name I can neither spell nor pronounce without help. Prepare yourself, now. You're about to see why I had to sell."

Gradually, as Marc took me from room to room, I understood. The villa had not been used as a residence, summer or winter, for over a hundred years. Generations of Corellis in need of money had sold off everything except the frescoes painted on the walls. Two of the frescoes were priceless, by Tiepolo, and were in need of restoration. There were no sculptures, no paintings, no rugs, not a stick of furniture remained. In its emptiness, the grandeur of the space was awesome. The structure itself was so basically sound that nothing short of an act of God—and maybe not even that—could have destroyed it.

"It's so sad," I said. We sat on the marble floor of the loggia and shared wine and cheese and fruit Marc had brought in a basket.

"Not really."

"It is, too! It's like . . . well, actually, it's not like anything in my experience. I have trouble even imagining what it must be like to have a family so old it's part of history. To own something so splendid as this villa and to have to let it go! It is sad!"

"Yes. Well, as for the family, old isn't synonymous with illustrious. You've met the surviving members, and we aren't winning any prizes. For culture, or anything else. Paolo, praise God, doesn't count. He's only a half brother."

"Oh?" I asked as inquiringly as I could, but Marc went on with other things.

"I'm doing what I can to preserve what we have left, and I had to make a choice. It wasn't much of a choice, really." He rubbed the back of his neck, a gesture I was coming to recognize was habitual when he felt stressed. "I can't live here, even if I could afford to do the repairs and to furnish it. And I can't sell the palazzo. The Lady would never give her consent, and although I don't really, legally, need her consent, I'd never do that to her. It might even kill her to have to live elsewhere."

I considered that in silence. She never left the palazzo. I understood his point. But I responded instead to a hint of wistfulness in his voice. "Um. Marc, would you want to live somewhere else? Beside the palazzo?"

He looked sharply at me. "Sometimes I think I would. But since it's not possible, I try not to think about it. No, the reality is that I'm stuck with my mother and with the Palazzo Corelli, which is going to crack like your famous American writer Edgar Allan Poe's House of Usher and fall into the canal if I don't do something about it. And that takes money, quite a lot of money. Therefore, I have sold the villa. It was necessary, I'm getting a good price, no reason to be sad."

"Maybe we could buy it back," I mused. I was off in a fantasy of my own, wondering if I had enough money to buy the villa from the unpronounceable Dutchman. I probably did. In my flight of fancy I didn't think about saving the money to make restitution to anyone. I was filling this marvelous villa with treasures, creating my own private museum. It was a dream, of course. I didn't realize what I'd said, or that I'd spoken out loud.

But Marc had heard me. "We?"

"What?"

"You said, 'Maybe we could buy it back.'"

"Oh. Don't pay any attention to me, I talk to myself sometimes. I was just daydreaming. It's a bad habit I can't seem to break myself of, saying my idle thoughts out loud."

A wonderful, warm smile spread across Marc's face. "I'm in favor of anything that results in your saying *we*. However, as to the thought, the Amsterdam man has plans to turn the villa into a hotel or something like that. Once the deal is closed I'll never be able to afford to buy him out, and I doubt you could afford it, either."

I began to gather up the debris from our alfresco meal. I didn't dare continue looking at Marc, with that smile warming me. He had been in my daydream and the after-image lingered in my mind: Marcantonio Corelli, with his long legs and beautifully bearded Renaissance face, stood on the villa's wide stairs; stood smiling, waiting for me.

"Oh, well, as I said, it was just a daydream," I shrugged. Shrugged the whole thing away.

DAYDREAMS, NIGHT DREAMS. I was still having nightmares. Perhaps I was driving my daytime fears into my subconscious, and they were coming out in my dreams. At any rate, I was definitely no longer as fearful during the days as I had been, and for that I was thankful. As for the nightmares, I didn't allow myself to dwell on them, didn't try to analyze them. Usually I couldn't recall them in any detail, anyway.

There was one exception: a dream I'd had twice in one week. It had all the earmarks of a recurring nightmare. It was like a dream within a dream: I dreamed I was asleep in my bed in my bedroom at the Palazzo Corelli, and there was someone or some *thing* in the room with me. I could hear it moving, feel it watching me, and my great fear was that the person or thing would touch me, unless I could wake myself up. In the dream I struggled so that the horrible intruder would not touch me, and in fact I *was* struggling to wake from the dream. When at last I did wake up I was wildly disoriented, not sure that I was truly awake, and with pounding heart and ragged breath I would search the shadows of my room for the intruder, search until I was sure that I was really in my room and not still dreaming.

I tried, these days, to dismiss both my daytime apprehensions and my bad dreams. But late one afternoon, something new and very disturbing happened. I felt that someone was following me. I tried to rid myself of the feeling. Told myself I only suffered from remnants of earlier groundless fears, or from echoes of nightmares.

That day I had spent several hours in the church called San Zanipolo, where I had made carefully detailed observations and notes on the Italian Gothic style. Zanipolo is a Venetian corruption of the church's real name, Santi Giovanni e Paolo. It is a very large church, full of history, including the tombs and monuments of many Doges. There was something in the atmosphere of that church that oppressed me, as if the place had seen too much of death and too little of joy.

I stuck it out nevertheless, and in the end I stayed too long. It was the difficulty of making sketches in the fading light that reminded me that I should leave. As I left the church I stopped to examine Verrochio's heroic statue of the Condottieri Colleoni on his horse. He had one of the most frightening visages I'd ever seen. In Zanipolo's twilight shadows I could imagine the statue coming to life, the great helmeted head slowly turning, the blank eyes glaring, the horse leaping from its base in slow motion.... I left before my imagination could do more damage. It was an effort not to look back over my shoulder to be sure that the statue hadn't moved.

San Zanipolo wasn't far from the Palazzo Corelli, but the streets between were narrow, twisting, and were growing dark. The back canals I crossed looked dirty and threatening. I would have welcomed some fellow pedestrians, but there were none. At least, none that I could see. But I felt someone behind me. Following me. The feeling persisted, no matter what I told myself, I simply could not shake it off. In the middle of a small, arched bridge I turned around abruptly. I saw nothing. Visibility was terrible, anyway—it was that time between day and night when the whole world has turned to shades of gray. I had an impression, a fleeting sense of a disturbed patch of air several feet behind me.

Fanciful! Said my rational mind. Maybe, maybe not, said another part of my mind, an unrational but wise part I hadn't had much use for since my children were small. I had alway known, then, where they were, even if I could not see them. In particular, I'd known if either of them was about to get hurt. I supposed all mothers had this sixth sense.

What I hadn't realized was that mine still operated, was operational now in Venice, as if it had been waiting on hold all these many years. My sixth sense told me at this moment that scarce seconds ago there had been someone behind me in that disturbed patch of air. Someone who did not want to be seen.

I tried not to quicken my steps, not to seem as alarmed as I felt. I heard the sharp, staccato click of my boot heels on stone pavement. How much farther to go? Too far. Not much as the crow flies, but the way this street twisted was amazing.

There! I definitely heard footsteps behind me. Rapid, hurrying, and so light that even as I identified the sound, it faded. I kept on walking, my ears sorting through the sharp raps of my own feet and background noises from inside the houses: a muffled blurt of rock music, the bark of a dog, squeals of children, a baby's cry; and above all this from some church floated faint baroque cascades of organ music. Through it all I strained to hear the hurrying feet behind me. Sometimes I thought I did, sometimes I didn't, but no matter what I heard I felt someone there. What could anyone want with following me?

To rob me, probably, though that made little sense. I dressed like a student, I carried no purse, only a large canvas bag filled with my notebook, a big sketch pad, soft pencils, and boxes of charcoal and pastels. What little money I had with me was in a small leather pouch on a belt around my waist. I didn't even carry a camera as many art students did, I preferred to make sketches. There was very little of value to a thief, but my notes and sketches were irreplaceable to me.

My sanity was also irreplaceable. As frightened as I was, my mind was working. My mind said that a robber would long since have swooped down on me and taken what he wanted. My mind said a rapist or some other kind of pervert would have attacked among the street's darkest convolutions, or would have thrown me from one of the little arched bridges into an alley-like back canal. Therefore, said my mind, if anyone was following me he was doing it simply to get on my nerves . . . and he was succeeding. Never in my life had I wanted to run, to bolt, more than I did at that moment.

But I did not allow myself to run. The street was widening, though it was no lighter because night had truly fallen. I knew where I was. One last zig to the right and a short zag to the left would bring me out on the street behind the Palazzo Corelli. I'd never been a brave or adventurous person, certainly not physically. That adrenaline rush that I knew some people craved had never done a thing for me except made me feel sick. My own children used to tease me about being timid: "Aw, Mom, don't be such a scaredy-cat!" when I steadfastly refused to do things like ride the roller coaster. Yes, I was scared now and I wanted to run as fast as I could to the palazzo, but I'd be damned if I was going to give the person following me the satisfaction of knowing that he'd succeeded in his attack on my nerves!

I listened hard. I heard the footsteps. I stopped; they stopped. I looked over my shoulder and saw shadows within shadows. Nothing moved. I walked on. My pulse raced but my feet kept a measured pace. When the street made its final zag I tucked myself into a dark space between two houses that was about wide enough for a cat, but a tight squeeze for me. I stood there, waiting with a hammering heart.

Out of the dark yawning mouth of the street's turning, more darkness gathered and grew. A shadow. Monstrously huge, identifiable as human by a head-shaped excrescence. Come on, I thought grimly, gritting my teeth, Come out, show yourself! Come out, but for God's sake don't come anywhere near me.

The shadow wavered, changing shape. I held my breath. Nothing happened, except that everything seemed darker than it had been before—uniformly darker. As if the shape

I'd thought was a shadow had spread itself out evenly over the paving stones, had crept up walls, insinuated itself through shuttered windows and into assorted spaces ... including my hiding place.

Of course, said my mind, relentlessly and blessedly rational, that isn't what happened. The person who cast the shadow turned—that was why it wavered—and walked back the way he'd come. So why hadn't I heard any footsteps?

Something brushed my legs and I choked back a scream. A cat streaked out of my hiding place and tore across the street, into that yawning mouth of darkness. I almost laughed with relief. "Go get him, tiger," I whispered. I had been right when I'd thought there was just about enough room for a cat, and there went the proof!

Much later, when I lay up to my chin in bubbles in my deep, old-fashioned bathtub, I gave a name to the feeling that lingered in me: disappointment. I'd wanted to see, to know who had followed me from San Zanipolo. Perhaps no one had. Perhaps it had all been in my imagination. Another trick, another illusion. Nothing else made sense. I could count the people I knew in Venice on the fingers of one hand, and none of them had any reason to follow me in such a threatening manner.

"I am *not* going to let this get to me!" I announced to the freshly bathed face in my mirror. Then I had to laugh at myself. The fierce determination in my voice and in the stubborn tilt of my cleft chin were totally at odds with the cherubic halo of curls around my head. I stuck out my tongue at my image, and then was instantly penitent. Only a few weeks ago I had looked in this mirror and had a sinking feeling that I didn't know who I was anymore. Now I was beginning to know this woman with the short, curly hair. She was the new Clea, and I realized with a little surge of pleased surprise that I liked her, much more than I had liked the old one.

I realized something else as I climbed into my antique bed and settled down to sleep: regardless of whether I had really been followed or it had all been in my imagination, at the end I had been more curious than afraid. And that, for Clea the formerly scaredy-cat mom, was nothing short of amazing!

Chapter Five

I opened the salon door for Marc and tried not to sound as exasperated as I felt. "I'm sorry to have to bother you with this, Marc. I can tell you've been working hard and I'm sure you have better things to do with your time at the end of a long day—"

He interrupted me, taking both my hands in his and brushing the knuckles with his lips. "At the end of a long day I can think of nothing I would rather do than be with you, Clea. For any reason."

His eyes glowed, and my hands tingled, I felt my face grow warm with the beginning of a blush and I turned my head away, guiltily. I had been avoiding him for days, and he probably knew it. If I could have solved my problem in any other way I would have continued to avoid him. My tingling hands confirmed the reason: I was trying my best to get at least a semblance of a normal life going, and I could never do that with him anywhere near me. Nor could I take him up on his offer to be a "friend." No matter what he said, the physical attraction between us was so strong that I couldn't believe he could stick to pure friendship. Perhaps I couldn't, either.

"Your message said you have a problem and need my help," he prompted. "I'm at your disposal."

"It's silly," I said, backing away. "I tried to take care of it myself but I just couldn't get anywhere. I'm sure it's not a language difficulty—I understand them and they seem to understand me, but I guess there's some kind of, uh, bu- reaucratic mix-up and I just can't seem to fight my way through it.''

Amusement played in his eyes and touched the corners of his sensual mouth. ''Suppose you tell me the exact nature of the problem, and perhaps then I will be able to untangle some of the bureaucracy.''

''Oh!'' I had backed into a chair, so I sat down in it. ''I didn't say in my note?''

''No, you didn't. Whatever it is, it has you in a rather pretty state of confusion.'' Marc slipped his hands in his pockets and leaned against a heavy old chest, smiling. He looked elegant yet at ease in the formal salon, still in his working clothes.

Not for all the world would I have let him know that I'd been mostly angry and not the least confused until he had come through the door. I set my chin and declared, ''It's the telephone. It's not working. I called them up from the li- brary at the Accademia and reported it, but I keep getting a runaround. They tell me my number is in service and I tell them it's not, and they ask me again where do I live and I say the apartment in the Palazzo Corelli and they go off for a while and then come back and say there's no problem on the line. I just don't understand it!''

''Hm.'' Marc frowned, drawing his dark eyebrows to- gether. ''How long has the phone been out of order?''

''I don't know,'' I confessed. ''I haven't needed to use it much. I don't know very many people here yet, and I've been writing letters to my children rather than calling them. But the other day I needed to call Professor Tedesco, and the phone was dead. I don't like to be without it, in case my son or daughter should need to reach me. I gave them the num- ber.''

''As I remember,'' Marc said, no longer relaxed or amused, ''there are two instruments, one in the kitchen and one in the Morning Room. I'll check the kitchen, it's closer." He strode out of the salon and I followed him. "You're right," he said with receiver in hand, "the line is dead. I don't understand this." He slammed it down and stood at the counter, rubbing the back of his neck and looking troubled.

"It's not such a big deal," I ventured. "Surely it's just some sort of a mix-up and you can straighten it out."

"I had these phones put in your name before I left for that trip I was on when you arrived. All the other telephones in the house work, so these should, too. Let me just check something out here." Marc took off his jacket and tossed it in the general direction of the kitchen table. He half missed, and it slid onto the floor.

"Men!" I muttered, picking up the jacket. It was a fine, silky-soft woolen fabric and unconsciously I stroked it as I folded it. I didn't put the jacket down immediately, I liked the feel of it over my arm.

"What?" Marc was taking pots out from under the kitchen counter.

"You take off your jacket, I presume so you won't get it dirty, and then you toss it on the floor. I was just making noises about that."

"Mm."

"Marc, what are you doing in there? I can only guess it's something to do with the telephone."

"I hope I'm fixing it. This would be easier if you had a flashlight. There should be one in a drawer in here, part of the furnishings since we're prone to power outages during the winter storms. Will you look?"

"Okay." I put his jacket over the back of a chair by the table and rummaged through the drawers. "No flashlight. I knew I hadn't seen one, but I never really looked before."

"That's all right. I think I've got it." He withdrew head and shoulders from the cabinet and sat back on his haunches. "Try it now."

I picked up the receiver. "There's a dial tone! What did you do?"

I wondered why Marc didn't look pleased with himself. Instead, his expression was grim, and he didn't answer my question. He said, "Let's check it out," and took the receiver from me, pushing numbers rapidly. "Hello, Giorgio. No, nothing is wrong. I'm in Mrs. Beaumont's apartment, just checking out her telephone. You don't know of any reason why someone would have disconnected her phone lines, do you? You didn't do it yourself for any reason? No, I thought not. I suppose it doesn't matter, since it's working fine now." He paused to listen, mumbled a reply I didn't hear, and hung up the telephone.

I hadn't heard Marc's reply because one single word blared in my head: I said it aloud. "Disconnected?" I felt a chill along my spine. "Why? How?"

"What I'd like to know is *who*," Marc replied curtly. "Let's go see about the other telephone." I trotted after him, listening as he explained. "This whole apartment was rewired when it was renovated. The connection for each instrument to the outside line is simple, it works on a plastic clip. All you have to know is where the outlet for the jack is. The one in the kitchen is sort of hard to find. I wanted a modern kitchen counter with cabinets underneath, but moving the outlet was a costly proposition. So we just upgraded the jack and brought the cord down through a hole we made at the back of the countertop. No wonder you didn't notice it wasn't plugged in. But here in the Morning Room....Look, Clea. I'm surprised you didn't notice that yourself."

"I—I just didn't," I gulped. I felt really stupid. Marc held the unconnected phone cord in his hand, plastic clip and all. It was almost exactly like the ones we have at home, and the jack for it was in a small white box on the baseboard which, though it was unobtrusive, was in plain sight.

Marc plugged the plastic clip in, picked up the receiver, listened, and held it out for me wordlessly. I listened to a dial tone, embarrassed. "Th-thank you," I stammered.

He dusted off his hands, looking at me critically. "You don't think you might have unplugged the phones yourself, or asked Zenia to do it? Maybe when you first arrived, and then forgot about it?"

"No." I shook my head. "I'm certain I didn't."

Marc's expression was speculative, and I couldn't fault him for that. He went back to the kitchen for his jacket, and once again I trailed after him. "Well," he said at last, shrugging his jacket into place and adjusting his white shirt cuffs one by one, "I suppose there's no harm done, but it's damn peculiar."

"Yes," I admitted. I felt strange, not sure if I should be embarrassed or alarmed or simply glad that the problem had been minor and now the phones were working. "Anyway, thank you for your help. Will you stay for a while? Perhaps a glass of wine?"

Marc smiled. He reached out and gave the back of my head a sort of tousling, friendly caress. "I've waited days for just such an invitation from you, but I can't tonight. The Lady is expecting me and, as Giorgio reminded me, I'm already late. Will you ask me again? Soon?"

"I will." I smiled in return. His smile could warm me like an open fire. "I promise, very soon."

"Good."

At the door Marc touched his lips to my cheek. "Good night," he murmured in my ear, his voice so low and intimate that it made me think of bed, of turning out the light, heads on pillows side by side, whispered endearments in the dark.

"Good night," I echoed in a throaty whisper. As I was closing the door he reached out a staying hand.

"Clea, is there anyone in Venice who might want to keep you from making or getting phone calls?"

"No," I replied. I was sure there wasn't, at the time. And at the time, I was also sure I hadn't done the disconnecting myself.

I RENEWED MY DETERMINATION to stick to a timetable for my independent study, no matter what. I had been in Venice for two whole months and I'd accomplished very little. Well—as Marc pointed out when I did invite him for a drink as promised—by saying I'd accomplished so little, I was putting myself down again. The fact was that I had accomplished a lot of things. I had my Italian flowing so fluently that now I thought in Italian a lot of the time. I didn't get lost so much. I was developing a "feel" for the city, which I found hard to describe to Marc, but he seemed to understand what I meant. And I had a sort of rudimentary social life, which consisted of lunches with people I met at the Accademia and an occasional evening with Marc. But, though I didn't say so to him, there were still a lot of unsettled and unsettling elements in my life and I was sure getting on with my studies would help. For me, a routine is reassuring.

Mornings I spent on book work or paperwork, sometimes at home and sometimes in the library. Lunch I always ate out. I resisted a persistent tendency to find one restaurant I liked and stay with it; I forced myself to explore. Usually I liked best the little cafés with tables outside along the *fondamenta*, but occasionally I would discover a small jewel of a place tucked away behind high walls in a side street.

My afternoons I devoted to art and architecture, following my independent-study outline. I was visiting all the churches first; later would come the palazzi and the museums, and finally the Doges' Palace, which I was saving for last. Occasionally I saw Maria Bonavita wandering distractedly through a church or standing in a *campo*, looking lost. She always carried with her a battered old Michelin Guide, which she could not read since it was entirely in Italian. She would neither part with it nor replace it with an English version because the Michelin had belonged to "my late husband, dear departed Mr. Bonavita."

Something about the way she said those words made me feel unspeakably guilty, and a little paranoid, as if the sprightly little white-haired woman deliberately wanted to make me uneasy. That was nonsense, of course; Maria could have no way of knowing I shared neither her sense of loss nor her lingering, loving respect for a dead husband. My guilt feelings were my problem, nothing to do with her. Still, I found myself uncomfortable around her, both because of her references to dear departed Mr. Bonavita, and because she was forever wanting me to translate the dear departed's guidebook. An encounter with Maria could easily set me back several hours in my work. I wanted a female friend in Venice, but maybe not at such a price.

On the whole my work was going well, I thought one afternoon as I sat at a table in the Piazza San Marco and watched the colors on the face of the basilica change in the changing light of the setting sun. Alabaster, amber, porphyry, cobalt, gold—lots and lots of gold. It was the busiest, most complex facade I had ever seen in my life. Horses over the doors on a cathedral, imagine! I wondered what Cotton Mather, that great Puritan from my home state of Massachusetts, would have said about this place of worship, and I smiled. Venice would undoubtedly have eaten straitlaced old Cotton alive, and would never have had indigestion. If he had come over here in his own century, they would have clapped a mask and domino on him and swirled him, raving, off into the crowd never to be seen again.

There was by heritage enough New England Puritan in me that I, myself, found San Marco barbaric in its splendor. But what else could you expect from people who had chosen their own patron saint, had adopted an obscure legend about him as gospel truth, and then had stolen the saint's bones to be the relics of their church? This church. I smiled again.

"Hey, haven't we met before?" The voice was male, the language American-colloquial. I looked up.

"You're Clea Beaumont, right?"

"Yes, and you're Paolo Corelli." Who else? Nobody else was that large, that blond or that tan. But his casual use of my language surprised me.

"You remember me!" he beamed.

"Of course I do. I won't be here much longer, but sit down, if you like."

"Thanks." He sat, raised one arm in the air and snapped his fingers without even looking for a waiter. He might look and sound like an American playboy, but that gesture was pure Italian aristocrat. He snapped his fingers and expected to be obeyed. And he was. As the waiter came he asked. "What's that you're drinking, coffee? It's the wrong time of day for coffee. Have something else, have a drink with me."

"No, thanks." I shook my head at the waiter and held my hand flat over the top of my cup. "I really must go soon."

"I bet you were thinking about some guy just then. Lucky guy! You must like him, you were smiling and talking to yourself."

"As a matter of fact," this time I smiled at Paolo, "I was thinking about your people, the Venetians. How they went to Alexandria and stole Saint Mark's bones and brought them back here. Only they didn't call it stealing. They called it the Translation of the Holy Relics."

"Yeah." Paolo grinned. "If we did it today, we'd say we liberated 'em. Same difference." He winked.

I laughed. Paolo seemed easy to be with, easier than his brother. In part this was because there was an absence of the sexual tension I felt with Marc, but it was also because Paolo seemed easygoing—where Marc was serious and inclined to formality. Paolo was casual in the extreme, he acted more American than I did myself.

When a lull fell in the conversation I asked, with what I intended to be a tactful hesitation. "You're, ah, Marc's half brother?"

"He told you that, did he?" The blue eyes glinted with a sudden steely undertone. "Well, sure he would. It's no secret." Paolo raised his arm and snapped his fingers for another drink, then tossed off what remained in his glass.

Curiosity won out over better judgment. I sensed that Paolo would talk, and I decided to stay for a while. I ordered a glass of white wine. Paolo interpreted my action as proof of his charm, and gave me a dazzling smile. Too dazzling. For the first time I was uncomfortable. But I went on. "You and Marc are so different. Even your English is different. He mentioned that he'd been at Oxford. Did you perhaps go to an American university?"

"Nope. Never been to college. I've just got a good ear for languages. Can't read any, except Italian of course, but I speak the main ones. English, French—used to read French too, now that I think of it, but not anymore—German, Japanese." He launched into a rapid-fire demonstration.

"I'm impressed," I said sincerely. "You must have traveled a lot, to have learned all that so well."

"Yes and no. I went to this Swiss boarding school for a long time and picked most of it up there. We had kids from everyplace. One I really liked, he was from Chicago."

"Oh." That explained a lot.

"The Japanese I learned in my business." When Paolo mentioned his business the steel came back into his eyes, and the easygoing manner hardened.

I wondered why. He wasn't dressed much like a businessman now, nor had he been the other time I'd seen him. First he'd worn the flashy white suit, now a bright blue sweater of heavily ribbed cotton, white pants and white rope-soled shoes. There was no gold at his neck this time, but his watch was gold and looked expensive. I decided a direct question would not be out of order.

"What kind of business are you in, Paolo?"

"Travel business. Tourists. There's big bucks in tourists these days." He winked at me again, and raised his glass, lapsing into Italian. "To the tourists! May they prosper and spend, spend, spend!"

"*Salute*," I murmured. I drank, without enthusiasm. A change had come over Paolo and I was suddenly wary. His wink this time had not been playful, it was knowing. Lascivious. As if the tourists existed only to be exploited, by him, and he counted me among them. I felt uneasy, but I stayed because of what he said next.

"I owe it all to big brother. Marc. No, not all. He got me started, set me up, but I've made my business into something Marcantonio Corelli never dreamed of. Hell, he wouldn't understand it if I drew him a map." Paolo continued to speak Italian, as if the English had been an act, part of an American persona he put on and off at will.

"I suppose it was good of him to help you, " I ventured, also in Italian. "I mean, from what I saw at the palazzo, there's some sort of estrangement between you two."

Paolo laughed. It was not a merry sound. "You noticed!" He raised his arm and snapped his fingers for yet another drink.

I declined, shaking my head for the waiter. It was quite dark now. I would have to take a vaporetto home because I wouldn't walk the distance from the piazza to the Palazzo Corelli at this hour. Still, I lingered. I said, "I'm sorry. I don't have any brothers, only one sister and I seldom see her anymore. She married and moved to California, which is a long way from where I live. But I often wish I had a brother, to be close to, maybe to lean on sometimes. It must be hard, sad for you, to have a brother right here and not be . . . not get along."

Paolo brooded over his drink. Mellow light from candles on the many little sidewalk tables could not soften his face. I'd meant well, but now I wished I'd kept my mouth shut— a position in which I too often found myself. When Paolo finally looked up, his eyes had changed again: the steel under the blue was white-hot, blazing. "He's *not* my brother," he said through clenched teeth, "he's half, do you understand, half! I'm a *bastard*! Didn't the esteemed, legitimate Marcantonio-the-heir Corelli tell you that?"

"No, he didn't. He only said you were half brothers. He didn't say how, but your name is also Corelli. I assumed..." I stopped, seeing my error. The resemblance to Eugenia was so strong, she was obviously his mother. How could I have been so stupid? I'd assumed Paolo and Marc were born of two different marriages, but then Paolo's last name would have been different. "I should have realized, Paolo. I just didn't think. It was very tactless of me to have gotten on this subject, at all, and I'm sorry."

"Well, never mind. All of Venice knows, anyway. The fact is, Marc and his father always hated me. I was the love child, you see. Mother, being the Lady, never pretended I was her husband's child. She could do as she pleased. And she never has told anyone, not even me, who my father was. Or is. So don't talk brother-sister-family to me! It's all sentimentality, nothing but crap!"

His bitterness was understandable, but I winced. I reached down beside my chair for the canvas bag, my carryall. I said, "Paolo, I never meant to open old wounds. And really I've stayed too long." I fished some money out of the pouch on my belt, shoved it under a napkin and stood up. "I think I'd best go now. Good night."

"I'd ask you to have dinner with me, but I realize you're already taken. My half brother has put his 'Marc' on you. Ha-ha! Get it, his mark?" His tone was both lazy and heavily sarcastic.

I had turned to go, but I stopped as suddenly as if he had shot me. I turned back to see Paolo rock his chair on its rear legs, a mocking expression on his face. I snapped, "What do you mean by that?"

"I mean Marc took the trouble to come all the way down to my office the day after I breached his inner sanctum, when you were there. He told me to remember that the house is off-limits, and he said the house's tenant was off-limits to me, too, whether she was in the house or out of it. Big brother has marked you for himself, Clea Beaumont, and he told me to stay away."

"But he doesn't...he can't..." I was so taken aback that I couldn't finish a simple sentence.

Paolo smiled, all charm again. "Of course, he can't. You're your own woman, Woman of the Nineties, right?"

"I certainly hope so!"

"And so is my mother her own woman, always has been in any decade, and the Palazzo Corelli is the Lady's house, regardless of wills and heirs and all that legal claptrap. Marc doesn't have much to say about who comes and goes in the palazzo. I go to the house whenever I want. I just avoid him. And the servants, too, of course. They're all his spies—although—" He didn't finish that thought. He looked directly at me. "As for you, Clea," he stood and threw a couple of bills on the table, "since you don't belong to Marc yet, how about that dinner? Have you been to Harry's Bar?"

"No." My head was swimming. "No, thank you. I just want to go home!" I walked away as rapidly as I could across the gray-and-white-patterned pavement of the piazza, and through the piazzetta. Past the clock tower and the great basilica, which rose against the dark sky like something out of the *Arabian Nights*. Every arch along the way was hung with a golden globe of light, and all this beauty was wasted on me.

Paolo kept up with me easily. "Another time, then? How about it?"

I continued my pace. "I'm really not interested in Harry's Bar, Paolo. Too many tourists."

"Okay, then, any place you want. I know them all. Dinner, any time you want. But soon. I promise you, Marc will never know." A new thought occurred to him. Apparently he found it alarming, for he grabbed my shoulder and pulled us both to a stop. "He'll never know unless *you* tell him. You wouldn't tell Marc we met today, or anything we talked about, anything I said, would you?"

From the corner of my eye I could see the quay and a waiting vaporetto. All I wanted was to get out of this situation and onto that boat. I had enjoyed talking to Paolo Corelli, briefly I'd even felt sorry for him, but all that had changed. I had not the slightest intention of becoming involved in a blood feud between the two Corelli brothers. Half brothers, whatever!

I rotated my shoulder and stared pointedly at Paolo's hand on it. He still held on. I said, not trying to keep the disgust I felt out of my voice, "I won't say anything because it's none of Marc's business whom I see, whom I talk to, or what we talk about. I won't go out with you, either, Paolo. I'm not getting involved at the moment. Not with you, not with Marc, not with anyone. Now, let me go. My vaporetto is waiting."

I broke from him and ran for the boat, hopping aboard just as it pulled away. Fortunately it was the right one—I hadn't taken time to look. Out of breath from running, I clung to the rail and did not take a seat. I wished I hadn't heard what Paolo had called after me, "See you at the palazzo!"

I shuddered. Somehow the idea that Paolo Corelli could walk about the palazzo without being invited, without even the servants knowing, gave me the creeps. How did he do it? He had grown up there, like Marc, he must know all the secrets of the house. I thought of Marc walking into total darkness on the fourth floor, saying, "I know this place like the back of my hand." Well, if he did, then Paolo did, too.

I was overreacting, and I didn't know why. I squeezed my eyes shut, still clinging to the railing of the vaporetto. Yes, I did know why: it was because holding onto me like that, pursuing me the way he had, Paolo had made me feel trapped—and that was a feeling I could not tolerate, not ever.

I opened my eyes and looked down, over the railing and into the water. Looking down was a mistake, a big mistake.

The waters of the canal were black: greasy, oily black. Slick and wet and sinister. They surged and heaved, as if with the motion of a giant black sea serpent coiling and uncoiling unseen beneath the surface. I was terrified.

Chapter Six

My body had its own set of reactions to Marc Corelli: a quickening of the heartbeat, a weakness at the knees, a tendency for voice and breath to catch in the throat, a compulsion of the lips to turn up at the corners in a smile I suspected must look goofy. As if those things weren't enough, all my insides seemed to liquefy and tingle at the mere thought that he might touch me; and if he did touch me, even the most casual touch, I felt as if I might burst into flame.

No matter how often my mind repeated that I would not become involved, no matter how firmly I insisted that I had forgotten Marc's declaration that he was falling in love with me, my body went merrily along doing its own thing. I certainly *tried* to control it. At the moment I was trying very hard—with my usual lack of success—and I was past caring, because the prospect ahead was too exciting. Marc was going to show me the Palazzo Corelli from top to bottom. He'd been very careful to tell me that he had the Lady's permission.

"In centuries past," Marc said, "this was the schoolroom. The English would have called it the nursery."

We were at the top of the house, on the fourth floor. This schoolroom was large, rectangular, whereas most of the rooms in the palazzo were more or less square in shape. A row of tall, arched windows ran along one wall. Sunlight fell through dusty panes in soft golden shafts, gilding low tables and small chairs fuzzy with their own dust. The room was hushed, shrouded in quiet, its generations of little Corellis long gone.

Marc crossed the floor, his steps making footprints. He said, "Come through here. This is the tutor's room. There's an excellent view from the balcony."

As I entered the tutor's room and waited for Marc to open the shutters and then the door to the balcony, I remarked, "You haven't used these rooms for storage, unlike most of the others on this floor."

"True. Of course you know Giorgio and his wife, and Zenia and Rosa, have the rooms on the other side of the stairs."

"Mm-hm," I nodded.

He folded the shutters back and light poured in, making Marc a dark silhouette against a sheet of gold. Dazzled, I caught my breath. He said, "I suppose I haven't touched this space because one always hopes that someday there will be more children. Come, Clea. The balcony is safe. I want you to see this view of the Grand Canal."

I joined Marc on the balcony. The unobstructed view gave one an illusion of being at a great height. Too, there was more of a breeze than I had ever felt from my own balcony outside the Morning Room. The breeze was fresh and cool and held the salty tang of open sea. I breathed deeply of it. My heart beat too fast, my knees were weak, I felt the goofy smile on my face. I fastened my attention on a panorama that might have come out of an art history book, and had to remind myself that I was here, this was not a dream, this was real.

"Venice can't have changed much in the last three or four hundred years," I said. "This looks exactly like one of Canaletto's paintings."

"Yes," said Marc behind me. "From up here Venice seems ageless. Timeless."

I felt him move closer. My insides were liquid, tingling. I called on my intellect—a poor defense, but all I had. I said, "The quality of the light is so remarkable. So...Italian. We don't have light like this at home. Nor, it would seem, do they in England. It must be that Venice, all of Italy, really, is closer to the equator and so the sun's light comes into the atmosphere at a different angle. The very air is golden. Clear, yet soft at the same time..." Marc touched me and I burst into flame. My voice died on my tongue.

His arm went around my waist and pulled me back against him. His long, strong fingers were splayed against my rib cage. I felt as if he were branding me through the thickness of my sweater, as if I might later remove my clothes and find the print of his hand burned into my flesh.

Marc bent his head to whisper in my ear. "I thought I was doomed to spend my life restoring this palazzo when it was, for me, no more than a mausoleum for the still-living...and then I met you on the stairs. You, Clea, are full of light, the kind of light you described—golden, clear, yet soft."

His lips brushed my cheek, the silkiness of his beard lay on the curve of my neck. I closed my eyes, melted by Marc's tenderness and by the heat of my own longing. An inarticulate sound escaped from my throat.

"Have I embarrassed you?" He released me, and I found I could, after all, stand on my own two feet.

"N-not exactly," I stammered, shaking my head. The breeze ruffled my hair and cooled my flaming cheeks. I looked up and met Marc's aquamarine eyes, incredible eyes in an incredible face. He was smiling, but those eyes were smudged underneath with shadows of sleeplessness, and faint lines of tension were etched across his forehead. "Have you been so unhappy?" I asked.

He inclined his head slightly—an admission.

I continued to look at him, thoughtfully, and realized how selfish I had been in withholding myself from him. I had thought only of my own concerns, made no more attempt to get to know this man other than to catalog my bodily responses to him. I had been running from my own desire, not from Marc. A spark of true caring, pure and bright, was ignited in me then and began steadily to grow. Through empathy I felt, though I did not understand, the burden Marc carried for his strange family. I said, thinking aloud, "The first day I came to Venice, I looked at these houses from my boat on the canal and I thought—more than that, I sensed—that their long windows were like eyes. But the eyes, hidden by shutters, did not look out at me. They looked in on themselves, on their own secrets. I think, Marc, that your palazzo has secrets that weight heavily on you."

Marc's fine nostrils flared with a deeply indrawn breath, while his eyes deepened and seemed to open inward, as if he would admit me through them into his soul. But the moment passed. He shoved his hands into his pockets. "You're very perceptive," he said, turning away.

He regained his usual veneer of formality as he closed the door to the balcony and fastened the shutters. "My own rooms are directly below these," he said. "Sometimes I stand on my balcony and look out, and I do see the beauty of Venice. At such times I can believe that the palazzo, and the family name, are worth preserving."

I nodded. "Of course." How could he ever doubt it?

WITH HIS HAND lightly touching my arm or the small of my back, Marc became one-on-one docent of my tour of the Palazzo Corelli. My instruction began on the stairs. "Did you know," he asked, "that grand stairways like this one we are descending were an invention of the Renaissance?"

"Yes, actually, I did. Before that, stairs were always attached to walls, or hidden in between walls. Where were the original stairs of the palazzo?"

"No one knows," Marc shrugged. "My ancestor Giovanni, who built the grand stairway, so completely changed the interior of the house that it is impossible to tell. There are supposed to be two of the other kind, between the walls, but I have never seen them. Servants used them in earlier times, and they were meant to provide secret escape routes in case of war, but as far as I know they were never used for that. Only Napoléon ever conquered Venice, and even then there was no real fighting in the streets and canals."

"The Venetians made a deal with Napoléon," I observed.

"Anyway, I don't know myself where the hidden stairs are. They were closed off, probably because they're unsafe. To move on," with a gentle nudge to the small of my back, Marc indicated the direction he wanted to go, "this floor has been the family's main living quarters for the past two hundred years. The Grand Salon you have already seen, so in the interest of time we'll pass it by today."

"Oh, but—"

"I know," Marc forestalled me with an amused curl of lip and a matching lifted eyebrow, "you'd like to spend some time in there. I remember. The Lady seldom uses the room, and she's glad to have you browse in the Salon as much as you like. Just have Zenia tell Giorgio when you plan to be there. I'm afraid you'll be disappointed, though. There's a lot of old stuff, but nothing valuable. I sold everything of any real quality. I had hoped, you see, to be able to keep the villa." Marc stopped and his hand on my arm stopped me. "Look up at the ceiling."

I did, and uttered a little gasp of awed surprise. The entire ceiling of the square open corridor around the grand staircase was coffered and gilded, in perfect condition. "You did all that? Restored it, I mean?"

"Yes. I had it done. Also plastered the walls. This was the next project after restoring the rooms that are now your apartment. And this..." Marc pushed open a door into a spacious, immaculate room whose main occupants were a heavy, boxy old grand piano and a graceful little harpsichord, "is the Music Room. Seldom used, as you can see. Recent generations of Corellis have not been very musical."

We left the Music Room and alternated between other rooms and the family portraits in the corridor. The smallest portrait was also the oldest. "Ugo," Marc said, "the first Corelli that we know anything about. He was a money-changer and in his lifetime he developed his business into a rudimentary form of present-day banking. He did not, however, loan money. Money-lending was another business entirely, in those times. Ugo began the palazzo, but he died and his son, the first Giovanni, completed the building."

The first Giovanni, whose portrait came next, looked very much like Marc. I commented on the resemblance, and asked if the light color of the eyes were not unusual in an Italian family.

"Not necessarily," Marc explained. "The original inhabitants of the islands that became Venice were not Mediterranean people. They came from the north, from the hills, driven down by barbarians. Light eyes are not so unusual, though my particular color does not seem to crop up very often."

I wanted to tell him how beautiful his eyes were, but I did not. We went on, from room to room and from portrait to portrait. We did not visit his mother's suite, her doors remained firmly closed. Marc's own suite of rooms, which he insisted that I see, comprised a bedroom and a study with an enormous bathroom that was part exercise room in between. His walls were all a mellowed off-white, the ivory shade of old candles. The woodwork had been scrubbed and then oiled to a golden glow. His furniture was contemporary, Italian-made, with clean, elegant lines. Most surprising to me was the carpet, wall-to-wall, so thick it was almost a shag, pale apricot in color—not a shade most men would have chosen but it was perfect, it added warmth and softness.

"My compliments to your decorator," I said. "I like the look of these rooms, even if it is a little surprising to find wall-to-wall carpet in a Venetian palace!"

"Thank you." Marc's eyes sparkled. "I'm no decorator, but I chose everything myself. I confess a weakness for the carpet. I like to go in bare feet, when I'm in the privacy of my own rooms."

I looked down at the floor, at my own feet, and suddenly I wanted to be barefoot, to feel that apricot softness under my toes. I wanted to lie in the big square bathtub with its Jacuzzi bubbles. "To ease the muscles after a workout," he'd said. A vision of how I myself would feel, bare-skinned in that tub with Marc, flitted through my mind and my body began to grow warm and I knew I was about to blush, so I fumbled for words and for the door, for a way out. "Thank you for showing me your place. Now, about the portraits . . ."

I heard Marc's low, intimate chuckle, but he didn't tease me or touch me, to my relief. He resumed his docent's role and I concentrated on the pictures. As art they were unremarkable, but as a family catalog they were fascinating. As I had anticipated, Marc's features appeared over and over, sometimes with the pale eyes, sometimes with dark. Very few portraits were of women; I guessed not all wives rated a place in the family gallery. About one of every four Corellis seemed to be a massive man, and I commented on this.

"Yes," Marc agreed, "it's a family trait, something in the genes. Every now and then the Corellis produce a 'giant.' Mother and Paolo are examples. Mother was not always so, ah, corpulent as she is now. When she was younger she was a strikingly handsome woman, as you'll see when we get to her portrait. Being of unusually large size was, I believe, thought to be an advantage for my ancestors, both male and female."

We reached Eugenia Corelli's portrait and I saw that, even making allowances for the artist's tendency to flatter, before she became obese she had indeed been a handsome woman. I turned to Marc. "Is there no portrait of your father?"

He averted his face, he would not meet my eyes. "No, there isn't. He—he died suddenly. Unexpectedly."

"I'm sorry. I would have liked to see his picture." More, I would have liked to know why someone as beloved as Zenia said the Old Master had been, didn't have a place next to his wife on the wall. Posthumous portraits were not uncommon.

"You would like to see a picture of my father?" Marc looked surprised, and genuinely pleased. He took me by the hand and pulled me along, back to a narrow door tucked into a corner, a door we had bypassed before. Because of its size and location I'd thought it was a closet. "I wasn't going to take you in here—you'll understand why. No one goes in here but me, and I keep it locked." He dropped my hand and fished a ring of keys from his pocket. "This was my father's workshop," he said as he unlocked and pushed open the narrow door.

"Oh!" I said. "I see what you mean." The tiny room was full of clocks, in all stages of repair and disrepair. But they had been there a long time and they were all silent. Otherwise, the room looked as if its inhabitant had just stepped out and would soon return. I looked over my shoulder at Marc, at the gentle sadness on his face, and knew it was this loving son who kept it that way.

"My father was a clock maker before he married Eugenia. After that, of course, he gave up his trade. But he used to bring home broken clocks the way some people bring home stray cats and dogs. He'd tinker with the clocks until he got them working again. Whenever he had too many, which was often, he'd go out on the streets and give them away. I loved to watch him work on the things, and it was fun, too, to go with him and watch him pick out a particular person, a stranger, to give a particular clock to. No one ever refused him, not that I saw."

"You loved him very much," I said softly.

"Yes, I did. There are photographs of him—I put them in here myself." Marc opened drawers in the big desk that took up most of the room. "Here. This is a good one."

The face in the photograph was chubby and sweet, almost cherubic, with salt-and-pepper curls spilling carelessly over the forehead and kind, myopic eyes behind round-lensed glasses. This man could not have looked less like the long-nosed aristocrats in the portraits if he'd tried. "He looks sweet," I said. "and kind. What was his name?"

"Giuseppi. Yes, he was sweet and kind. Everybody loved him. Everybody, that is—" Marc took the photograph from my hands and turned his back to me while he returned it to the drawer "—except my mother. And Paolo."

"Then why did she marry him, if she didn't love him?"

"Because," said Marc enigmatically as he urged me through the door and locked it once more, "she is the Lady."

I kept quiet as long as I could, which was until we reached the next floor down, my own floor. "Is that one of your secrets, Marc? Why your mother married your father? And why is she called the Lady?"

"I don't like to talk about my father," said Marc grimly. He went ahead, opening doors on the opposite side of the second floor from my apartment, and left me to follow. "These are guest rooms," he said, "none too well furnished at the moment, but that doesn't matter since we seldom have guests to fill them. When the family was bigger, aunts and uncles and cousins lived down here. Maybe I ought to make another rental apartment, I don't know."

His refusal to talk about his mother and father had only piqued my curiosity. I tried to think how I might get him to tell me more. I glanced cursorily into the guest rooms, closed doors Marc had opened, and then I ventured, "When you love someone and they die, it's easier if you talk about them. How long ago did your father die?"

"A long time. I was sixteen, and Paolo was twelve." Marc's shapely mouth was pressed into a forbidding line. "We'll go down to the ground floor now."

We went down the final flight of stairs to the hall, with its mosaic-tiled floor, slender columns and curved, painted ceiling. Marc explained, "People used to do their business on the ground floor of their houses. This hall was a money exchange—a bank, if you want to call it that. They would set up long tables, wooden planks on trestles, during the day and at night take them down again."

"I wondered why it was so big and open, what it was used for. I guessed it was some kind of reception hall."

Marc took a small flashlight from his back pocket and directed its beam into the curved vault of the ceiling. Faded and decayed though it was, the colors painted there leaped into life. "The ceiling is a fresco representing the four seasons. Unfortunately, as you see, the damp is near to destroying the ceiling as well as the walls. I have no idea how to stop it, and cannot afford to call in an expert." He switched off the flashlight and pocketed it again. The vast room seemed all the darker without its small, intense beam.

"It's a wonder they could see to count their money," I grumbled, squinting at the gloom.

"I can let in more light," said Marc, and obligingly he opened both sides of the big front door. His footsteps echoed from the tiles as he crossed the expanse of floor to open the back door and the shuttered windows onto the walled garden.

"Oh!" I exclaimed. The change was dramatic. In my mind's eye I saw the hall not as it was now, grayed and cracked and peeling, but as it must have been in Renaissance Venice. I saw people milling about the slender columns, making a hum of conversation amid the clink and golden flash of coins exchanged at long tables, and the painted ceiling vaulting its colors over all. A feast for the senses. My neck ached as I strained upward, trying to make artistic order out of what seemed a tangled mass of vines and leaves and human limbs and faces. The four seasons? That was what Marc had said and he should know, but the more I looked the more it looked to me like an unknown artist's vision of Apocalypse come to the Garden of Eden.

As will happen when one views a huge ceiling for too long, turning and moving this way and that for a better view with head thrown back all the while, I lost my balance. I staggered and cracked my right shoulder sharply against a column. My "Ouch!" was involuntary.

Marc, off with his own thoughts several feet away, turned his head at the sound. "Are you okay, Clea? What happened?"

"Nothing." I rubbed my shoulder, too preoccupied to notice if it hurt or not. Something was odd, something was wrong here, but I didn't know what. I sneaked a furtive look upward, and almost cried out again—not in pain this time, but in alarm. But I bit my lip and held back the cry. I could not possibly have seen what, for a moment, I thought I'd seen: a pair of eyes looking down at me. Real eyes, among the painted ones which peered through the leafy branches and tangled vines all over the ceiling. No. It was just that this ceiling gave me the creeps. And that was not out of the ordinary, not at all. Lots of things in the Palazzo Corelli gave me the creeps. I shrugged and walked over to where Marc was standing.

"Thanks for the tour," I said.

"There's more. Are you game?"

"Game for what?"

"I remembered your fear of the dark. That's why I brought the flashlight. Haven't you ever wondered what's under these houses? Under Venice?"

"Y-you mean," I grasped my aching right shoulder tightly in my left hand, "there's something *under* here?" I didn't like the sound or the feel of that. I preferred my original impression: beautiful Venice, *La Serenissima*, floating magically upon the waters. I didn't want to know that lovely vision was an illusion. I didn't want to think about what might be under this palazzo, under Venice.

"Of course there is." Marc spoke patiently, as if to a child, and began shepherding me again. "All of our buildings rest on huge beams, piles, driven deep through the soil of the original islands until they reached bedrock. So of course there's an underground chamber, what today we call a basement. And here are the steps."

The steps were revealed when Marc pushed on a panel, which looked like part of the wall. "A secret panel," I said doubtfully. My practical, twentieth-century self did not approve of entering dark flights of steps on the other side of secret doors. But Marc beckoned and I didn't want to appear as timid as I felt. Gingerly, I started down. "Maybe, ah, maybe this is one of those hidden stairways you told me about?"

"No," said Marc, ever patient, "these steps go only from the hall to the underground chamber, nowhere else. There's a vault down here, where they kept the money. I inspected it years ago, when I inherited. I guess I was hoping for piles of forgotten gold coins, which were not there. Then I had the vault sealed off."

Down we went, and down. Marc's flashlight didn't illuminate much, but at any rate there was nothing to see. There was plenty to smell, and to feel. The smell was wet and fusty. I felt cold, clammy, and claustrophobic. Don't feel, I told myself, think! I thought about what Marc had said. "You mean the Corelli bankers had their bank vault under the palazzo? And they didn't want anyone to know where they kept the money, so they concealed the door and the steps behind that secret panel."

"Yes. Here we are—careful on that bottom step."

I joined Marc and was glad when his arm went warmly, protectively around me. The "basement" revealed in a sweep of flashlight beam, seemed as vast as the hall above. Where that had slender columns, this had huge beams faced in brick, and row on row of curved brick arches. I let out a sigh of relief. Everything seemed solid and substantial, more than strong enough to hold the weight of the great house above.

My relief was only momentary. Marc began to walk forward, but I hung back. I wished I were somewhere else. I sensed a presence somewhere in the surrounding darkness—and it was not the rats whose rustling, scurrying sound would have been easy to identify even without the occasional telltale squeaks. I thought of the real eyes that had seemed to peer from the hall's painted ceiling; I remembered the night I'd been so sure I was followed through the streets. This felt the same.

"Wait!" I whispered, urging Marc to a standstill. For an instant I heard a rhythmic, breathing sound, amplified by the arches above. Then it stopped and I heard nothing, not even the rats' rustle. Nevertheless, I whispered again, "We're not alone down here, Marc. Someone else is here. I . . . I feel someone's presence. Don't you?"

"That's impossible, Clea," said Marc, his normal tone of voice loud in the huge, hushed underground chamber. To satisfy my fears he played his flashlight beam full-circle around us. "There is nothing here but rats, and they won't bother us. You aren't afraid of rats, are you?"

"No, I'm not afraid of rats," I murmured. But I was not reassured, and I shivered.

Marc's arm tightened around me. He said, "Your imagination is working overtime again, that's all. I was going to show you the old vault, but perhaps we'd better skip it. I know you're cold, I can feel you shivering. We'll go up and sit in the garden, in the sunshine, and I'll tell you the rest."

"I vote for that!" I said heartily. If I never saw this basement again, it would be fine with me!

In the garden we sat side by side on the stone bench and I turned my face gratefully up to the sun. The breeze in my hair felt wonderful. Marc stretched his arms over his head and expelled a long breath.

"Thank you," he said, looking over at me with a smile on his lips and in his eyes, "for letting me take you through the house. Now you have some idea what it's like to try to maintain one of these old places."

"Yes. It was an honor, Marc. I should be the one to thank you for showing me your home." I was beginning to understand how seriously Marc took his family responsibilities. The tour of the palazzo, the smattering of family history, the heritage evident in the portraits, all this made me realize how Marc must feel. This one, lone, striking and often solemn man was the last of the Corellis. It all came down to him. I felt honored that he would share any part of his burden with me.

"*Carissima*," he said huskily, reaching out to tangle his hand in my curls, "what are you thinking, to make you look at me that way?"

"I was thinking that it can't be easy to be Marcantonio Corelli. In a very real way, you have the weight of centuries on your shoulders."

"You do understand!" he exclaimed softly, wonderingly, as if that were a miracle.

I smiled; I wanted to touch him, so I closed my fingers over his hand, which rested on his knee, the hand that recently had been in my hair. "I think I do, a little. Your brother is illegitimate and for some reason you don't trust him, so he can't help you. Your mother is, well, I guess she lives in a world of her own, somewhat removed from reality, so she can't help, either. You loved your father, but he died when you were very young to have to take on all this. No wonder at times you seem so remote, formal, proud—that distant manner is the armor that enables you to stand alone."

"God sent you to my house, to me," Marc said, the look of wonder still on his face. Hesitantly, as if I might break or dissolve into the air, he brought his face to mine. His pale eyes seemed to plead with me—don't break! don't disappear! And then his gaze went to my lips, and his own mouth softened, opened.

I hung on that moment, my heart beating fast, faster, waiting for his kiss. His mouth closed over mine softly, in a long, gentle, almost reverent kiss.

When we parted, Marc said, "Thank you, Clea. From the first, I knew you were different. Other women have not..." He turned his head away and a faint red flush appeared along his cheekbones. "I beg your pardon. It's unspeakably rude of me to mention other women; nevertheless it is true that no one has understood the way you do. They see the palazzo as a prize and me, the last male Corelli, as—I don't know what they really do see, but not the person I am underneath the appearance. Oh, Clea...!" He seized my hands and held them tightly, a look of such love and longing on his face that it took my breath away.

I remained silent, with my heart in my throat. I did not want him to say that he loved me, and yet I did; I did not want to hear from him words of commitment, yet I already felt my own commitment to Marcantonio Corelli growing, a steady, strong conviction in my breast. It's too soon, too soon, I thought. Just as my old fear of intimacy was about to rise up between us, making me want to snatch my hands away, Marc released his hold.

A faraway look had come into his eyes. He gazed not at me, but beyond me, as he spoke. "You asked why my mother is called the Lady. Why she married my father if she did not love him. My father himself told me, not long before he, ah, died."

This was a memory evidently too painful for Marc to sit still. He continued to talk, but left my side and paced restlessly as he spoke. "My family were nobles, they had bought their way into the Book of Gold by the fourteenth century. But the Corelli name was struck from the Book in Napoléon's time, they say because that particular Corelli—whom, by the way, I strongly resemble—would not agree with the others of the council to accede to Napoléon's demands and let him bring his ships into the lagoon. That was not so long ago, less than two hundred years. The family's prosperity did not suffer, they simply returned to banking and, in fact, were probably better off for it. But my mother, even as a small child, wanted the title that otherwise would have been hers. She was an only child, born to her parents late in life, and she knew she would inherit. In Venice, a woman could have the title if there were no direct male descendents, and there was none. Eugenia Corelli wanted to be *La Duchessa*; since she could not she decreed that she would within her own household be called the Lady instead. She was also determined that the Corelli name should not die. You have, perhaps, heard of Archangelo Corelli, a musician, a contemporary of Vivaldi?''

"Yes," I nodded, "I have."

"Like most musicians, Archangelo was poor. His branch of the family eventually left Venice and settled in Verona. Their relationship to the Venetian Corellis is distant, something like third cousins. I think the truth is that my mother would have preferred never to marry. But she wanted to keep the Venetian dynasty going and she knew of the Verona Corellis, so she went to Verona and found my father. He was an unmarried male named Corelli, which was all that mattered to her.''

Marc stopped in front of me, rubbing the back of his neck. He was deep, deep in his own thoughts, his own conflicts. "There are wedding pictures, I saw them once. The Lady is majestic, quite beautiful in an overwhelming way. My father was half a head shorter, not a match for her in size or temperament, but he was grinning like an idiot. I think he loved her, even though he knew she didn't love him. And he would have been happy enough, he probably was happy until Paolo came along.... ''

Marc wandered away abstractedly, to stand at the wall with his back to me. When he neither turned nor spoke, I went and stood behind him, laying my cheek on his broad shoulder blade. Marc did turn then, his arms went around me and pressed my cheek to his chest. I heard his heart beat, felt his suppressed emotion and could not tell if it was sadness, or anger.

I raised my head. I inquired tentatively, "Because Paolo was not his child . . . ?"

Marc looked down at me. He spoke softly, with great control. "Papa—he liked me to call him Papa when we were alone—Papa would have loved any child, his own or not. But Paolo was . . . difficult. That is another story for another day, Clea." He moved me away from him and looked at his watch. "I have to go, I have other things I must do today. I'll walk upstairs with you."

As we neared the top of the stairs, I realized that I felt differently about the palazzo now. It was less a mystery, more a home with a long history, and I told Marc this.

We stopped at my door and Marc leaned his arms against the door frame, capturing me within. He said, "Clea, I'm sorry to have to tell you this: I have to go away for a few days. A business trip."

"I'm sorry you have to be away," I breathed. "I hope your trip goes well."

"So do I." His face was very close to mine. "I'm glad I got to spend so much of this day with you. Will you miss me, *carissima*, while I am gone?"

"Yes," I whispered. My lips trembled at his nearness, and I caught my lower lip in my teeth. I cast down my eyes.

"What a woman-child you are," Marc murmured. "I cannot believe you have children of your own. Nor can I bear to leave you, Clea, *mia cara*, but I must."

When he kissed me, as I knew he would, suddenly I could not bear to let him go. A surge of emotion such as I had not felt in years swept over me and I clung to Marc. I returned his kiss with such passion that I felt embarrassed later, after he was gone.

Chapter Seven

It was the first of November, and it was raining. When I looked out of my window it looked as if God, or Mother Nature, had shrouded Venice in a gray veil. I felt dull and depressed, and more than a little unsteady on my feet. Perhaps I was coming down with a virus. Or perhaps I'd had the dream again and just didn't remember—I certainly didn't feel as if I'd slept very well.

I felt lousy and the weather was lousy, and Marc had been gone four days. Altogether a lousy situation, but never mind. I'd feel better after a cup of coffee; I always did. I ignored the blue flannel bathrobe I'd left at the foot of my bed the night before, and rummaged through the wardrobe for my yellow terrycloth one. A day like this definitely needed a bright yellow pick-me-up!

Zenia was in the kitchen. Her bright face and black-button eyes were more than I could bear this morning. I mumbled a greeting and accepted a glass of orange juice, and then I had an inspiration: I sent her to tell Giorgio that I would be spending the morning in the Grand Salon, and I told her to go on and do her marketing after that.

I sighed with relief when she was gone. Not that I didn't like Zenia, but that I liked being alone better. Especially in the morning. Zenia was a wonderful cook—of everything except breakfast. She either could not or would not learn to make coffee my way, nor would she give me the simple breakfast of toast and fruit that I preferred. I stumbled around the kitchen, more groggy than I'd realized and glad she was not here to see me so clumsy.

At last I had the coffee made and leaned against the counter while I drank the first cup. Then I took my toast and a second cup of coffee to the Morning Room, thinking with satisfaction that all I had needed was the coffee. I felt better already. I opened the shutters and sat at the table, looking out on the gray day. November 1, All Saints' Day.

I thought about the night before, the Eve of All Saints—Halloween, to me. There had been a street carnival and Maria Bonavita had persuaded me to go with her. I might have enjoyed the carnival in different company, I reflected. Immediately I regretted the thought and chided myself for being so uncharitable. Maria was just a little old lady, she couldn't help being set in her ways.

I drank more coffee and thought some more. Zenia had told me, rather shyly, that all the native Venetians would turn out for the carnival on All Saints' Eve, because what they were really celebrating was the end of the tourist season. I had wanted to see this, Venice reclaimed by the Venetians. Some people wore costumes, everyone wore masks—even Maria, though the elaborate white cat's head provided by her hotel looked ridiculous with her royal blue polyester suit and sensible shoes.

I wore all black, a long black wrap skirt and a black turtleneck top, and I bought my mask from a street vender. It was a wonderful multicolored fantasy, half bird and all fairy-tale, it covered all of my face except my mouth and chin, and it had a beak encrusted with silver sparkles. Watching the other people had been fun, but it would have been more fun without Maria's constant critical comments. Nor did she like the gondola races, which I thought were wonderful; if she could have been quiet I might have been able to imagine what such races had been like hundreds of years past.

Be honest, I said to myself. What was really wrong was that I wanted to be with Marc. With Marc I would have danced, like the others, in the streets. With Marc I would have stayed out until midnight to watch the fireworks fired from the Lido out over the lagoon. I would have done the same, I realized, if I had gone with my student friends from the Accademia. Instead, I had gone with Maria, I hadn't danced, and I had come home early.

The coffee had made me clearheaded and I asked myself, why had I done that, why had I gone to the carnival with Maria Bonavita? Because she had asked me, and I felt sorry for her. Because she was elderly, and an American, and she seemed so lonely and out of place. But if she felt lonely and out of place, then why did she stay here? There was nothing to keep her in Venice, she didn't even *like* Venice, so why didn't she go home to good old New Jersey?

I shook my head. When would I ever learn? There was no reason for me to feel sorry for Maria Bonavita. She was probably no different in New Jersey than she was in Venice; nor would she be different in Paris or London or Athens—all places I had not yet seen and would like very much to see some day. Maria Bonavita was mean-spirited, that was her problem, and it became my problem whenever I was with her. In the Piazza San Marco she didn't see the splendid symmetry of the arcades or the glory of the basilica, she saw pigeon droppings. I could imagine her standing between the paws of the Sphinx and seeing nothing but camel dung in the shadows of the Great Pyramid. No doubt she would be able to stand before the rose window of the magnificent Cathedral of Notre Dame in Paris and snarl at the street children, just as she did here: "Get away from me, you dirty little thief!" While I, just as soon as she had turned her back, would give them pennies to buy ice-cream cones.

Was Maria as critical of me as I was, at this moment, being of her? You bet she was. She watched me like a hawk,

I was sure of it. So why in the world did I continue to spend time with someone like that?

She's old, said my persistent conscience, she deserves respect. I don't want to hurt her feelings by refusing her.

I examined this declaration from my conscience and found it to be true. I just didn't have it in me to break off my acquaintance with her. I might be able to turn aside an occasional invitation, just as I was able sometimes to avoid her, if I saw her coming before she saw me. But for better or worse, I did feel sorry for her and nothing was going to change that, so I might just as well stop ruminating about it.

One of these days, though, I thought as I was getting dressed, I would tell Zenia that I didn't want her to come to my apartment before ten o'clock in the mornings. I would tell her that I could get myself up and get my own breakfast, and that I preferred to do so. Not today—I didn't like to hurt Zenia's feelings, either. But I would do it soon.

I put on brown wool slacks and a rust-red cashmere sweater, and used the tortoise shell band to hold my hair back off my face. The curls were getting long, I needed another haircut. I looked critically at myself in the mirror. I was pale, too pale. The disturbed sleep was telling on my face. A little blusher would fix that. I brushed it on my cheekbones and flicked a dab under the thumbprint indentation in my chin. A wave of dizziness washed over me unexpectedly and I swayed on the dressing-table bench. If I'd been standing, I would have fallen.

"What is wrong with me?" I said aloud. "Maybe I really am getting sick," I mumbled. My face in the mirror looked all eyes, and the eyes were scared. I turned my head away, got up carefully, and held onto the bedpost while I slipped into my shoes. If I was coming down with something, it had been on the way for quite some time. This morning was the worst I'd been, but most mornings I felt groggy and dizzy and uncoordinated until I got going. An illness that I could succumb to and then have it over and done with would be a relief. Perhaps that would happen. Then again, perhaps it wouldn't. Perhaps as long as I lived in the Palazzo Corelli I would have those bad dreams, so that my nights were disturbed and I would end up sleeping unusually heavily toward morning, as one does after a disturbed night. Maybe I did need Zenia to wake me, after all. With a chill I realized that I hadn't awakened without her calling me in so long that I wasn't sure when was the last time I had awakened on my own. That wasn't normal, that wasn't healthy.

I climbed the stairs on my way to the third floor, the family quarters and my destination, the Grand Salon. At the top of the flight I stopped for a moment, and looked at the portraits, which stared back at me. Why did I assume that the bad dreams that disturbed my nights were somehow connected with this palazzo, that they would go away when I no longer lived here? I walked up to one of the pictures, which resembled Marc, and studied the face, looking for reassurance in the image of one who, if he were here, would reassure me. I realized that I wanted to tell Marc about the bad nights, about the strange recurring dream that there was someone or something in the room with me. I wanted to ask him if there had ever been stories about the palazzo being haunted. But that was ridiculous, I wouldn't dare!

Marc's ancestor had the same sensual mouth—his curving lips seemed to smile at me with a sort of knowing derision. If I told Marc about the bad dreams, he would want to know more, would want to know if there was anything in my life other than his wonderful old house that could cause me to rest uneasy. And of course there was. There was the possibility that I had caused my own husband's death. There was that anonymous note, which still hung heavy, heavy over my head even though so many months had passed. No, I couldn't say anything to Marc.

This will pass, I said to myself. I squared my shoulders and with a little nod of my head to the ancestor, I went down the corridor to the Grand Salon.

The double doors stood open. I went through them, and wondered if I should close them behind me. It occurred to me then that someone else might be in here. I took a few steps, adjusted my eyes to the impressive length of the room and the rich clutter which assaulted all my senses.

"Hello?" I called out. My voice sounded small in this huge place. No one answered, and I didn't see anyone. I decided that I would prefer a little privacy for my perusings, and went back to close the doors. They were huge, more than twice my own height, but in spite of that they swung easily on well-oiled hinges and closed with a click that sounded rather final. Nerves! I thought, silly me. What I ought to be remarking is that these big doors are so much easier to handle than my own!

I took my notebook from under my arm and a pencil from the pocket of my slacks, and went to work. I didn't want to feel like a voyeur, and yet I wasn't at all sure what I would find here in the Corellis' Grand Salon, or what there would be to make notes on. For the sake of proceeding in an orderly fashion, I marched down the whole length of the Persian rug and started by examining the fireplace at the far end of the room. Renaissance, I decided. In truth, it was remarkable for its size rather than its beauty, and there was quite a draft standing in front of it. I soon moved on, and in no time at all had lost myself in all the treasures that Marc had called "junk."

My own ignorance was a handicap, but nevertheless I was fascinated. Especially by the ornamental glass, which was clustered on a long table in front of a huge gilt-framed mirror. I recalled reading that Louis XIV had caused an international scandal of sorts when he hired Venetians to make the mirrors for Versailles—they weren't supposed to make the mirrors outside of Venice, but had been unable to resist the money he offered. I wondered if this mirror might be of the same period. The decorative work on the frame looked as if it might be.

I began to sketch objects that interested me and of whose origins I was uncertain. Many of them had to have come from elsewhere, not Venice; which was natural, since the Venetian Republic had made much of its great fortune through trade with the East. Marco Polo, I thought . . . and moved on through the huge room.

I had no awareness of time. I hadn't worn a watch and oddly enough there were no clocks whatever in the Grand Salon. Perhaps it wasn't so odd—this was after all the Lady's domain, and clocks probably reminded her of the husband she hadn't loved. I didn't care about the passing time, I was far too occupied with my discoveries. I had just regretfully closed a book of seventeenth-century maps, thinking that I could examine it more closely another time, when a small flash of gold caught my eye. It must have been the angle of light through the window and the exact tilt of my head, for when I looked and tried to find the golden object, I could not. But I remembered the general area from which the flash had come. I was curious, because Marc had so clearly said that he had sold everything of value.

In our guts we all know that gold is intrinsically of value. I think that is what drove me to search for the source of the flash of gold. I found it by instinct or blind luck: not that it was hidden, but that the exquisite little thing was far back on a shelf of what the French call an étagère, mixed in with a motley collection of bric-a-brac.

The gold object was a small salt cellar, delicately, cunningly carved and molded in the shape of a cherub whose wings enfolded a tiny bowl lined with cobalt glass. Surely this was real gold? I reached carefully among the other things and picked up the salt cellar. It fit perfectly in the palm of my hand. On close inspection its perfection increased. I had never seen more beautiful work. It couldn't be Cellini; if it were, it would be worth a small fortune. Even if it had been done by one of Cellini's pupils, it might still be quite valuable. Perhaps Marc didn't know what he had here!

I was in the process of turning the salt cellar over in my hand to look for the craftsman's mark underneath, when I felt suddenly alert. I wasn't sure if I heard a sound, or what, but instinctively, feeling unaccountably furtive, I replaced the gold salt cellar on the shelf exactly where I had found it. I backed off a couple of steps, my ears straining, and still I heard nothing. I glanced toward the double doors, which remained firmly closed.

Me and my big imagination, I thought. But I left the possibly priceless gold object where it was, and turned to a new page in my notebook. I would sketch it, I decided. Then I could do a little research before I said anything to Marc. There was no point getting his hopes up if the thing turned out to have no value. I sketched quickly from memory.

The double doors of the Grand Salon swung open soundlessly on their well-oiled, well-balanced hinges. I heard nothing, but a sixth sense warned me that I was no longer alone in the room. I felt a prickling on the back of my neck, which was so uncomfortable that I looked up, even as I told myself there was no one there. But this time, there *was* someone there, and I gasped involuntarily and almost dropped my notebook.

"P-Paolo?" My voice quavered. It had to be Paolo, I was sure even though the man was some distance away. He was so big, a giant, and though I knew him, still I was frightened.

"What are you doing here?" Paolo asked sharply.

"I have permission," I replied, drawing myself up to my full, if relatively insignificant, height.

"Whose permission?" Paolo strode angrily down the rug toward me. "Marc's?"

"No, Eugenia's. She said that I could look around in here any time I want." I sounded and felt defensive. "I'm an art-history student, you know. This is a wonderful opportunity for me to study a family collection."

Paolo had reached me and now he loomed close, too close. I stepped back and tucked my notebook under my arm. "Not much of a collection," he sneered. But his eyes darted this way and that, as if he were trying to assess what I had seen.

I took courage, feeling that I had been silly to let Paolo frighten me. After all, I had more right than he to be here. "That's what Marc said," I concurred, "but to me, it's fascinating. I didn't realize how ignorant I am of all but the broadest categories of art. There are so many different things in this room and all of them—well, to be honest I guess I should say most of them—seem wonderful to me."

"Uh," Paolo grunted. "What's that you've got there?" He reached for the notebook under my arm, but I shied away and took it firmly in both hands. I didn't know why, perhaps it was just my normal possessiveness of my notes, but I had no intention of letting Paolo look at my notes or sketches.

"It's just a notebook—" I tossed my head "—you know, student stuff. Nothing interesting, just things I write to remind myself. I have a good eye, but a horrible memory." That wasn't true; the truth is that I have an unusually good memory for visual detail. But I didn't like the way Paolo was looking at me, with his eyebrows narrowed and that steely glint, which turned his blue eyes to a cruel gray. He seemed to place too much importance on my presence in the Grand Salon, and I didn't want to call any further attention to myself. I only wanted to get away. "I was about to leave anyhow. It's getting late and I have an appointment."

"Uh." Paolo made that indeterminate grunt again. But he gave way when I moved resolutely, and allowed me to walk past him. From the corner of my eye I saw him scan the room again, and then with a couple of strides of his huge legs he fell into step beside me. He asked, "You have a lunch appointment?"

I had no appointment and no idea what time it was, but to this man I lied without compunction. "Yes."

"Too bad. I was going to invite you to have lunch with me and the Lady."

I stopped and looked up at him. He could change moods like a chameleon. Now he was friendly, beaming, and he looked so harmless that I had to wonder why he seemed so threatening before. "That's why you're here, to have lunch with your mother?"

Paolo winked. "I told you before, I come when I like. Of course, right now it's no problem because big brother is away again."

"He's away on business," I remarked, and then bit my tongue. I wished I had kept my mouth shut. I didn't want Paolo to know how well I was getting to know his brother.

"Yeah," Paolo grinned. "I hear his business isn't doing too well these days. He's likely to be away a lot. Too bad, too bad!"

We reached the doors, and my curiosity got the better of me. "Is that just wishful thinking, Paolo, or do you know for a fact that Marc's business isn't doing well?"

Paolo gestured me through the doors. "You'd be surprised what I know, Clea Beaumont." He turned and closed the doors behind us. I waited, sensing that he would say more, and he did. He bent over me and before I could move away he took my chin firmly in his big hand. "I have a lot of contacts, a lot of important contacts. It's a fact that Marcantonio-the-heir Corelli isn't doing too well these days."

I felt my cheeks color. I blinked at Paolo, but I wouldn't back away, I wouldn't give him the satisfaction. "I don't understand why you two brothers can't resolve your silly quarrel," I said. "It would surely be so much better for everyone, especially your mother."

"Never." Paolo brought his face closer to mine. His expression was intense, compelling. "Break your lunch date. Eat with me and the Lady. Forget Marc."

"I can't." I kept my voice firm. "Some other time, perhaps."

"Okay." He let go of my chin, and I resisted an almost irresistible need to rub it, to rub away the feel of his fingers. He repeated, "Okay, but we'll do it some other time. I'll tell the Lady, and I'm going to hold you to it, Clea!"

"Ah, sure!" I backed away, annoyed with myself. I'd been making excuses to get myself out of what felt like a tight spot, and instead it seemed I was only getting in tighter. Now, when the invitation came, I wouldn't dare refuse.

DURING THE NIGHT a storm broke, the first of the winter season. It was a thunderstorm, which woke me with its ominous booming. I heard also the howling, thrashing wind. The entire palazzo seemed to moan in protest. I pulled the covers over my head, but was unable to get back to sleep. You would think, for a person with my reputation for timidity, that I would have been frightened by thunderstorms, but the opposite was true. A great storm has always held fascination for me. So, when I found myself wide awake and counting the seconds between the booms and the flashes of lightning, I got out of bed and went to my window. I opened the shutters and was greeted by a fresh, windy invasion. There was not much to see, but I stood there for a while anyway, enjoying the wind and the sound of the rain as it rushed down over the rooftops. I looked down into the dark garden below. Pan was getting very wet, I knew, but I couldn't see him. I decided to go to the Morning Room where I could look out over the canal.

In contrast with the relatively dark streets, the canal was well lit by large globes on tall standards outside of every house and public building. The Grand Canal was like a surging, living beast. Boats rocked dangerously at their moorings. The wind whipped my nightgown about me and flung the rain in my face. I got quite wet but I was too excited to care. In stark, white flashes of lightning I could see all the way across to Giudecca, and beyond to the lagoon itself. The waters were dark, roiling, white-capped. I stood watching until at last I became too cold to continue, and then I closed the shutters, went back to my room, and changed into a dry gown. I went back to sleep feeling warm and cozy, with the sound of the receding storm lulling me like a baby.

I awoke ahead of Zenia's call. To my surprise, when I looked at the battery-powered travel alarm by my bed, it was only seven-thirty. I didn't think to be surprised by my clearheadedness or the alacrity with which I sprang from the bed; I thought only that last night's storm surely must have produced the *acqua alta* about which I had heard so much, and I wanted to see. I supposed I shouldn't go downstairs in my bathrobe, though no one was likely to be around at this hour. I pulled on gray sweatpants and sweatshirt, crammed my feet into sneakers without socks, splashed my face with cold water and gave my hair a quick, hard brushing, and ran for the stairway. Zenia hadn't been anywhere in my apartment—it was too early even for her.

I paused on the landing to turn on the balustrade lights, then went down the stairs carefully, curiously. At the stair's turning I looked down into the reception hall. Someone had been up before me, and with the same thought; Giorgio, probably. The mosaic floor was indeed covered with water, I couldn't tell how deep. Giorgio had been ready, though— he had placed wooden planks on some kind of supports from the bottom of the stairs to both back and front doors. I felt awkward, strange, as I walked upon the planks to the back door, opened it, and saw that the planks continued through the garden. I walked the whole of the way to the gate, feeling like a child doing a balancing act even though the plank was more than wide enough for my feet. It was the strangeness of it which made me feel that way.

On my progress through the garden I noticed that the invading water became shallower. I had not realized it, but the garden and the street behind the palazzo were on almost imperceptibly higher ground. It was, apparently, enough higher to make a difference, for the planks ended at the gate and in the street beyond, there were no platforms for people to walk upon. A family, man, woman and child, sloshed by through two inches of water, wearing knee-high rubber boots, the kind the British call Wellingtons. They saw me at the gate and waved to me cheerfully, and I waved back. Apparently this family did not find the *acqua alta* daunting in the least.

Zenia was not yet in the kitchen when I got back upstairs, and I hummed to myself as I made coffee and put bread into the toaster. When she arrived I was in the Morning Room with my toast and coffee and a big orange I intended to peel and eat after I finished the toast. She brought the newspaper, as she always did, and said as she handed it to me, "Good morning, *Signora* Beaumont. You are up so early. I hope everything is all right? There is nothing wrong, that you should be up so early?"

"No, nothing is wrong," I replied. "On the contrary, I feel better than I have in, I don't know, days. I was excited by the storm, I wanted to see what the high waters had done, so I jumped out of bed as soon as I awoke."

She looked at my toast and my orange critically. "You should let me fix you a better breakfast, *signora*. After all, you were not here for dinner last night, and you never eat lunch here. I begin to think that you do not like my cooking, *signora*."

I had noticed before that if Zenia was a little annoyed with me, or anxious about her own performance, she would not call me Clea but reverted to formality. Usually I pointed this out to her teasingly, but this time I did not. She acted not so much anxious as petulant, which surprised me. I had never seen her act that way before, and I didn't like it.

I tried to be friendly but firm as I said, "You must not be so sensitive, Zenia. I do like your cooking, but you must realize that I like to have dinner out occasionally. Last night I simply didn't want to stay home and watch more television. I get tired of game shows, and for me the novelty of 'I Love Lucy' reruns in Italian wears thin after a while, so I went to dinner and a movie. Believe me, none of that is any reflection on your cooking!"

Zenia hung her head; she didn't respond to my faint attempt at humor, though she and I had often joked over the quality of local television. I reminded myself that she was little more than a child, younger than either of my own children. I said, "Zenia, please sit down here at the table with me for a moment," and I waited until she had done so. "Since it already appears I've hit a sensitive spot with you, I'm going to go on and tell you something that I know you won't quite like, but I hope you'll try to understand."

Zenia's head came up; there was a flash of alarm in her eyes, which seemed to me all out of proportion to what was going on here, but I persisted. "Zenia, I would be much happier if you could start your day with me a couple of hours later. You usually come at, what? about eight o'clock?" she nodded, the black eyes wary. I went on. "Then let's say that from now on you'll come at ten, instead. You see, I really do like to be on my own in the mornings. I just can't get used to having you here so early, and I do prefer to get my own breakfast."

Her protest was immediate, and strong. "No, *signora*! I, I can't do that. *Signor*—I mean, the Lady would be so angry with me, she would think I displease you, I would be in trouble!"

"I can tell her myself, if you like, what a wonderful cook you are and that it's me, it's my problem that I like to be alone in the mornings."

"No, please, no!" This idea seemed to alarm her even more. "Please do not say anything to the Lady! I—I will do as you say, b-but it will be so, it will seem so wrong. What am I to do for those hours, when everyone in the house will be working except me?"

Although I didn't understand it, I saw that Zenia's distress was real. I would have thought that she would be happy to have a couple of hours to herself, in which she could do anything she pleased. I felt like twelve kinds of bad guy when I noticed that there were tears in the corners of her eyes.

Desperately I cast through my mind for a solution and fortunately, one came. I remembered that Giorgio was majordomo, the Italian equivalent of a butler. I suggested, "I will have a word with Giorgio. I'll tell him that I'm just an eccentric old American woman who likes to start the day by herself. Perhaps we could make it a part of your routine to do the shopping first thing in the morning, and if there is extra time you could shop for Giorgio and his wife, too. I should think she would be glad of an extra hand."

"Well . . . maybe that would be all right. Giorgio isn't so bad, he would probably understand." With the resilience of youth, Zenia brightened. "And it is true that I would like to do the shopping for the entire household. That would be a big responsibility, and my sister Rosa would be jealous. Yes, Clea, I think that will be okay!"

"Good." Inwardly I sighed with relief. "Then it's settled."

"Yes." Zenia stood up and paused to look once more at my small breakfast, which I had just begun to eat when she came in. She said with a degree of satisfaction, "Your toast is cold. Shall I make more?"

"Thank you, that would be nice."

When Zenia put a fresh plate of toast before me, she lingered. "There is just one thing, Clea."

"Mm." I looked up from the newspaper. "What is it?"

"I do hope you won't eat dinner out too often. You see, what I really want is to learn to be a cook, a really good cook. I do not want to be just a maid all my life. So you will try not to eat dinner out too often, please? So that I will not get out of practice?"

Her tone was exactly that of a pleading child, and I smiled indulgently at her. "I promise you I will eat dinner here almost every night. I'm not going to go out in the evening that often, you may be sure of it."

I sought out Giorgio before leaving the palazzo that morning, told him what I had decided with Zenia, and found him both agreeable and easy to talk to. So I lingered and chatted about last night's storm and the high water. He said this was nothing, a small storm only. Much worse ones would come later. He looked pointedly at my feet in the high leather boots I had bought a couple of months before. He said, "If I may make a suggestion to the *signora*, it would be best to have rubber boots. When there is only a little water we do not put the platforms out on all the streets, but even an inch of water will ruin those boots."

"Alas, Giorgio," I agreed, "I'm sure you're right, but I don't have any rubber boots. Can you suggest where I might buy some?"

He smiled, and with a lift of his chin and a twist of his shoulders, became the gallant gentleman that is possible for any Italian male of any age or station to be. "If you will permit, I will take you in the boat to the very place, and there will be no need to get your feet wet until you have the proper kind of boots for water!"

I accepted gladly, took leave of him long enough to don my dawn-colored wool cape, and we set out. Along the way I learned much more about the *acqua alta*.

"It gets worse every year, *signora*. Perhaps these new machines they are building will help, but—" his shrug was eloquent with skepticism.

"You mean the project they call MOSE, the dikes that will lie on the floor of the lagoon until they raise them up."

"Yes, that is it. *Signor* Marc is a member of the consortium, but even so, I cannot think but that we have tampered for too long with the lagoon. Perhaps we are doomed."

"Oh, Giorgio, surely not! But I didn't know Marc was part of the New Venice Consortium. That's rather exciting, and good for the family, don't you think?"

Giorgio did not comment, once again his shrug was eloquent.

"There is something I don't understand, Giorgio," I said, "perhaps you could explain it to me. I heard that Venice is no longer sinking."

"That is true."

"So what I don't understand is, if Venice is no longer sinking, why is there more frequent high water than there was in the past? It doesn't make sense."

"Some say the oceans of the world are getting higher all the time, so the tides are higher. Others say that when the big corporations came after the War, the World War Two, and dredged channels in the lagoon, that made it so that the tides do not come in and go out the way they used to. I do not understand either, *signora*. If you ask the Young Master I am sure he will explain better than I. I am just a servant, getting old, but I remember when I was a boy these canals were not so filthy, the tides washed them clean every day, and we did not have the water coming into the houses so much, or into the streets and the Piazza San Marco." He shook his head sadly. "I may be ignorant, but still I fear that Venice is doomed. I will never see the Venice I once knew, never again. And many of us feel the same."

It was a sobering thought, and one that Giorgio obviously believed. I couldn't think of a response, and I looked into the canal beneath our boat. The high water was receding now, and taking with it a lot of trash even here, on the Grand Canal.

"Ah," Giorgio smiled, his gallantry returning, "but I should not say such sad things to a pretty lady. The sky clears above, you see? It will be a fine day, and here is the place where you can buy the rubber boots to protect your feet. Shall I wait for you, *signora*, and take you back to the Palazzo Corelli?"

"No, thank you. You've been a great help, and informative, too. When I have my new boots I'll go on to the Accademia. And Giorgio, thank you for being so understanding about Zenia. I know how anxious she is to do her job well. My way of doing things isn't what she is used to, and I'm sure that makes it difficult for someone as conscientious as she is."

"Do not trouble yourself over Zenia, *Signora* Beaumont," said Giorgio, his generous mouth set in a firm line.

"She will always land on her own two feet, like a cat. Zenia is not at all like her sister Rosa."

I wondered for a while afterward what he had meant by that enigmatic remark. Was Zenia perhaps not the innocent child I thought her? Well, if she wasn't, so much the better for her, I supposed.

I bought my boots and went on about my business at the library. Later, when I was on my way back to the Palazzo Corelli, I thought what a good day I'd had, how much better I'd felt all day long. I decided I must have had a lingering, low-level virus and shaken it at last. It did not occur to me, not then, that my good day had followed a day and a night in which I had eaten none of Zenia's cooking.

Chapter Eight

It was hard to do, but I did it. I was tired of being nice and considerate of people who didn't care one iota how I felt; and besides, there was something about these two Corellis together in the same room, towering over me, that had the opposite effect of intimidation—it made me a fighter. I took a deep breath and said, "No, Mrs. Corelli, I mean Eugenia, I don't think I'll be coming to lunch with you and Paolo again. At least, not unless Marc is here also."

Eugenia looked at Paolo, and her eyes widened in an expression that was almost a parody of disbelief. I was sure I had offended her; nevertheless I lifted my chin higher.

"What do you mean?" she asked.

Paolo bent nearer to me, with a smile that was both dazzling and cunning. "You don't seem to understand, Clea. My mother has just made you the most exceptional offer. She wants to show you her own private collection. It is so private that only I have seen it. Marc doesn't even know these treasures exist!"

I wavered. I reached for my wineglass and took a sip, too late remembering I had decided not to drink anymore because I didn't like the taste of this wine. Clearing my throat I suggested, "Perhaps I could see the collection now, since I'm already here? I'm really uncomfortable doing this behind Marc's back."

Eugenia Corelli narrowed her eyes; they glittered, almost lost in the expanse of her face. "No, not today. I am tired now." She raised a beringed hand dramatically to her forehead.

Paolo leaned back in his chair and stared at me. Several times during this luncheon he had made remarks, which suggested that he himself was interested in me, and that he had told his mother so. Now that I had brought Marc into the conversation, Paolo must be wondering about my relationship with his half brother, wanting me to say more.

I decided to oblige him. "Please understand, both of you, that I'm grateful for your hospitality and all you've already done, and I truly would feel honored to see the private collection. But..." I hesitated, unsure how to find the right words. I took a quick breath and went on. "Your, ah, family dynamics have me confused. Marc has been very kind to me, and to a certain extent I feel disloyal even being here with the two of you right now."

"What is this," Eugenia said to Paolo, "this family dynamics?"

Paolo shrugged, though by his facial expression I was sure he knew exactly what I was talking about. "I haven't the slightest idea, Mother. Perhaps, Clea, you will explain yourself to the Lady."

I clung to the edge of the table through the tablecloth as if it were a lifeline. "I am referring to the fact that I know Marc, as head of the household, has said that Paolo is not supposed to be here in the Palazzo Corelli. I know there is bad blood between these two brothers, I know that somehow you two do not like Marc, and I do like him, very much. So you see, it puts me in an awkward position."

"Ahh," said Eugenia, with a satisfied sigh, "that is nothing. Nothing of importance. It is easy to explain. Marcantonio is not a good son. He chooses to ignore his mother's wishes. You are liking the wrong one, Clea Beaumont. My baby, my Paolo, he is worth ten of Marcantonio! I am the Lady, it is what I wish that matters! And I wish that you should forget this silly little friendship you seem to feel for Marcantonio. You are a sensible woman. A little plain, perhaps, but you are smart, and a smart woman does not have to be beautiful.'' She bent to me and compelled me with her gaze, as she covered my hand with her damp, doughy fingers. ''Also, you have good blood in you, new blood, American blood. We Corellis need new blood. I approve of you. You come again, you will see. I will show you my treasures, and you will know what it is like to be a Corelli of Venezia!''

The compliments, such as they were, were wasted on me. I persisted stubbornly. ''What have you got against Marc?''

Eugenia's grip on my hand tightened. ''He is cold, that one. He can be so charming when he wants to be, but he is at heart cold and unfeeling. Whereas my Paolo, he is full of life! You come again, yes?''

My mind was racing. Mainly I wanted to get out of there. Sharing the same room with those two giants was beginning to make me feel that they took up all the air and did not leave me enough to breathe. But there was a part of me, too, that conceded they might know Marc better than I did. ''I don't know, I'm not sure...'' I said. Then, I had a new thought: Seeing Eugenia's private collection was not necessarily disloyal to Marc; rather, if he didn't know of its existence, perhaps he should. Someday, when I understood better what was really going on in this family, I might decide to tell him. I bowed my head, admitting defeat. ''All right. Thank you for the invitation. I'll be glad to come, grateful for the opportunity to see the collection.''

Eugenia and Paolo Corelli beamed at one another, the huge black-haired mother and the huge, blond son with identical looks of pleased self-satisfaction on their faces. ''Good, good!'' crowed Eugenia.

Paolo looked at me as if he had scored a victory and I was the prize. ''You won't be sorry,'' he said.

''I'm sure,'' I said. I pushed back from the table. ''Now, I'll thank you for a delicious meal and leave you. No,

Paolo," I gestured for him to keep his seat, "you stay here with your mother. I'll get back downstairs on my own."

I held myself carefully as I walked to the door—something, either the tension or the awful wine, had made me queasy in the stomach. But in spite of my eagerness to be away, I paused with my hand on the door. There was a question to which I longed for an answer, and perhaps one of them could give it. "I presume you want us to have this next lunch before Marc returns. He has already been away for quite some time. Do you know when he's coming back?"

Eugenia waved a plump hand in careless dismissal. Clearly, she didn't care. Paolo said, "My contacts will let me know when he is to return. You don't need to be concerned about him, Clea. I advise you to forget Marc entirely, put him out of your mind."

"Yes," said the Lady, "yes, put Marcantonio right out of your mind! Who knows, he may never even come back!"

WHEN I GOT BACK to my rooms, my queasy stomach rebelled. I lost my lunch in the bathroom sink. Afterward I felt better, if weak; I felt emptied out, cleaner. I lay down to rest for a while, and to think. I thought about Marc. I knew, if Eugenia and Paolo did not, that he would come back; his mother's remark had just been some sort of wicked wishful thinking. He had said he was falling in love with me, and I didn't believe he would disappear out of my life without a word. Nor did I believe he would abandon his mother, whether she appreciated him or not. I knew that I was powerfully drawn to Marc, but could I trust my feelings? I had been wrong before about men, more than once. Memories of past mistakes, past unhappiness, reared their ugly heads and made me doubt myself.

I twisted my head back and forth on the pillow, blinking away tears. I wished mightily that Marc would return. I wished that the world and the past, his and mine, would just go away. I wished there was no such thing as responsibility and reality; I wished that for a time, no matter how brief, Marc and I could live in the beautiful illusory world that was Venice. Wishing these things and seeing Marc's face in my mind, I fell asleep.

Zenia woke me for dinner, asked if I was feeling well and I admitted I wasn't. I got up anyway, splashed cold water on my face, and went to the table set in the Morning Room. My heart was in the right place, I wanted to eat at least some of the meal she put before me, but I could not. The meat was veal cooked in a wine sauce, which smelled reminiscent of the wine we'd had for lunch. One whiff of that and my insides rebelled. I picked up the plate and took it to the kitchen, where Zenia sat on a high stool at the counter reading a magazine.

"I'm sorry," I said, "I think I've had a relapse of the flu or something. I just can't eat this."

She looked at me skeptically. Her cooking was becoming a bone of contention between us and as much as I regretted that, there wasn't much I could do about it. She slid off the stool and regarded the plate that I'd placed on the counter. "You wish me to fix you something else, *signora*?"

"No, thank you. I...I'm going to take a bath. You go on home. I'll see you tomorrow morning, ten o'clock."

Zenia pouted. "I do not much like this coming late, *signora*," she said. "Giorgio has not given me the shopping to do. I do not like to be idle."

"I don't feel well enough to discuss it, Zenia. And we've been all through that anyway. I'm sure you and Giorgio will work it out. Good night." She just stood there looking at me. I smiled, and she didn't return the smile. I repeated, with a tone of finality, "I'll see you in the morning, Zenia."

"Yes, *signora*," she said at last, and flounced out. I watched her go and wondered when it was that Zenia had decided she didn't like me anymore. I couldn't blame her. My "ways" as she called them, were just too different.

"Well," I muttered to myself as I scraped my own untouched plate into the garbage, "it takes all kinds of people to make up the world. It doesn't hurt Zenia to learn that at an early age." I felt some regret. Such a lesson was not at all what I had wanted her to learn from me.

I didn't want a bath, that had been an excuse. I went to my bedroom and changed from the wrinkled dress I'd napped in, to my blue robe over a Victorian-styled white nightgown with lace at its high neck and long sleeves. The gown was new and so were my slippers, which were dove gray and of the softest leather. They felt good on my feet. I brushed out my hair and realized that stirring around had made me feel better. I was hungry now.

Back in the kitchen I rummaged in the cabinets and found a can of tomato soup. While the soup heated I grilled a cheese sandwich in a frying pan, turning it carefully with a wide spatula until the bread was golden brown on both sides. I poured mineral water to drink, and put coffee on for later. The simple meal tasted wonderful—I ate sitting on the stool at the counter. When I was done I washed up the few dishes and took my coffee into the Morning Room. I opened the shutters and drank my coffee as I watched the lights and heard the sounds of Venice drifting up from the Grand Canal below. I felt well-fed and content, and decided my earlier stomach upset had been due to tension and not to anything I'd eaten or drunk for lunch. Still, I doubted I'd be able to smell or taste that particular wine with any enjoyment in the future, I'd always associate it with queasiness.

Left to my own devices, I had a quiet, rewarding evening. I read over my notes for a while, saw that in spite of the many distractions and my rather haphazard way of doing things, I had indeed made progress and learned a great deal. I resolved to set up an appointment with Professor Tedesco soon to have him check my work; then I read a novel until I was pleasantly drowsy, and went to bed.

I WAS HAVING THE DREAM AGAIN. I could see and feel myself lying in the bed with its canopy over me. I struggled,

struggled to wake from the dream. There was a figure looming just beyond the edges of my vision, I was sure of it. I seemed paralyzed and I fought against it in the panic of the nightmare. The canopy was descending, pressing down on me, it would smother me...there was a giant hand pressing the canopy down, there had to be! I strained every nerve and every muscle, I had to move. I had to breathe, I had to see my oppressor. No matter how horrible the sight, I had to see!

I woke, I felt my eyes fly open as in the same moment I lifted my head and the upper part of my body. Still in my mind was the command, "I must see!" With every fiber of my being I looked into the darkness and saw a shadow moving away from my bed. A dark shadow, darker than the surrounding dark, nearly shapeless. As I watched, my own gasping breath harsh in my ears, it simply faded away and left me unsure whether that was something I had really seen, or a remnant of the dream. I had to know!

I was wide awake now, and determined to do something, anything. Anything was better than lying here one more night and willing myself back to sleep in the wake of the dream. I got out of bed and my feet found my slippers in the darkness, but I didn't pause to pull on the robe. Nor did I turn on the light. If there had been someone in the room and that someone had disappeared, there was only one place he or it could have gone—out the door. The door was closed, and though I knew I had not heard it close, I flung it open. In my soft slippers my feet moved swiftly, soundlessly, my eyes already accustomed to the dark. I fairly flew through the familiar rooms of my apartment. There was no one, nothing, the rooms were still as the grave.

I tugged open the door from the salon to the corridor and left it gaping wide. There was grayish light falling from high above the stairs. I leaned over the railing and caught a glimpse of something dark on its way down—a form, a human form, or human-like; it moved swiftly. Even if it were a ghost I was determined to follow. I hadn't believed in ghosts before coming to the Palazzo Corelli, but since coming here I was no longer certain what I believed. No, that wasn't true, not quite: I believed in knowing what it was that tormented me in the night! I followed the form, my feet whispering on the stair treads down, down, down. Near the bottom of the steps I stopped, straining my eyes. I had lost it, the dark form was gone.

More slowly now, clinging to the railing, I descended the remaining steps. Had it really been a ghost? Had the thing simply vaporized, or whatever it is that ghosts do, disappeared into thin air? I both wanted and did not want to believe that. I stood at the base of the stairs and tried to focus my eyes in the almost complete darkness of the high-ceilinged chamber. I could make out the columns, like tall wraiths spaced about the room. The ceiling was lost in blackness. There was no dark form anywhere that I could see.

But there was one part of the chamber I could not see from where I stood: the windows along the back of the palazzo, and the door to the walled garden. I should never have stopped, I should have kept on running in pursuit of whatever it was I pursued, because now that I had stopped I was most reluctant to continue. My adrenaline-fed burst of courage had deserted me. I shivered, I was cold. And I was afraid.

I've come this far, I said to myself, I must go on. If there is someone, something behind the stairs I need to know. This is no time to get the willies!

Scrratch! The sound was harsh and loud in the silence of the dark palazzo. Yet it was familiar, a commonplace, this-worldy sound . . . if I could only place it. I crept around the stairs, and my heart almost leapt out of my chest! There was my ghostly figure, the dark form of unknown origin, standing in front of the door to the garden.

The sound came again, the scratching, and then a tiny flare of orange light, illuminating a human profile. Suddenly, all the information came together for my senses, and

I exclaimed "Oh!" as my legs almost gave way, I was so weak with relief.

The figure's dark head snapped around, and I could see the lighter shape of his face, his familiar face. "It's me, Marc," I said in a shaky voice, "I didn't mean to frighten you." The irony of the words got to me—me, frighten him!—and I began to laugh in relief. My laugh sounded more than a little hysterical, even to me.

"Clea?" Marc came rapidly to me. "What are you doing down here? Why are you up at this hour of the night?"

He put his arm around me and I dug my fingers into the cloth of his robe. It was navy blue terry cloth, that was the darkness of my ghostly form. In his other hand he held a pipe. That was the sound I'd heard, the scratch of the match as he lit the pipe. I said, my voice still unsteady, "I, I had a bad dream and when I woke up I thought I...well, it's hard to explain. I thought there was a, an intruder or something, and I went out into the corridor to look and I saw someone on the stairs so I followed and, well, thank goodness it was you!"

Marc kissed my forehead. "You're a puzzle, *carissima*. I thought you were afraid of the dark, and yet you follow someone who might be an intruder! And what do you suppose you would have done if I'd turned out to be a thief?"

"I don't know. I wasn't thinking. Actually if I thought anything it was that you might have been a ghost. Do you have any ghosts in the Palazzo Corelli?"

Marc tucked me more closely into the curve of his arm and began to walk toward the door of the garden. He chuckled. "No ghosts that I have seen or heard of, though for a place of its age, I suppose the palazzo must have a few whether I've heard of them or not."

He opened the door and led me out into the garden. The night was refreshingly cool but not cold, considering the time of year. A golden wash of light was shed by a pair of lamps that flanked the gate on the far wall. I looked up at a velvet black sky where stars were bright points around a pale quarter moon already low in its descent. I breathed deeply, stretched my arms, and looked up at Marc. "What are you doing home? I didn't know you were coming back tonight! And, for that matter, what are you doing up? I should think you'd be exhausted after your long trip."

Marc tousled my hair. He didn't answer, but took my hand and brought me to sit beside him on the concrete bench. The fountain splashed musically behind us, and Marc pulled on his pipe, sending a soft stream of smoke from his lips to curl over our heads. It should have been a relaxing moment, a magical moment in the Venetian night, but it was not. I could feel tension in his body, and a weakness that was the residue of suppressed fear in my own. Finally he said, "I couldn't sleep. I came down here to smoke, and to think. Somehow, tonight, my own rooms seemed oppressive. I wanted to get out from under the roof of the house—if that makes any sense."

"It does," I nodded. Unfortunately, it made all too much sense to me.

Marc smoked in silence. I didn't interfere. It was enough for me that he was home, that I was with him. Slowly my own tension eased. I became aware that I wore only a nightgown of cotton, which was on the thin side, though with its high neck and long sleeves it was sufficiently modest. I wrapped my arms around myself for warmth. As if he had noticed, though he seemed lost in his thoughts a million miles away, Marc lifted his arm to encircle me and pull me close against his side. I snuggled, letting my head rest on his shoulder. I loved his strength; I felt I could sit like this with him forever.

Gradually the tightness of Marc's body began to ease. I moved my head to look up at him, and his lips came down to my upturned face. They closed over mine with infinite tenderness, softness, so gently. The kiss was long, both comforting and seeking comfort. I felt an intimacy of a kind I had never felt before, with anyone, and for once this intimacy did not frighten me. I yielded, I gave what his lips asked for, and the sweetness of that kiss flowed back and forth; from me to him, from him to me, in a moment that went on forever.

"I'm glad you came after me in the middle of the night," said Marc when at last we drew apart, "even if you did think I was a ghost."

I smiled, and stroked his beard, loving its silky yet wiry texture. I said, "I missed you. You were gone a long time."

Marc's arm tightened around me, he put aside the pipe from his other hand and pressed my head to his chest with strong fingers. He held me there like that, as if he would never let me go. When he spoke his voice was hoarse, breaking. "I need you, Clea. Dear God, how I need you! And yet I, I have so little to offer you. My life is falling apart!"

I pulled away. "Marc? What do you mean?"

"I don't know. I wish I did." His face in the gold-washed darkness was all planes of light and dark shadows, and he looked more than ever like an El Greco: dignified, sad, mysterious. "When I was trying to get to sleep just a while ago, I think I went a little crazy. I started thinking that some gypsy must have put a curse on me. I can't think of any other way so many bad things could be happening all at once! That was when I decided I had better get up, move around, smoke, try to get a handle on this thing."

"I don't believe in gypsy curses."

"Neither do I!" His laugh was harsh, without mirth. "But that's as good an explanation as any I can come up with."

"Why don't you tell me what, exactly, has happened."

"I'm not sure I can."

"Look, Marc," I took his hands firmly in mine, "you said you needed me. Okay, I'm willing to be needed, I liked hearing that. M-maybe," I hesitated, it was hard for me to say what I was about to say, "maybe we need each other. But we aren't going to get very far in any kind of a relationship if you can't trust me enough to tell me what's going on."

"You're right, of course," said Marc gravely. Some of his old formality was back, but I didn't mind. I knew it was part of his way of coping. He straightened up and I let go of his hands. He said, "You remember that I thought I had sold the villa to the Dutchman?"

"Yes, the one with the unpronounceable name."

"Well, I didn't tell you, I didn't tell anyone, but the closing did not take place as scheduled. His lawyers postponed, and then they postponed again. I had business to do elsewhere, in Hamburg and in Paris, and so I went also to Amsterdam to see him, to find out what was the delay. He has cancelled the deal, Clea. His laywers got him out of it on a technicality—they claim I didn't make a complete disclosure of the condition of the property, and yet I did. They claim to have found faults that I didn't even know were there! There was nothing else I could do in good grace except to acquiesce. In time, perhaps I can find another buyer."

"Oh, no! I'm sorry, I know you were counting heavily on that money."

"Yes, I was. And that was only the tip of the iceberg, believe me. Everywhere I went, doors that have formerly been open to me were all but closed. People with whom I've formerly had cordial business relations were barely polite, and not interested in hearing me out no matter what I had to say. It's as if I've been blacklisted all over Europe, and I could not find out why! There is no rhyme nor reason to this, I swear it."

"A misunderstanding..." I murmured, knowing I was totally inadequate, such things were way beyond my ability to understand.

"That, my dear Clea, is the understatement of the century! I will have to put my own people on it, to find out why this is happening, and I came back to Venice to do that. Then...something else happened. I did not know whether or not to tell you, though when I finally got back here to-night there was nothing I wanted more than to go straight to your apartment, just to hold you in my arms....To tell you or not, that was one of the things I intended to think about when I came down here earlier."

"But now I'm here," I urged, "I'm with you. You must tell me, Marc."

"I will sound crazy, paranoid."

"I know you aren't crazy, and I've never seen any evidence that you're paranoid. Go on, please."

"Very well. I almost died tonight."

A silence fell between us. I couldn't believe my ears. A cold chill, a memory of another who had died right before my unremembering eyes, gripped me. I was unable to speak, move, make a sound. I sat like a stone and waited for Marc to continue.

"I would have drowned in the lagoon, if I were not a strong swimmer. It was an accident, perhaps. Or perhaps not. I have it well looked after, and yet when I was far out into the lagoon the boat suddenly took in water. Rapidly. It was as if all the cocks had been opened at once, which is, of course, impossible; likewise impossible for such a great leak to spring so quickly. I believe the boat must have been tampered with, but I will never be able to prove it. I doubt I, or anyone, could find it now in all the muck on the bottom. My boat sank and I swam almost all the way to Giudecca before another boat saw me and picked me up."

I grasped at straws, trying to deny that he had been in such danger. "I thought the lagoon was shallow, too shallow for a person to drown...?"

"In some places, yes, though there is so much muck on the bottom that I doubt one could stand. But there are also deep channels, which have been dredged, and it was when I was crossing one of the channels that the boat went down. I suppose if someone were clever enough, and wanted badly enough to be rid of me, that it would be possible to time a device that would breach the hull at the time it normally takes to reach one of the channels. But I cannot believe that there is anyone who hates me enough, who has any reason to want me dead. Or even, if being in the channel was just by chance, to frighten me with a boat accident. I have no idea how it was done, I heard no explosion...." Marc fell silent, ruminating.

Slowly, aware that I might be about to open Pandora's box, I spoke. "I can think of someone."

Marc's head turned. He looked full at me, and the light from the lamps was caught in his eyes. "Who?"

I swallowed. My voice was little more than a whisper. "Your brother. Paolo."

Chapter Nine

"No." Marc's response was so fast that it seemed automatic. "No, not Paolo."

I observed that Marc had spoken without thought, and I wondered how often in the past he had defended his half brother against the accusations of others. I challenged him. "Why not?"

Marc had looked away, rubbing the back of his neck. Now he looked back at me and I could feel the chill in that glance. I knew if I had been able to see his eyes they would be like pale aquamarine ice. "More to the point, I might ask why you, Clea, should think that he would do such a thing. You do not know Paolo. Or do you?"

I shivered, not just from the coldness I sensed so suddenly in Marc, but also because we had been out in the night for some time and I was chilly without his arm around me. I crossed my arms over my breasts and said, "It's very late, Marc. I probably shouldn't have said anything. Maybe we should leave this discussion for another time."

"You're cold," he observed, "you're shivering. I'm sorry, we'll go in." With that quick change to gallantry of which he was capable, Marc stood and offered me his hand, which was warm, and the shelter of his arm, which was even warmer. He said in a low voice, "You aren't exactly dressed to be out in the night, even on a relatively mild night like this. I like the gown you're wearing." He touched the lace at my throat. "It's old-fashioned, yet it becomes you."

"Thank you," I murmured.

Inside the door Marc turned me to him, holding my shoulders in his hands. "Please forgive me if I sounded harsh just then. My nerves are on edge, my emotions are rather volatile at the moment."

"Of course they are," I agreed, and clamped my teeth down over my lower lip, to prevent my saying any more. I had said enough, probably unwisely.

But Marc had other ideas. "I know it's late. I also know that I will not sleep tonight. I'm still much too stirred up to sleep. What about you, Clea? If you are too tired, then we will as you suggested continue this discussion at another time. But if you are as wide awake as I am...."

I could feel Marc's need to go on, he communicated it to me somehow without words, just as he had communicated so much in the kiss—a need for closeness, a need for support, a need for, well, love. I told him the truth. "I don't want to sleep."

"Aagh!" Marc groaned softly, pulling me to him, holding my body pressed full against the length of his. "I don't know which I want more, *carissima*, to talk or to make love to you and simply forget everything that has happened!"

I felt his body stir and harden, and my own body, always so responsive to his merest touch, thrummed and swirled inside. Not so many hours before I, too, had wished that I could simply be with Marc and make the world go away. Yet I was relieved when, with a heavy sigh, he stepped back and said, "If we do not talk this through now, we will only have to do it later. I think it best that we do so tonight. I must know why you said what you did about Paolo. Are you willing?"

Reluctantly I nodded, "I guess so."

"Come to my rooms, then. I can make a small fire in the fireplace. We'll have brandy, or coffee if you prefer."

"All right. I think brandy is a good idea."

I WAS GLAD not to have to go back to my apartment; that awful dream was still with me, I realized as we climbed the dark stairs. The light walls and the apricot glow of Marc's carpet were welcome, and gave chase to the last residue of my bad dream. He gave me brandy in a short, round crystal glass, and I asked if he had another robe I could wear, or failing that, a sweater to put around my shoulders. He quipped, "What? You want to cover up all that loveliness?" and I blushed as his eyes roved over me and I realized that in the light, my gown was more revealing than I'd thought. But I nodded, and he brought a robe of dark green velour whose velvet softness I welcomed. Much too large, it swallowed me, but I knotted its sash and rolled up the sleeves and settled comfortably with my brandy on the couch while I watched Marc build a modest fire in the fireplace.

He moved with a lithe, unconscious grace I admired. I saw that beneath his navy blue robe he wore pajama bottoms of a lighter blue, but no top. The robe gaped as he moved his arms and I glimpsed the dark hair of his bare chest. A thrill went through me. I sipped my brandy and allowed myself to fantasize how that hair would feel to my fingers, the hardness of the muscle beneath. Marc crouched to add a small log to his fire and I noted the long, lean lines of his thigh. My imagination soared. My fears of being intimate with this man were melting away, especially when he glanced at me over his shoulder with a curve of his beautiful mouth, as if he knew what I was thinking. I felt my own lips curve in return. I nestled, settling more deeply into the cushions, as warm and content as a purring cat.

Marc finished his task, got brandy for himself, and sat not next to me, as I would have wished, but in a chair nearby. He raised his glass to me, and for a moment his eyes softened in a look of such tenderness that it took my breath away. Then he drank, crossed his legs at the knee, adjusted his robe—the formality had returned. "Now we will continue our conversation," he said.

I sighed. "Must we? I'm so comfortable here."

"Yes, Clea. We must. You yourself said that if we are to have any kind of a relationship we must trust each other. I want you to tell me what you know about Paolo that would cause you to think he could want to do me harm."

"He...hates you, Marc. He's jealous of your position as the heir to the Corelli fortune."

"Fortune! Hah. Paolo well knows there is no fortune."

"Well, then, to the name, to the palazzo. He seems terribly conscious of the fact that you're legitimate and he's not. I'm not sure 'hate' is the right word, but there's certainly something abnormally intense about his resentment of you."

"All right, I'll grant you that. Paolo has always wanted to be Number One. But his business is doing extremely well, and it was I who set him up in that business. Without me he would have nothing. He has nothing to gain by doing me harm." Marc was quiet, sipping brandy, staring at nothing. Then he said, "Unless...I think you had best tell me how you know these things, Clea."

This was difficult. What if Marc should misunderstand? I twisted the sash of his robe around my finger and hoped I could find the right words. I wanted to be careful what, if anything, I said about Eugenia; I guessed that Marc was unaware of the feelings toward him that she had expressed to me. "I saw Paolo in the piazza a couple of months ago, he invited himself to join me, and he had a lot to say. For example, he said that you had come to his place of business and warned him to stay away from me."

"That's true, I did." Marc's eyes narrowed. "Paolo has a poor track record where women are concerned. He, ah, uses them. He is in the travel business, and he has a reputation for, you might say, seducing women tourists. I didn't want him to try any of that on you. Has he?"

"Not exactly. I haven't been out with him, if that's what you're thinking. But that same evening he told me that he would see me here, at the palazzo. He said he comes here when he wants, that you can't stop him. And that seems to be true, Marc. He is here far more often than I think you realize."

"Damn!" Marc got up from his chair, paced across the room and back. "The servants are supposed to tell me if Paolo comes here without my knowledge."

"I have the impression that he's able to get in and out without them knowing."

"That's impossible! Giorgio is faithful, he would know if anyone came in, and besides, no one could get in without a key unless Giorgio or Rosa let him in. Rosa, too, is faithful. I trust them both."

"Well, then, maybe your mother gave him a key. I don't know, all I know is that I've seen him here several times. The last time, well next-to-last, he surprised me when I was looking over things in the Grand Salon. You remember, your mother gave permission. Anyway, Paolo made such a nuisance of himself that I agreed to have lunch with him and your mother. And we did that, just today." I looked at the clock on the mantel and saw the time—it was almost three in the morning. "Yesterday," I amended. I gulped nervously at my brandy and watched Marc over the rim of the glass. His bearded face was expressionless.

"And how did that go? I've wanted you to spend some time with the Lady, but I didn't have in mind that Paolo should be there, too. In fact, you are quite right. I had no idea she was entertaining him in my absence."

"They were both very nice to me," I said carefully, "your mother especially. But I was uncomfortable being there without you, and I said so. It's—it's hard to get around the two of them. They sort of ganged up on me—or at least, that's how I felt. I agreed to do it again, have lunch with them." Seeing the thunderous look that came over Marc's face I hastened to add, "But I had an ulterior motive. It seems your mother has her own private collection of art objects, and she said she would show them to me next time.

A-apparently you've never seen this collection, Marc. But Paolo has.''

Marc muttered an explective under his breath. I didn't quite catch the word, but I didn't need to, his expression and his body posture said it all. "I thought I had put an end to that! Paolo is bad for the Lady, Clea. You can't imagine how bad. She has a—a streak of abnormality in her and he feeds it. What the devil am I going to do?" With his clenched fist he pounded on the arm of his chair.

"I think you might recognize that he's dangerous, not just to her but also to you. I don't really know the man, Marc, but I'm sure there's a lot more to what's going on in this family than you've ever told me, and whether I like it or not, I seem to be caught up in it."

Marc leaned forward in his chair, his arms on his knees, the glass half full of brandy clutched so tightly that his knuckles were white. There was a nakedness in his eyes that tore at my heart. "Clea, you've never said that you return my feelings for you. You're not, surely you're not...equally interested in my brother?"

"Marc! Oh, Marc, you're not thinking straight!" I left the couch and went swiftly to kneel next to him and wrap my arms about him. I couldn't bear that look on his face, or the anguish in his voice. "Didn't you hear me say that Paolo is dangerous? I'm actually a little afraid of him, I'm certainly not the least bit attracted to him! Look at me, Marc." I waited until he had raised those clear blue-green eyes, so full of longing, to mine. "The only reason I seem to be getting caught up in this strange family of yours is because of you. Because of you, I stay in this house even though I sense there are things happening here that I don't understand. Oh, I've made other excuses to myself, but that's all they are, excuses. It's because of you, because I, I care for you more than I like to admit, more than I'm ready for...."

There were tears in my own eyes as I took Marc's face in my hands and kissed him. I wasn't even sure what I had said, I knew only that I had said what was in my heart because I couldn't bear to see him look at me that way. I couldn't bear to think about him all alone, fighting his solitary battles when his very family, whom he sought to preserve, seemed to be against him.

"Clea, *mia cara*!" Marc pulled me into his lap. There were tears in his eyes too as he kissed me again, and then we simply sat, holding each other. The clock on the mantel chimed with a clear, pure tone: once, twice, thrice.

"You are right, *mia cara*," said Marc, not moving in the circle of our mutual embrace. "Paolo is dangerous. He killed my father."

I was so shocked that I almost jumped out of Marc's lap.

"No, *carissima*, don't move," Marc went on, "let me continue to hold you while I tell you the story. I have never told anyone before, for obvious reasons. It will be a long and not very pretty story, but I will tell you the whole truth."

I stayed as I was, with my arms twined about Marc's shoulders, my cheek in the curve of his neck, his beard caressing my temple and his arms tight about my waist, and I listened.

"I was, as you may imagine, a rather quiet, studious child. I did well in school, played some sports, and was altogether an unremarkable boy. The Lady had little use for me, little affection for me, but my father made up for everything. I was close to him, I spent as much time with him as I could, as far back as I can remember. My mother's malicious tales of Papa's peasant origins made no impression upon me, even when I was old enough to understand why she would tell me such things.

"Paolo is four years younger than I, and from the very beginning he was quite different, almost a polar opposite of me. Of course, for a long time I knew only that he was my brother, no one had ever told me he had a different father. So there was I, dark, quiet, gangly, and here was this sunny-looking little brother, a strikingly handsome child to look at, but he had a hellish temper. My mother spoiled him, the servants did, too; yet Paolo seemed to hate me from as far back as I can remember. He was mean and sneaky, and he was a little thief. If I complained of his behavior, if I tried to get back the things he took, I was accused of being jealous and ungenerous. For a long time he had even my father fooled. But I suppose all that is of little importance to the story, I'm just getting caught up in old memories.

"To go on, Paolo grew rapidly, and by the time he was twelve and I was sixteen, he was almost as large and as strong as he is now. His behavior was a problem. He was no longer so popular with the servants, who had too often been the targets of his bad temper, as I was. He didn't do well in school, either; he had problems with authority, and since he stole things in school as he did at home, he got in trouble a lot. The Lady would hear none of this. She adored him—he could do no wrong in her eyes, no matter what. She had shielded Paolo from knowledge of his illegitimacy, but of course that was a mistake, because he found out the truth at school. And it sent him into a torrent of destructive behavior—he was twelve at the time.

"From then on his hatred of me increased, and he also turned that hatred on my father.

"One day, in a senseless rage, Paolo attacked my father. He battered him with a bronze statue of a horse. He didn't just hit Papa over the head with it, Clea, he knocked him down and then he kept hitting him, again and again. I was the first to come into the room when I heard Papa cry out and heard the sound of his falling. That first blow may have killed him, I don't know. When I got there and saw what was happening I tried to stop Paolo. I grabbed at his arm, but he was too strong for me. He shook me off and kept on hitting, hitting. I'll never forget the look on Paolo's face, in his eyes. He looked absolutely insane. I yelled for help and the servants came, but by then it was much, much too late. Papa was... his head was just a bloody mess there on the floor."

"Oh, God!" I exclaimed in a whisper.

"I don't remember anything of that day after that. The Lady took control of everything. She got the family doctor to call it a natural death, I don't know how. Probably she paid a huge bribe. She bought the silence of the servants, too. I knew what she did was wrong, but she intimidated me by holding the family name over my head. She told me that I was the heir, that everything, money, property, would come to me when I came of age at twenty-one but until then, she was in charge, and her word was law. To her credit, I will say that she held up quite well in that crisis, and she was hard on Paolo. She arranged for him to go away to Switzerland to boarding school and told him that if there was even a whisper of trouble there, she would bring him back to Venice and turn him over to the police. The threat was, apparently, sufficient. Paolo never distinguished himself academically at that school, but he didn't get in trouble, either. I seldom saw him after that. I soon went to Oxford myself.

"I wasn't quite satisfied, though. I knew some day Paolo would come back, and I couldn't forget that insane look in his eyes, or the fact that he had always been subject to almost uncontrollable rages. I had looked for that bronze horse all over the palazzo, and I hadn't been able to find it. My first summer home from Oxford, while Paolo and the Lady were away on vacation together, I paid some street children to dive for the statue in the canal near the palazzo. I figured that was what Paolo would have done with it, he was never very imaginative and that's what everyone does with things they want to get rid of—they throw them in the canal. By sheer luck, or God's will, the divers found the horse, and I kept it.

"When Paolo finished school at eighteen, the Lady sent him on an around-the-world tour. Her version of the Grand Tour that wealthy gentlemen took in earlier times. I had the inheritance by then, and I knew we could ill afford it, but I didn't protest. I didn't want him at home, either. Finally, he did come home. He seemed happy to settle in and be a playboy, but I couldn't allow that. I got him jobs but he didn't keep them, and he resented my interference. I became concerned.

"Although on the surface Paolo's behavior wasn't all that bad, I sensed that his rages had simply gone underground, he was as mean as he had ever been, the difference was that he had learned to be more cunning. And his influence on the Lady was terrible. She seemed to have forgotten what he had done. Once again, as when he was a child, she believed Paolo could do no wrong. She was living in some sort of twisted fantasy world. Paolo encouraged her. He took her out into the nightlife of Venice, and she . . . well, she made a spectacle of herself.

"I decided that I had to take matters in hand. I was twenty-four then, Paolo, twenty. I got out the bronze horse, which I had hidden for years. I called Paolo in and confronted him with it. He remembered that horse, all right. He actually turned pale. I told him that without a doubt his fingerprints were still all over it—I didn't know if that was true, but I did know Paolo wasn't smart enough to debate it—and that even though our mother seemed to have forgotten what he had done, I had not. I told him, in essence, to shape up or else. He did, for a while, at least on the surface. But his strange influence on the Lady still continued. The two of them were driving me nuts, Clea."

"I can imagine," I said.

"So, for right or wrong, I asked Paolo to move out of the palazzo, to tell the Lady he wanted his own place. Of course he wasn't cooperative, even though I could tell he was scared. He tried to make a deal. He would move out if I would give him the bronze horse. I negotiated, and ended by setting him up in his own business with the understanding that he would live elsewhere, and visit only on special occasions. I never suggested to the Lady that she should not go to see him. But as far as I know, she never has. She adjusted to his being gone, but she became reclusive. That has been a blessing after her outrageous behavior in public with Paolo at her side. Seven years it is since Paolo moved out, and the Lady has been much calmer. She seems healthier, I mean mentally, without his constant influence. That's about all there is to say. More than enough, to judge by the dryness of my throat."

Marc shifted me off his lap and I moved back to the couch, while he went to the wet bar.

"I don't know what to say," I said. "That's an incredible story. It's . . . horrible."

"Read a few history books," said Marc over his shoulder. "Worse things have happened in *La Serenissima*. Many worse things. Would you like a glass of water, or more brandy?"

"Water, please."

I felt completely wrung out, temporarily unable to think. I knew it would be some time before I could process all that Marc had told me. We sat side by side on the couch and watched the fire die. The clock struck one clear note: the half hour, three-thirty. It seemed to me that half a century had passed, rather than only thirty minutes. We didn't talk. Marc put his arm around my shoulders and I rested my head against him until I grew drowsy. Then, suddenly, as I was on the verge of falling asleep, I sat bolt upright. "Marc, what has happened to the bronze horse? Where is it now?"

He looked at me curiously. "It's in my safety-deposit drawer at the bank. Why?"

"Are you sure it's still there?"

"If safety-deposit drawers are still safe, it is. And it certainly should be. That's my bank, Clea, I work there. No one can get into that drawer except me, and everyone at the bank knows me. Now, why did you ask?"

"Because something is going on here in the Palazzo Corelli, I'm sure of it. And someone tried to kill you tonight, and nothing you've just told me proves to me that Paolo didn't do it."

"Then, my tousle-headed friend," Marc rumpled my hair tenderly, "I just went to a whole lot of trouble for nothing. Let me make the picture crystal clear for you. Paolo is afraid of me. He owes his business to me. He would not stand to inherit anything even if I died, since he's not one hundred percent Corelli. Now, do you understand?''

I wanted to see this his way, I really did, but I couldn't. However, I realized that I, too, needed to sort some things out. Things I hadn't told Marc. I didn't know if I could trust my own feelings and instincts. For example there was my recurring nightmare. Why was I having that dream? Did it have anything to do with the palazzo or not? And there was the mystery of the gold salt cellar: I'd seen it, sketched it, yet when I went again to the Grand Salon, it was gone. Why? Where was it? I had searched and searched...and I was doing entirely too much of that these days. I lost things in my own apartment all the time, only to find them in a place much different from where I thought I'd put them. Maybe I was the one who had something wrong with me; certainly I'd been feeling sick a lot of the time. I'd have a good day or two and then it would start all over again. Considering all that, who was I to say that Marc's judgment was off?

"Well, Clea, what are you thinking? I can almost see the wheels turning.''

"Nothing, really. I'm too sleepy to think straight, and I see you are, too. Why don't you walk me downstairs to my apartment. Maybe everything will look different, better, in the light of day.''

Marc nuzzled at my neck, he touched my earlobe with the tip of his tongue, and a delicious shiver ran through me. "I have a better idea,'' he said. "Come to bed with me. I don't really relish the idea of walking down all those stairs, not to mention back up again.''

I was tempted. I touched his nose with my fingertip, and then his lips. Such wonderful, expressive lips. The tip of Marc's moist tongue met my finger, and I savored the tingling for a moment before I took it away. "No, not tonight. Some night, maybe. Probably. But not tonight. Come on, you'll live through one trip down the stairs.''

"Cruel woman,'' Marc said, but he was laughing.

My door was still wide open. "Did you leave your door open like this?" asked Marc.

"Yes, I did. I just ran out, you remember, I told you I thought someone had been in my room, but it was only a bad dream."

"Yes. I don't think it's such a good idea to leave your door open, though, even if the palazzo is locked up for the night. Promise me you won't do it again."

"I promise." I held my face up for a kiss, which was brief, but sweet. "Wait," I said, "let me give you your robe back. If Zenia found it here..."

Marc chuckled, a low, wonderfully suggestive sound. "What do you suppose would happen if she found not just the robe but me, in your bed?"

I made a face in answer, and handed him the robe. "Good night, Signor Corelli."

"Good night, Clea, *mia cara*." He turned to go, but I reached out for him, touched his shoulder, and stopped his leaving.

"Marc, one thing more before you go."

"Yes?"

"I do think there's something going on here, and I do think it's serious. I also think it's going to take both of us to figure it out. Promise me, please, that you'll keep an open mind? And you won't close me out? That we can work on it together?"

"Clea, I promise you that of all the things I might ever do, closing you out is not one of them. All I ask is that you make me the same promise."

"I do, Marc. I promise."

Chapter Ten

After Marc left, I slept like a rock for five hours and woke feeling unusually refreshed, ready to take on the world. While my coffee brewed I went through the apartment humming, throwing open all the shutters to let in the sun. Since I'd asked Zenia to start work later, the opening of the shutters every morning had become a favorite routine. I never tired of the view from my windows; every day it seemed a miracle to me that I was in Venice. Over and over again I marveled at the sheer age of the city; I found it wondrous beyond words that without city planners, with architects who knew nothing of modern engineering, this place could have come together with such dignity and balance. Not to mention that here it stood, where by rights there should have been nothing but a collection of little islands and marshes. That Venice should exist, at all, that was the real miracle; that she still existed after hundreds of years was almost beyond belief—and every morning, here was the evidence before my very eyes.

By the time Zenia arrived at ten I had eaten, dressed hastily in tan wool slacks and a black sweater, and was ready to throw on my long wool cape and breeze out the door.

"You are feeling better this morning, Clea," she observed.

"Yes, thank you," I smiled, and silently made my own observation: I was back in favor again—she was calling me Clea and not *signora*. "I'm off to the library."

"You will be here for dinner, I should cook tonight?"

"Yes, Zenia. I plan to be here for dinner. Now, I really must run. I lost almost the whole day yesterday, and I have to make up for it."

"Goodbye, Clea. Oh," she called after me when I was already almost out of the door, "the Young Master returned last night. I thought you might like to know."

Just in time I stopped myself from saying Yes, I know, and said instead, "Good, I know his mother will be glad to see him. *Ciao*, Zenia!"

I walked swiftly through the streets and found that I was smiling at the people who passed, and many of them smiled back at me. Streets and bridges that had once seemed so strange to me were now familiar, I felt at home. I felt like a native, and like the natives I could rejoice that there were far fewer tourists now; it seemed that our city had been returned to us for a while. On the long stretch of the Accademia Bridge I stopped and looked back over the Grand Canal in the direction of the Palazzo Corelli. The scene was busy, colorful, charming. I felt the sun on my face, smelled a delicious, cool freshness in the breeze, which ruffled my hair and playfully lifted the fringe of my cape.

I'm happy, I thought in amazement. With all that has happened, with the terrible things that Marc told me last night, and some unresolved if not quite so terrible things in my own life, still I'm happy! And far, far back in my mind there was a little whisper telling me why. "I'm in love," the whisper said.

I grinned, and hefted my canvas bag higher on my shoulder. For once I wasn't going to tell myself that being in love was not at all the thing to do, that nothing could come of it, or all the many things I usually told myself to get my mind off of Marcantonio Corelli. He needed me, he had said. He was a strong, desirable, virile, vital man, and yet he needed me. For the moment I would allow myself to feel the joy. The days to come would take care of themselves as they came.

My good spirits endured throughout a busy day, which included an impromptu lunch with Maria Bonavita. I suspected she had been waiting for me, since I encountered her on my way out of the Accademia, and I didn't think she had been there to see the paintings. For the life of me I couldn't understand why she was still in Venice; she might be enjoying herself in her own negative way, but whenever I saw her she seemed to be at loose ends.

I decided to ask her as tactfully as I could. "Maria, you've been here for several weeks now, and you do seem a little, ah, restless. Have you thought about going home?"

Her bright blue eyes sharpened behind their glasses. "How interesting that you should ask, my dear. Why, just this week I met the most charming young man. He's going to make me a whole new itinerary!"

"Oh? So you're planning to do some more traveling?"

"Yes, indeed. I couldn't possibly go back until after Christmas. There would be too many sad memories being alone at Christmas, without dear departed Mr. Bonavita."

"I understand," I said, with a pang of dismay. Myself, I hadn't even thought of Christmas, though it was now only about six weeks away. Instantly I felt guilty, as I so often did when I was with Maria. But she was continuing to talk and I chased away reminders that I must make plans, must call the children.

"My new travel agent is so knowledgeable and capable. You must know him, Clea."

"I don't think so. I don't know any travel agents in Venice. I made all my own travel arrangements before I left home, I haven't needed to see anyone here."

"Well, if you don't know him I think it's very odd, considering the name of that place where you live. He isn't just an ordinary travel agent, my dear, oh, no, not at all. He owns his own travel business. His name is Paolo Corelli,"

Maria pronounced, with a slightly smug look on her pink-cheeked little face.

"I, yes," I swallowed hard, taken by surprise, "yes, I do know him. Not well. He doesn't live at the Palazzo Corelli."

"He doesn't? With the same name, and all? Well, that is odd, isn't it?"

Not as odd, I thought, as that out of all the probably hundreds of travel people in Venice, you should come up with the very one I least want to have to talk about. I cleared my throat and said carefully, "Actually, his brother, Marcantonio Corelli, has become a friend of mine since I've been here. I understand that Paolo has his own apartment somewhere."

Maria bent forward over the table, white curls bobbing. There was nothing she liked more than a bit of gossip, and she was loving this. "Big palace like that, you'd think there would be plenty of room, wouldn't you, and young Paolo wouldn't need his own place."

I refused to play. "I really don't know, Maria. I've never given any thought to the living arrangements of the Corellis." I had to bite my tongue from saying that it was none of my business, nor of hers, either.

"Humph! Well, I hope your friend Mr. Marc-whatsis is as nice as my young travel man. He's getting me on a cruise to Hong Kong and Japan."

I finished off my last bite of sandwich, glancing at Maria across the table. She was wearing pink today, and if it were not for a hint of maliciousness in her bright eyes, I would have thought she belonged nowhere except in a photo feature on grandmotherhood for an American women's magazine. Maria, in Hong Kong? It boggled the mind. I said casually, "That sounds really interesting. When will you be leaving?"

"Oh, I don't know. Mr. Paolo hasn't finished planning the trip yet. But it will be a good, long cruise, so I can be sure that the holidays are long past when I get home to Boston."

"Yes," I murmured, and took my last swallow of mineral water. Then what she had said hit me. I almost squeaked. "Boston? I thought you were from New Jersey."

"Oh, dear." Maria was flustered. She fidgeted with the brooch at the lace collar of her blouse and her eyes darted away from me. "Did I really say that? I, well, I—" she sighed then, seemingly with relief "—I confess I've been thinking a lot about Boston lately. I just didn't want to say anything about it to you. That's where you're from, isn't it, Clea?"

"Yes, it is. We've talked about Boston, if you remember."

"Of course I remember, and I told you Boston was my home, it's where I always lived until I married Mr. Bonavita. I confess that lately I've been thinking I might move back there." She bowed her head, but she sneaked a look at me over the tops of her glasses. "You see, I really don't want to go back to where I lived so happily with my husband now that he isn't there anymore. I can't think of that as home now, and so more and more I've been thinking of my old home, of Boston. That's why it just came out, I guess. How embarrassing. I hope you don't think I'm a foolish old woman. Although, I suppose I am."

"No, no, of course you're not." I comforted her, and I accepted her explanation, while at the same time I couldn't help but think that I didn't particularly like the idea of running into Maria around the corner from the Egyptian Room at the Museum of Fine Arts, or in the Public Garden, or...anywhere.

We paid for our lunch and parted, and I admitted that lunch with Maria had taken some of the shine off my day. I squared my shoulders and went on. I had one last church to visit, San Giorgio Maggiore. I had left it this long only because it's not that easy to get to—it sits in isolated splendor on its own little island, the Isola San Giorgio, across the Bacino San Marco. I stood on the Riva della Schiavone, looking at the great white-domed church across the water, and debated. Should I tangle with vaporetto schedules, or should I do a daring thing and hire a gondola? I had never yet been in a gondola, and though it was such a "touristy" thing to do, I had often secretly wanted to try it.

I dared. I hired a gondola. All by myself, just to get across the water. I told the gondolier my destination, climbed in gingerly, but not without noticing a certain degree of appreciation in the gondolier's dark eyes. He adjusted his wide-brimmed hat with its bright red, long-tailed band, and we rocked away. I thought: If he sings to me, I'm going over the side! Then I forgot to be cosmopolitan and cynical. In the sleek, dark little boat, Venice took on a whole new perspective. We glided through the water; I felt like a swan, so graceful and slow was the movement. The Bacino was, at the moment, not crowded with other boats. On that brief trip I felt for a while as if I were transported back into the past, I knew some of the pleasure and pride the old Venetians must have taken in their city.

The ride was over all too soon. I thanked the gondolier and tipped him outrageously. My high spirits had returned. I climbed the broad steps and went into the church, mentally cataloging what I knew about it. The architecture was Palladian, sixteenth-century; there had originally been a Benedictine monastery on the site; there were two or three Tintorettos and a fourteenth-century wooden crucifix that was supposed to be remarkable. I wandered around first, as I usually do, just to get the feel of the place. One thing I had learned through visiting so many churches: they all felt different, each was unique. San Giorgio Maggiore was grand, imposing, formal, and had a clean sort of openness about it.

A few minutes later I was ready to begin sketching and note-taking. I reached into my canvas bag for my notebook and my high spirits crashed. The notebook was gone! It simply was not there! My other notebook, the one with lined paper which I used for my library research was there, I had used it just that morning; so was the first sketchbook I had used and abandoned because it was wide and cumbersome to handle. But the unlined notebook with all my recent on-site notes and sketches was gone. The other clutter I carried—soft pencils, charcoal crayons for shading, art-gum erasers, a well-dented small box of tissues, a big comb, a narrow plastic zippered case in which I kept a lipstick and pressed powder and a toothbrush and toothpaste and various other necessities—all of that was there. My hand went to my waist to be sure I hadn't lost the leather belt with its pouch, even though in my head I knew I had it because I had just paid the gondolier. In a sudden moment of panic, I felt that if I had lost that notebook I could lose anything!

I told myself not to worry, the notebook was probably back at my apartment. The sensible thing to do was to use the old sketchbook and worry about finding the notebook later. I tried. I started at the back of the long nave and took out the old sketchbook, but I couldn't keep my mind on the work. The familiar, reassuring process that could usually blot out all else just didn't work this time. In the back of my mind I knew why: because losing anything at all was not like me, I was not a person who lost things and yet it had been happening so frequently of late. Up until today I'd lost nothing of importance, and true, whatever I missed usually turned up again. But this notebook was different. The loss of it would cripple my work.

Who was I kidding? I rubbed my hand over my forehead and squeezed my eyes shut and open again, as if those actions could straighten out the mess inside my head. It wasn't my academic work I was worried about, it was the other sketches, the ones I'd made in the Grand Salon at the Palazzo Corelli. Those sketches had been in that notebook, too. I knew I would not have a moment's peace until I'd searched everywhere there was to look for the missing notebook.

I shoved the sketchbook and pencil back into the canvas bag and ran out of the church of San Giorgio Maggiore, down the steps, as fast as I could. There was a vaporetto at the quay and I waved and shouted although I had no idea if it was going up the Grand Canal in the direction I needed to go, or not. The boat waited and I hopped on. It was going to the Grand Canal, but the long way around, through the Giudecca Canal first. We would approach the Palazzo Corelli from the opposite side of the way I usually went, but that was good enough for me. A boat in the hand is worth two in the bush, I thought as I dug the fare out of my pouch.

I was too anxious to sit down. I clung to the railing, my hands tight from the tension in my body. My thoughts were tumbling. Yet, in the midst of all this, I recognized that I was thinking clearly. There had been all too many days when my head felt fuzzy, when to be concerned about a lost object was just too much trouble. Lost! An empty, black space opened up inside me and threatened to swallow me whole. Lost, like those lost moments out of time on the day my husband died. Was it happening again? Was I losing things because there were blocks of time that I couldn't remember?

"Oh, God!" I whispered. I stood on the deck of the vaporetto, my knuckles turning white as I clung to that railing, and I prayed as I had not prayed in all the many churches I had visited in past months. Please, God, I prayed, don't let me be losing my mind. Let there be some other explanation for this!

THE VAPORETTO SWUNG AROUND, making a wide arc of wake in the water as it headed into the north end of the Grand Canal. The stop nearest the Palazzo Corelli was, of course, on the wrong side of the canal. That was something I hadn't thought of, and in my frustration and impatience I stood there, looking at the palazzo such a small distance away across the water, and I wanted to cry. Then the trained architectural observer in me took over, reminding me that I had never really looked at the palazzo from this perspective before. It was interesting. I looked upward, and located my own small balcony off the Morning Room. I continued to look up, and then for some reason I thought of what Marc had told me about the boys he had hired to dive in the canal, and how they had found the bronze horse. The murder weapon, as I thought of it. Ugh! How could Marc be so sure that his half brother was cured of the violence that had caused him in childhood to commit such a crime?

I took a step backward, and focused on the palazzo again. Yes, like the other great houses on the canal, the Palazzo Corelli too looked as if there were secrets hidden behind the shuttered windows. In this case, I was sure looks did not deceive. There was something going on in there, I was sure of it. Perhaps I was jumping to conclusions to assume that Paolo was behind whatever was going on, but still I was convinced. We had only to find proof, Marc and I.

I HURRIED TO THE NEXT BRIDGE over the canal and from there picked my way carefully along the wooden boards, which made a narrow canal-side walkway to the front door of the Palazzo Corelli. Since I so seldom came this way I had a little trouble with my key, but at last I got it to work and I rushed through the hall and up the stairs to my apartment. I burst through the salon door at top speed, slipped a little on one of the rugs, and was calling Zenia before I entered the kitchen where I guessed I'd find her.

She was there all right, and not alone. On her face was an expression I recognized: the child caught with his hand in the cookie jar...only worse. The person with her was Paolo Corelli. And I was furious.

"What the hell are you doing in my apartment?" I yelled at Paolo.

In answer he smiled that lascivious smile, raised his eyebrows and inclined his head slightly in Zenia's direction.

She cowered behind the counter. Her face, which I thought should have turned scarlet, had blanched instead.

She was obviously speechless. I had no intention of letting her off the hook. Reasonable or not, I felt as responsible for her as if she were my own daughter. I fixed Zenia with my sternest gaze and asked, "Did you invite him in, or did he force himself in here?"

"I, oh *signora*. I . . ."

"Of course she invited me," said Paolo smoothly. He turned his head in Zenia's direction and winked. "Zenia and I are good friends, aren't we, Zenia?"

She gulped, if anything whiter-faced than before, and nodded.

I threw my heavy canvas bag down on the kitchen table, where it made a satisfyingly loud thump. With my hands on my hips I faced them both. "And you thought, because I almost never come home in the middle of the afternoon, that my apartment would make a good, safe place for your hanky-panky?" I glared first at one and then the other. Zenia continued to cower; Paolo looked smug. He was enjoying this! The very thought of him with Zenia made my skin crawl. "Out," I said to Zenia, "and just be grateful you're too young to know any better. Go and wait for me in the Morning Room. I want to talk to this man alone."

She edged around the counter, staying as far from me as she could, then fled in the direction I had sent her.

"I know how trite this sounds," said Paolo, his voice like silk, "but you're beautiful when you're angry, Clea."

I had been outraged before; now I was beyond that. My voice was low, controlled and deadly. "You're despicable, Paolo Corelli. Zenia is little more than a child, and this is the twentieth century, not the Middle Ages. There's no such thing as droit du seigneur. And even if there were, I don't appreciate you fooling around in my living quarters! If you're going to violate Marc's ban and come to the palazzo to see your mother, that's one thing, and I guess I can't stop you. But you are not welcome in my apartment. You understand? Never, ever, do I want to see you here again!"

I was shaking when I finished my speech. Paolo stood unmoved, except for a steely opaqueness which had come into his eyes. He said, "Are you finished, or do you want to insult me some more?"

"I'm finished. I'll see you to the door."

"Not yet. Okay, so Zenia has the hots for me. Is that my fault?"

"It is, if you encourage her."

"I could tell you it's none of your business."

I gritted my teeth and spoke through clenched jaws. "For the last time, it's my business when you invade my home! And this is my home now, make no mistake about it. You're not wanted here, and if you don't leave this very minute, I'll tell Marc how often you've been in the palazzo against his wishes. You wouldn't like that, would you, Paolo? Marc is back now, I suppose you know that."

"Yes, I know, Zenia told me. You had better not say anything to him, Clea, that's not in my plans." Paolo took a step toward me and I backed up but there was no place to go. I already stood against the edge of the kitchen table.

Nevertheless, I raised my chin and challenged him. "He had an accident. I suppose you know about that, too?"

Paolo's eyes flashed, a look I could not read. He took another step toward me and suddenly my anger no longer protected me, I realized full well the size, the physical power of this man. His tone was threatening, much more threatening than mine had ever been. "How did you know about that?"

"He told me, of course." I lied, my pulse racing. "I saw him on the stairs this morning when we were both on our way out." Then something occurred to me. I didn't think Marc would have told Eugenia about his accident. "How did *you* know, Paolo?"

His eyes narrowed. He looked as if for two cents he'd strangle me. "I heard on the street. The man who picked him up is telling about it all over town. It isn't too often an uptight perfectionist like Marcantonio Corelli makes a stupid mistake with his own boat and ends up in the lagoon."

I bit my tongue, I let it pass. Paolo and I stared at each other, neither of us spoke, both of us were breathing heavily. Stalemate.

When I was calmer I said in my normal voice, "Will you leave now, please?"

"In a minute." Paolo stuck his hands in the pockets of his trousers, moved his large head on that column of neck in the way one does to loosen muscles, and managed to smile at me. It was an engaging smile, as if none of the previous ugliness had even happened. "Yeah, I was having a little fun with Zenia. I apologize. I won't do it again, I don't want you to be mad at me. But I was going to ask her to give you a message, that's really why I came to your apartment."

"Oh?"

"Yeah. The Lady and I want you to come to lunch again day after tomorrow. She'll show you her private collection then. Will you come?"

"Doesn't it make any difference to you that Marc is at home now, that just as I came home early and surprised you, he could come home at lunchtime and find you here?"

"Nope. It's not likely to happen. Besides, the Lady will have a table set for us in her own study, that's where she keeps the collection, and nobody goes in there but her. I doubt Marc has ever been through that door. I have, of course, but I'm special." His smile was dazzling, all white teeth in a still tan face.

There was something particularly awful about Paolo's ability to display such charm where only moments before he had seemed so dark and threatening. He was special, all right, but not in the positive way he meant. I had to gather up all my self-control to say, "All right. I'll be there, day after tomorrow. Same time as before?"

"Same time. That's good, Clea. Now, you can walk me to the door."

I FORGOT TO CHASTISE ZENIA. I forgot to look for my notebook. I forgot everything except a need to get back some peace of mind. The confrontation had exhausted me; I'd never been any good at confrontations. Oh, I could stand up for my principles when I had to, but afterward I always felt like I'd been flattened by a truck. I decided to take a long, hot bath; when I almost fell asleep in the deep tub, I decided to get out and take a nap before dinner.

Zenia woke me. It was already dark outside; I had napped for a long time, yet when I got up I felt unrefreshed. I didn't dress, but kept on my terry-cloth robe, which was unlike me. I didn't care. I tried brushing my hair but the thick curls resisted the brush. It was too much like work, and I just let it be. I'd gotten another haircut recently, it didn't look too bad. Besides, there was no one here but me. Zenia would leave as soon as she saw that I approved of whatever she had cooked for dinner.

I went to my preferred place for meals, the oval table in the Morning Room. Zenia served chicken in some kind of mushroom sauce, flat green beans with slivered almonds, and angel-hair pasta with butter and parmesan. She had placed a bottle of white wine on the table. I preferred mineral water, which she knew, but I said nothing about it. "Everything looks good, Zenia," I said.

"Grazie," she replied. She watched me anxiously, twisting her white apron in her fingers.

Then I remembered that I had left her here, in the Morning Room, after seeing Paolo out of the apartment. I supposed I must say something about the incident. Wearily I regarded her. "He's not good for you, you know, Zenia," I said.

She nodded, her black eyes darting, unable to meet mine. I went on. "He isn't supposed to be in the palazzo, there has been some sort of trouble between him and Marc, whom you call the Young Master. You know that, don't you?"

Zenia nodded again. She seemed resigned to anything I might say.

Even through the weariness my curiosity pushed at me. "How often, Zenia? How many times has Paolo Corelli been with you in this apartment?"

Looking at the floor, not at me, Zenia replied. "He has not been here before, *signora*. Today is the first time."

I couldn't judge if she told the truth or not. I would have had more confidence in her if she had met my eyes. "Look at me, Zenia," I said.

She did, twisting the corner of her apron round and round. She blinked, and said, "Your dinner is getting cold, *signora*."

I sighed. "You are only going to make yourself miserable if you continue to let a man like that fool around with you. I'm not your mother—"

"I have no mother, *signora*. Rosa and I are orphans. The Lady took us in to work for her when our parents died."

I felt a sharp pang of sympathy. More kindly I said, "I wish I could forbid you to see him again, either here or anywhere, but I know it would do no good. Even if you were my own daughter, you're too old to listen to me. But what I can do is tell you what I told him, that he is not allowed in this apartment ever again. Do you understand that? This is my home. No matter what his relationship with his brother and his mother may be, I don't want Paolo Corelli here. I don't like him, and I don't trust him. If you do, then you're a foolish young woman. That's all. You may go now, Zenia."

"Yes, *signora*," she said.

From the corner of my eye I saw Zenia pause in the doorway and look back at me. I knew that she wanted to be sure I would eat the food she had prepared, so I cut into the chicken and took a bite. Yes, that was what she had waited for; she left.

The chicken was good, but I thought I detected an undertaste of that wine that I didn't like. The Corellis must have a huge store of the stuff, to use it so often for drinking and cooking. The taste was faint enough that I could ignore it, and I was hungry, so I went on eating. I didn't feel like getting up and going into the kitchen for mineral water, so I poured a glass of the wine Zenia had put on the table. Stolidly I worked my way through the meal.

Sometime later, I was sitting at my dressing table and looking at myself in the mirror. With a shock, I realized that I didn't remember coming in here! The last thing I remembered was taking my dinner dishes to the kitchen...and now, here I was. In between, nothing. My heart rose into my throat, my hands went damp and turned ice cold. I gripped the corner of the dressing table to steady myself as I rose, and staggered over to look at the travel clock I'd kept by my bed since I no longer had Zenia to wake me in the mornings. It was ten minutes after eight. It had been around six when I'd sat down to eat my dinner. I couldn't have spent more than half an hour eating, so even allowing for the time I'd talked to Zenia, there was over an hour I couldn't remember!

Lost, lost! Lost beats out of time! It had happened again, just as when my husband died, only now there was no reason! Maybe it had been happening all along. Maybe that was why I lost things and then found them again right here in this apartment. Maybe I was wandering around like a lost soul, moving my own things and not remembering, not even knowing that I was losing bits of my life!

I sank down on the bed, horrified, and buried my face in my hands. I was too shocked even for tears.

The telephone rang. I heard it, faintly insistent, ringing and ringing. On uncertain legs I went to the kitchen and answered. "Hello?"

"Clea," said Marc's voice, "I knocked on your door a moment ago but you didn't hear me."

"I'm sorry," I murmured. The sound of his voice penetrated my dull horror. It was good. I waited for more of the welcome sound.

"If I'm interrupting anything, I'll call you back."

"No. No, I was, was in the bedroom. It's a little hard to hear a knock on the salon door from there." Or had I heard? Had Marc's knock been what brought me out of wherever I'd been, was that knock the last thing that had happened in the time I didn't remember?

"I, ah—" Marc paused. There was a wonderfully intimate note in his voice when he continued "—I'd rather not talk on the phone when you're so near. I have a few things to tell you. May I come down there?"

"Yes, please. I'd like that."

"Good. I'll be there immediately."

I ran my hand through my hair. I knew I looked a mess, but it couldn't be helped. I should have asked for more time, I needed to get myself together, I felt so . . . strange. Weak. Disoriented. I shook myself, literally, the way a dog shakes water off his coat. It helped, it restored my circulation, and I felt a tiny bit better. Coffee, I thought. I'll make coffee, Marc will want some, too.

Before I had time to put the water on, I heard Marc's knock. I went as quickly as I could into the salon and pulled open the door. "I'm sorry," I said, "I'm not dressed, I know I look terrible, I was about to make coffee, but I haven't started it yet. If you don't mind coming into the kitchen . . . ?"

"*Cara mia*," Marc smiled, brushing my cheek with his lips and my neck with his beard, "you did that the very first night, do you remember?"

"I did what?" I looked up at him and slowly I warmed, warmed to his smile, to his gentle touch as he caressed the back of my neck.

"You kept apologizing when you opened the door. You had already won my heart even then. With me you have never to apologize, for anything."

"Oh," I breathed. Life flooded back into my body, I could feel my blood coursing through my veins, feel the color come back into my cheeks. "Well, then, come on. You can watch me make the coffee."

"Is it Ethiopian?" Marc asked. He sat on the stool at the counter while I measured beans into the coffee grinder.

"Not this time. This is from Kenya."

"Um."

"Have you had dinner?"

"Yes. The Lady and I finished eating a little while ago." Marc waited while the sound of the grinder filled the room.

"What did you want to tell me?" I asked, leaning against the counter next to him while we waited for the water to boil.

"I have been thinking about the things we talked about last night. I checked my safety-deposit drawer at the bank. The bronze horse is still there, Clea. I thought you might want to know."

"Well, that's something."

"It means that if Paolo crosses me, I still have the evidence to use against him. Or Paolo thinks that I can use it against him, which is the same thing."

"But someone did tamper with your boat. And if you were dead, your evidence wouldn't be much good, would it?"

"I thought of that," said Marc gravely, rubbing his beard. "We'll get back to that later. I'm a businessman, Clea. I couldn't spend too much time today dealing in speculation when there were more urgent matters to attend to."

"Your business, you mean." The water was boiling now, and I poured it over the ground coffee in the filter cone while I listened to him.

"Yes. I took a junior staff member into my confidence. He will see what he can find out about the change of heart I experienced in those who were glad to work with me in the past." I had put coffee and cups on a tray. Marc said, "Here, let me carry that for you. To the Morning Room?"

"Yes, thank you." I followed him.

"No, let us not sit at the table. Here," Marc said, gesturing to one of the love seats. "When I've had a cup of this coffee, which smells so good, I'll build a fire. If you like."

"I like. I'm just not very good at doing it myself."

"You need some of those little portable tables in this apartment," he observed, putting the coffee pot on the floor. "I'll see that you get some. Now. Where was I?"

"Business decisions," I supplied.

"Mm. Yes. The other thing I had to take care of today," Marc continued, "was reporting last night's accident to the insurance company."

"Did you tell them there might have been foul play?"

"No. I would have, if there had been any hope of recovering the boat for proof. But there isn't. We went out into the lagoon and looked, Clea. It seems that the boat did sink over the Mestre Channel. It's too deep. They won't attempt to bring it up. Without proof, there is no point in making such an accusation. I would feel like a fool. The insurance agent assumes the boat was damaged below the water line and that it must have happened while the boat was docked at the yard during my trip. He will negotiate with the insurance company of the dockyard, that's not my problem. At any rate my insurance will pay, so tomorrow I will go to look for a new boat. I thought perhaps you might go with me."

"Me? Why? I know nothing about boats, I'll be no help to you."

"Well, for one reason, I would like your company." Marc smiled, and then grew serious. "And for another reason, Giorgio will come with us. I will need him to drive our boat back if I get a new one."

"Marc, I don't understand. How can Giorgio drive a boat you sank?"

"Giorgio will drive the family boat. It was my own boat which sank. You don't think we would have only one boat, do you?"

Now it was my turn to laugh. "Oh, Marc. Where I come from, we don't drive boats, we drive cars. We sail boats, and they're a luxury. Nobody has more than one. Besides, you've said you're concerned about money..."

"This is Venice, boats are to us what cars are to you. I must have my own boat, *cara*, and I confess I have an ulterior motive in asking you to go with me."

"Aha."

Now Marc's face was now very serious indeed, in spite of our lighthearted banter. "The final thing you said to me last night was that you are convinced there is something going on here in the palazzo. That we should work together to find out what it is. You said also that Paolo has often been here, that he has a way of entering without the servants' knowledge."

Immediately I sobered, recalling how I had come home to find Paolo in my apartment. With Zenia. I said, "Yes."

"We will have Giorgio with us tomorrow, away from the palazzo. Away from here, he will speak more freely. My mother's influence will not be the all-pervasive presence that it is under this roof. We will talk to him, Clea. We will find out what he knows."

I nodded vigorously. "Now I understand. That's a good idea, Marc."

He squeezed my shoulder with strong fingers. "I thought you would agree." He searched my face, in his own eyes a look of incredible openness and vulnerability. "I am sorry these bad things are happening, but I cannot tell you how glad I am that you are here. I need your support, Clea. I have never been able to admit that to another human being before."

I reached out and touched his cheek. He had moved me too much for words.

"Shall I make the fire now?" Marc asked softly. I nodded, and curled myself into a ball. My energy was so low, so low. I rocked a little, back and forth, and watched Marc build a fire, just as I had watched him the previous night. But my body did not now have the same responses it had had then. My senses were dulled. I supposed, too, that my emotions were numbed from the horror I'd felt over not remembering that block of time...although now that seemed a faint memory. Perhaps I had imagined it? No, I had not. I felt miserable, totally undeserving of such a beautiful man.

While Marc knelt in front of the fireplace, building the fire, he continued to speak. "I care more for you with every day that passes. When I was away, I wanted to call you every night, like a schoolboy with his first crush. I want to share everything with you, I trust you as I have never trusted a woman before."

I held my knees in a death grip. I remembered that only this very same morning I had been happy, standing on the Accademia Bridge in the sunshine. I had told myself I was in love with Marc Corelli. And I was. But just as his house had secrets, so I also had secrets I must keep. At least, until I myself understood what was going on. Marc and I could work together at solving the mystery of what was going on in the palazzo, but who could find my lost moments of time for me? No one.

"You mustn't love me," I said in a breaking voice. "There are things about me you don't know. Things too terrible to tell you."

Chapter Eleven

Marcantonio Corelli loved with a beautiful simplicity. Now, two days later, I looked back and marveled at how easily he had dismissed my declaration that there were terrible things he did not know about me. He had simply said, "I thought earlier that you looked as if you were not feeling well, but I did not say so because saying so can make one feel even worse. Now, I say that it is an illness speaking, not you. If you were yourself, *mia cara*, you would not say these things. You would realize that there is nothing—understand, *nothing*—that could be too terrible for me to hear about you."

I had protested, but Marc would have none of my protests. He had said, "I know there are things in your past that you do not wish to tell me, and I do not care. I care only that those things have hurt you. Perhaps you do not yet have enough distance from them, and the memory hurts you still. It does no good to tell me not to love you, Clea. It is too late for that. Perhaps some day you will be able to love me. Until then, I hope you are my friend, as I am yours and always will be. When you are ready, I will be your lover."

With this astonishingly unselfish promise, Marc had kissed me on the forehead, and offered to leave. I asked him to stay, to sit with me for a while by the fire, and he did. The feel of his presence, the simple, undemanding warmth of his body next to mine, gave me a kind of all-pervading comfort I had not known since childhood.

Later, after he had gone and I was falling asleep in my bed, I thought I understood why it was so hard for Marc to accept what seemed so obvious to me, that his half brother was the one most likely to wish him ill. And though I had not yet said so, his mother was not much better. Marc was a romantic, and an eternal optimist. Probably somewhere deep down inside himself, Marc still believed that Paolo and the Lady, brother and mother, would some day care for him as he no doubt cared for them. He didn't let them walk all over him, but he waited and he hoped, and in the meantime he did what he could to provide them with what they needed. They were family. I had never known a man like Marc. If I had not also seen another side of him, the side that was vulnerable and hid his needs in a cloak of seeming arrogance and cold formality, I would have thought him too good to be true.

We had gone with Giorgio, as planned, to look at boats. He was not as helpful as we'd hoped he would be. He denied that it was possible for Paolo Corelli to have a key to the house, and further denied having seen him any time except when the Lady had expressly announced that Paolo was to be present for a meal.

Marc had accepted Giorgio's statement, and looked at me as if to say, I told you so. I was not so easily satisfied. I'd taken a different tack. I asked Giorgio, seemingly out of the blue, if there had ever been tales of ghosts in the Palazzo Corelli. He'd looked uncomfortable, looked to Marc for a sign that he could speak freely, and when Marc had nodded permission, Giorgio said unfortunately there were such tales. His wife, Anna, believed them. It was said that Umberto Corelli, one of the "giants," had committed suicide by drowning himself in the canal. This man's portrait was not hanging on the walls, and Marc had not heard of him. Umberto's ghost was said to walk the halls at night, lamenting whatever it was that had caused him to take his own life.

Under my further questioning, we learned that though Giorgio had never seen this ghost, Anna believed that she had seen it. She said it was not white, as ghosts are thought to be, but dark. A huge, dark, shadowy presence. Rosa, too, thought she had seen the ghost. And Giorgio himself had "heard things." What sort of things? I'd asked. Sounds, noises in places that there should be no noise—in the walls. He had actually thought rats must have come up from the basement and gotten into the walls. He had put out poison, but no rats came to take the poison. They had all heard such sounds in the walls from time to time, and had learned to live with them. Sometimes they heard, too, the sound of heavy steps, and did not investigate, assuming this to be Umberto's ghost.

"Does the Lady know?" I'd asked. "Yes. She laughs at any ghosts, and says she herself is giant enough that she need not be concerned," said Giorgio.

I thought the business about the ghost was very interesting. Marc found it amusing; he had been more concerned about the possibility of rats in the walls and had asked a considerable number of questions about that while I pondered other possibilities. I suspected that Zenia was the person who was letting Paolo into the house, but I said nothing to Giorgio or to Marc about this because I didn't want to get her in trouble. I was afraid she might even lose her job, and that would be terrible for her.

Eventually Marc had turned his attention to the real reason for our outing, and we looked at boats. I learned more about small motorboats that day than I ever thought I would want to know, and Marc did buy one. He sent Giorgio back on his own, then took me for a long, glorious ride through the lagoon. We'd gone all the way out to the Lido, where the prototype of the MOSE lies on the bottom of the sea ready to raise its huge platform to become a floating dam between the Venetian Lagoon and the Adriatic. I'd prompted Marc to talk about the work of the New Venice

Consortium. Of course, Marc being Marc, he was optimistic for the future of Venice.

Those hours that we spent alone in his new boat had been wonderfully refreshing. I'd found it harder than ever to return to the palazzo. Harder still to leave Marc, but I had to get ready for my luncheon with Paolo and Eugenia. Ready to be closeted in the Lady's private study with those two giants, ready to see her precious collection. I had seldom been more ambivalent about anything. I did not want to go, and yet I did. Marc knew about this luncheon and its purpose, I had told him. I intended to tell him everything from now on—about the palazzo, that is. My own personal demons I must still keep to myself.

I dressed with care for Eugenia. I knew she liked strong colors, so I chose the brightest of the three dresses I had bought in my flurry of fall shopping. It was emerald green, a synthetic material, which felt like velveteen. Perhaps it was too dressy for a lunch at home in the middle of the week, but Eugenia herself would surely be decked out like an Oriental queen. The dress had a kind of updated Renaissance look, with a full skirt gathered to a high waistline under the bosom, and small covered buttons up the bodice to a wide, rounded collar trimmed in satin piping of the same color. The skirt was mid-calf, and the sleeves were gathered just below the elbow in a cuff trimmed with the same satin piping as the collar. I thought the color of the dress was good with my tawny shades of hair. But my face was too pale, it looked like I felt: weak. I was a long way from feeling my usual self, though I'd slept for two nights without dreaming . . . at least, as well as I could remember. Not to worry, I told myself, a pale face is easy to fix. I put on more makeup than I usually wore, and was ready.

"I'm going upstairs for lunch," I told Zenia. She was dusting the salon. She had been exceptionally quiet for the last couple of days.

"Upstairs? With Signor Marc?" Her curiosity gave her face some of its old perkiness.

"No, with the Lady. And Paolo Corelli will also be there, I am told."

Zenia's black eyes flashed before she turned her head away. Was that jealousy which flashed in her eyes? She said, "I hope you enjoy your meal, *signora*."

"So do I," I said rather grimly on my way out the door.

THE MEAL WAS ELEGANT, and interminable. The two Corellis did not disappoint me—they were as repulsive as I had expected they would be. If I had not known Paolo, I might have been impressed with his broad-shouldered blond good looks. He wore a suit, gray and probably silk, and his tie was sapphire blue, which deepened the blue of his eyes. Eugenia had on one of her caftans. This one was iridescent, a shimmering pallette of exotic colors, like a peacock's tail. Her hair was the usual elaborate combination of loops and braids. But her face! Truly, she did not look well. Hers was not a healthy fatness, she seemed bloated. When I was not hoping that she wouldn't touch me, I found myself wishing that she would get some medical help.

She paused in her own gargantuan repast to observe, "You aren't eating, Clea."

"Yes, I am. There's just so much more food than I usually have in the middle of the day," I said.

"She's too thin," Eugenia said to Paolo. "Don't you think so, son?"

"She looks just fine to me," said Paolo with one of his winks. "But you must finish your meal, Clea. The best is yet to come!"

I looked at my plate. My head was swimming, and my stomach more than a little uncertain. The pasta was my best bet, I thought, the least likely to send my digestion into further revolt. I twirled my fork in the pasta, grinned foolishly at both of them, and ate.

For a while there was silence, everyone eating. I distracted myself with an observation of the surroundings, forcing myself to make a mental catalog so that later I could report everything to Marc. He had told me that Paolo was right, he hadn't been in his mother's private study since he was such a small child that he no longer could recall what it was like.

The room was smaller than most rooms in the palazzo. The walls were of dark paneled wood. There was one window, and it was barred with decorative grillwork—for security, I supposed. The deep window embrasure revealed that the walls were thicker here than in my own rooms, or in Marc's, and I suspected that the wood panels actually fronted cabinets built against the walls. There were no paintings, no clocks, no statuary or ornamental glass—and no shelves on which to place them. There was a fireplace at one side of the room, and a large, handsome desk on the opposite side. Our table was round, not large, about the size of a game table, and it was in the middle of the room under a chandelier composed of three glowing glass globes. I thought idly that it looked like a sign for a pawn shop.

I ate pasta, and I drank wine. I ate a few mushrooms, drank more wine, and wished I dared to ask for a glass of water. I felt the Lady's eyes on me, and looked up just in time to catch her break the stare and look away. I wondered why she was staring. Paolo refilled my wineglass from one of the three individual carafes on the table. I smiled thanks. I was drinking more than I should have, more than I usually did, but I was so nervous and I thought the wine helped. Certainly something was insulating me from them; they were talking and I didn't really hear what they were saying, nor did I care. They might have been miles away.

The first warning came with a tinny taste at the back of my tongue. It was not the same, and yet it reminded me of that wine I didn't like. I made a mental note of it, and gave my attention to Eugenia because she was bending toward me, speaking.

"Paolo will clear the table now. I do not allow the servants in this room, except for Rosa to clean once a week. Now, Clea, is the time. I will show you my treasures!"

"Yes, please," I said eagerly. The sooner I saw, the sooner I could leave.

With a flourish of her massive white arms and a swish of her skirts, Eugenia rose from the table. She went to the paneled wall opposite the window, turned, and smiled back at me. I thought of a huge, evil little girl: See, I'm going to show you my pretties, all the things I have and you don't! Then she placed her hands on the panels and one by one they opened.

Eugenia's collection was glass, all glass, in a dazzling array of colors and shapes. "Through all the centuries the Corellis have collected the finest glass in the world, not just from Venice but wherever glass was made. Here, these are the oldest..." she gestured to the top shelves, where the objects were smaller, darker. "This one is Egyptian," she said, taking down a square of glass, which she brought to me. She allowed me to hold it in my hand—part of a box, probably it had been a jewelry box, in dark blue and green. It was heavy, obviously old, but I knew nothing about glass myself and could not have said if it was truly Egyptian.

Eugenia brought me object after object until my head was spinning. I had not known there could be so much variety: goblets whose stems were worked with leaves and flowers, some with twisted human forms, some with faces; plates so large they were a marvel of construction, plates swirled with an incredible array of colors; bowls of every size, some in whose depths ingeniously cut scenes appeared, some etched with portraits. There was one whole section of cabinet that held only glass spheres of various sizes from smallest to largest, some hollow and some solid, of every color and combination of shades of color that I could possibly have imagined.

Everything was quite beautiful. In fact, it was dazzling. As a collection, it seemed complete, one of the finest specialized collections I had ever seen. And there was nothing at all sinister or strange about it. I was lulled, reassured. I drank more wine, I smiled, I did not even mind that Paolo stood too near my chair and just out of my range of vision.

But in my lulled state I drank deeply, and I saw Eugenia's predatory smile. She rubbed her hands together, gloating. And I tasted again, more strongly, the tinny taste. A *wrong* taste. Another warning. I weighed it in with the warning I'd stored, and together they added up. They told me something I should have realized long before: I was being drugged! The separate carafes, the feeling that I'd been packed in cotton wool, the uncertainty of my stomach; not to mention the off-again, on-again bouts of feeling ill.... I could not think about this more at the moment, Eugenia and Paolo must never suspect that I knew!

Eugenia was still rubbing her hands together. She said over my head to Paolo, "Now, now we will show her the rest, yes, my son? See, she likes my things, she is appreciative. We can show her everything, can we not?"

"It all belongs to you, Lady. Show her whatever you like," said Paolo. He moved from behind me and once again took his seat at the table. He had sounded casual, but he was tense with anticipation. His fingernails made marks on the tablecloth where he rested his hand.

"These, these are the best." Eugenia opened a final panel, in the center of the wall. It was so narrow that I had thought it a center molding which did not open. Inside this panel, which was at most six inches wide, were shelves. And on each shelf, an exquisite stemmed goblet. Each goblet was of a different color, though their stems were clear. Simple, yet stunning. I did not know how stunning until one by one Eugenia took the goblets from the shelves and brought them to the table. She and Paolo forgot me, I might as well not have been there. They gloated over their treasures.

From the red goblet Eugenia's pudgy fingers, fat white grubs, drew a red jewel. "The ruby!" she declared, holding it up to the light. It was deep, blood-red, the size of a pigeon's egg.

"Let me hold it, Mama!" Paolo demanded. And suddenly, I understood what this was all about. This was greed. Nothing else. Pure greed.

I watched the two of them as the performance was repeated, time after time. There was a sapphire in the blue goblet, cut in the shape of a hexagon at least an inch in diameter. In the green goblet, a huge rectangular-cut emerald. In a purple goblet, an alexandrine the size of a chicken egg. I blinked back pricking tears as Eugenia cooed over an aquamarine the color of Marc's eyes. An opal, from an opalescent goblet, striking fire and reminding me of its dangerous reputation. She had them all—garnet, topaz both blue and gold, amethyst, a pearl so big it looked fake. And the prize of them all, so magnificent that it took even my breath away, was a goblet of citron-yellow that contained a pear-shaped yellow diamond, which filled the hollow of Paolo's huge palm.

Fascinating, and revolting. Eugenia and Paolo Corelli were Greed Incarnate.

And I had to get out of there before whatever they had given me could take complete effect. I didn't know what they had planned for me, or if they had planned anything, but I had consumed more of whatever drug they were giving me than ever before and I wasn't going to be able to hold my head up much longer. I prayed that my legs would work. Perhaps, I thought fuzzily, they were sufficiently preoccupied with their precious toys that they would not notice my leaving.

I got my feet in position. I steadied my hands surreptitiously on the table. Neither Paolo nor Eugenia paid any attention to my movements. Mentally I gathered myself before I acted, and then I slid sideways out of my chair in an action more fluid and rapid than I could have hoped for. I made not a sound. I had actually reached the door when Paolo turned his head. He barked, "Where are you going?" But he held the diamond in his hand, and I knew that was my advantage. For the diamond also held him; he was reluctant to give it up, and he would have to, if he wanted to follow me.

I opened the door before I answered him. "All of a sudden I'm not feeling well. You must excuse me." Then I ran. It felt more like swimming because my legs were like water, but I knew by the portraits, which blurred as I passed, that I was really running. I carromed off the stair railing, then grabbed it and swung myself around. Would Paolo come after me? He hadn't so far. Maybe I was worried about nothing, but still I had this urgency to get away, back to my own apartment.

I let myself half fall down the stairs, holding onto the railing so tightly that I felt I was wrenching my arms from their sockets. Down, down; I whipped around the landing and stumbled down, down again. Surely now I was safe. I had better be; I could barely see. My head was pounding as if Thor were loose in there with his hammer. Thank God I had left the salon door unlocked since I was only going upstairs, no way could I have been able to do anything so complicated as work a key in a lock!

I fell, in the salon. Well, I thought lying there, I had known those perilous little oriental rugs were going to get me someday. My cheek lay against the bare floor. It felt cool. Perhaps I would just lie there, go to sleep.

Enough of me was conscious that I realized I was not alone in the room. I lifted my head. I saw Zenia's feet. She had not made a sound, not made a move to help me. That was significant, I knew, but my mind had quit working....

"No!" This great refusal roared up out of me, from a well of strength I did not know I possessed. "No!" I roared again, and got to my knees. I glared at Zenia. "You will help me to the bathroom," I told her, in a voice so imperious it sounded like somebody else's.

She helped me. I said, "Thank you, now get out!" and I slammed the door on her. Then I sank to my knees in front of the toilet. More than anything I wanted to rest my head on the cool porcelain and go to sleep, but I knew that I must not.

I had never had to induce vomiting, either in myself or one of the children. In my normal state, if anyone had asked me I would have said that I couldn't make myself throw up. But I did. Probably just in time, because my vision was filled with black patches and I knew I was close to losing consciousness. Again and again, I heaved the drugged contents of my stomach into the toilet bowl. When nothing more would come up, I could see again. I pulled myself to my knees; then, shakily, to my feet. Flushed the mess away. Washed my face in cold water. I didn't look in the mirror over the sink, I didn't want to see what I looked like. I did look down at my dress, thinking that I had probably ruined it. I hadn't; to my still-garbled mind that seemed a good omen.

When I opened the bathroom door Zenia was there, just outside, twisting her apron in her hands. Her face was covered with tears. "Clea," she pleaded, "why didn't you let me stay with you and help you? You were so sick!"

Now it came to me, the thought that had evaded me when I lay on the floor of the salon. If I had been drugged over a period of weeks, which seemed likely, then Zenia had done it. She had put whatever it was in my food. Yet here was the girl with so many tears that not only her face, but the front of her dress was wet. I didn't have the energy to deal with her. I just shook my head and waved my hand vaguely. "Some things a person has to do alone," I mumbled. "I'll be all right now." I started toward my room. "If you really want to help then let me be by myself. Go upstairs, go out, go anywhere, but go!"

"Y-yes, *signora*," she stammered.

"And for God's sake, Zenia, lock the door after you!"

I SLEPT, of course. I had gotten most of the drug out of my system, but not all. I had to sleep the rest away. There were dreams both good and bad. When I awoke, my bedroom was gray with twilight. I turned my head on the pillow toward the window. The sky outside was a uniform dark gray. Clouds, the whole sky nothing but clouds. It had been sunny when I had gone upstairs, but now there would be a storm. That was all right, that was good. The rain could wash everything clean again. Perhaps I would go outside and stand in the garden in the rain, and the rain would make me feel clean again, too. I slept once more.

When next I awoke all was dark, and the rain was falling. A moderate rain, big drops by the sound of it, not much wind. I sat up in bed, felt for the lamp and turned it on. An enormous sense of relief flooded through me. I had been drugged! That accounted for everything, including the strange, almost hallucinatory dreams. It accounted for the loss of memory, for the things lost and found again, for the vague sickness which came and went. But why? Why should anyone drug me?

Not just anyone, I thought, as I got up slowly, tested my legs and found them steady. Mostly what I felt now was a great emptiness in my middle. There was bound to be something safe for me to eat in the kitchen. No, not just anyone. Zenia had to have done it, when I was in my apartment; and today upstairs it had to have been Paolo. With his mother's knowledge and cooperation? Impossible to know. Should I tell Marc? If I told him, would he believe me? Or would he think me paranoid?

I wasn't going to be able to figure anything out until I got some food into myself. I took off the green dress and put on my blue flannel robe over bare skin. I appreciated its softness. Appreciated too the softness of the dove-gray leather slippers. The truth was, I appreciated being alive, and sane.

A little later, over a bowl of canned minestrone and saltines from a new, never-before-opened box, I put together as many pieces as I could. Everything made sense, provided you accepted as fact that I had, indeed, been drugged. I called the Corellis, knowing that Rosa would most likely answer the phone. She did, and I asked to speak to Marc.

When he came on the line I said, "Can you come down here, please?"

I didn't have to say more than that, his response was, "I've been hoping you'd call. I'll be down right away."

As soon as I opened the door, Marc took me in his arms. He hugged me to him, then held me off at arms' length and examined me. "Zenia told Giorgio you were sick—it seems you sent her home early. And Giorgio told me. I didn't want to bother you, but I did want to know if you're all right. Are you?"

"Yes," I said, taking his hand and pulling him after me to the Morning Room, "but I have a lot to tell you. And I'm not sure you'll believe me."

I began with the bizarre tale of his mother's collection. Marc frowned. He knew as well as I that the goblets with their fabulous jewels were in themselves worth a fortune. If his mother had told him about them and had been willing to sell a few of them, he would not have had to sell the villa. I could see wheels of thought turning in his mind, but he made no comment. I went on, telling him how I had realized that the food or the wine or both were drugged.

Marc's black eyebrows rose as I continued. Disbelief? I tried not to care, I put everything together for him as I had put it together for myself. I told him of finding Zenia and Paolo together, that she was obviously infatuated with him and would do anything for him. I felt sorry for her, I did not want her to lose her job, I said, and yet I could not have her in my apartment again.

"Of course not," Marc agreed. "I'll find you another maid. I'll think of some explanation."

Oh, these Corellis! Life without a maid was as unthinkable as life without one's own personal boat. I said, "Marc, believe it or not, I can live without a maid. I don't want another one. I would much, much rather be by myself for a while. It will be a relief to be alone."

"If you're sure." He looked skeptical. He stroked his beard and gazed critically at me, and once more I was afraid that he might think I was making all this up. Then he asked the question I had asked myself. The question I wasn't sure I could answer. "Why, Clea? Why should Paolo get Zenia to drug you? Why should he do it himself right under the Lady's nose?"

I took a deep breath. "I think he is up to something, something you told me yourself that he did as a child—stealing. I think he's a thief. Big-time. Very expensive, rare things. I think he brings them here, hides them in the palazzo under your nose and your mother's. There is one thing I haven't told you yet, but it fits. When I was looking at the Grand Salon, I found several objects I thought were potentially quite valuable. Because you had said that you'd sold anything of real value, I sketched them. I hadn't yet had a chance to tell you about them because you were away, when I discovered that the notebook in which I'd done the sketches was missing. I thought I'd lost it. Now, I think Paolo has it. I think Zenia let him in here and he took it, because I had made a record of some of his stolen objects. I think when Giorgio and Anna and Rosa have heard things and seen things they thought were Umberto's ghost, it was Paolo coming here to hide his loot. To put such objects in the Grand Salon was very clever, really. There is so much in there already that only a nosy person like me would ever notice."

"Hmm. Yet you said that your strange dreams, and your feeling sick, and all that, started before. It hasn't been that long ago that I got you the permission to go into the Grand Salon."

"Yes, I know. Not everything fits." I was silent, thinking of the things that didn't fit. I looked up at Marc, my eyes wide. "There's another thing that doesn't fit, but I suppose it could be important. I'd almost forgotten."

Marc raised an eyebrow.

"Very early on there were times when I was walking around Venice, still not comfortable with the streets and unsure of my way, and I thought I was being followed. One night in particular I'll never forget—I was coming home from San Zanipolo. I know I was being followed that night. I hid, hoping to see whomever it was, but he was too smart. He backed off, and all I saw was a shadow. I couldn't tell if it was a man, or a woman, or what."

"Clea, I don't like this."

I shrugged. "Oh, that business of being followed wasn't so bad. Not nearly as bad as the forgetting and the sickness and the dreams. I forgot about it. I paid no more attention. I thought at the time that whoever it was, was doing it just to scare me. To give me a bad case of nerves. When I didn't go to pieces, I guess he stopped. That could have been Paolo, too."

"I don't know," Marc said, rising from the love seat. He paced and rubbed the back of his neck. "I suppose, from the way you've explained this, that it does make sense. Other people who have rented this apartment did not get involved with the family. They came and went; none stayed longer than a month; they never went upstairs. But you, because of my interest in you, you have been all over the house. That very first night we took the clocks upstairs, into a part of the house where no one usually goes."

"Um-hm. That's the explanation, Marc, it has to be. Paolo has done all this to keep his hiding places safe. He was trying to make me leave the palazzo. I don't think he ever meant to physically harm me, he just wanted to scare me away. Wants to scare me away. He won't stop. I wonder what he'll do next?"

Marc leaned against the fireplace mantel and stared into the flames of the fire he'd made. Outside the wind was picking up, driving the rain against the windows. He turned to me. "You have to leave the palazzo. I don't want you to be in danger. I still don't believe Paolo tried to sink my boat; if that was an attempt on my life, it doesn't fit in any way with what has been going on in the palazzo. But if he really has been trying to make you leave, and he figures out that you're on to him, he might . . . try to harm you.''

"I'm not leaving," I said stubbornly. Marc stared at me; I stared back at him. I broke first, I said. "Paolo may be a success as a thief but he basically isn't too bright, is he?"

"No. In fact, I don't see how he could be bright enough to be a successful thief. Someone else must be working with him."

"Okay. Zenia doesn't know that I know I've been drugged. I've been sick a lot lately, that's all she thinks I know. In fact, that's what I said to her, that I was sick. And she and I have had a rocky sort of relationship from the beginning, because of something you'll find hard to understand. I really do have trouble having a maid, Zenia is better at being one than I am at having one. She may not think it too strange if I just dismiss her. She'd even understand that I might not have the nerve to do it myself, that I had to tell you and ask you to tell Giorgio. So, even if Zenia reports everything to Paolo, he still doesn't have to know that I know. I can be careful. We'll have to keep watch, Marc. We have to catch Paolo in the act of stashing his stuff, or else we have to find where he's keeping it. I doubt, after my sketches, that he puts anything in the Grand Salon anymore."

Marc gave the back of his neck one final, hard rub, then came and crouched in front of me so that his eyes were level with mine. He studied me, as he sometimes did, as if those blue-green eyes could penetrate through my own eyes into my soul. Finally, reluctantly, he agreed. "All right. If you're sure that's what you want to do."

I nodded. "I'm absolutely sure."

He stood up, opening his arms to me, and I went into them. He nuzzled my hair, my cheek, my neck. Then he held me so tightly that I could hardly breathe. He said, "I hope to God that you aren't going to be in any real danger."

Chapter Twelve

All night the wind moaned and the rain pelted the windows. I slept and woke and slept and woke and slept again. When I woke for the last time there was silence, and my room was filled with shafts of pink gold—the light of dawn piercing through the shutters. I got up, opened them and looked at the sky across the rooftops. Beautiful! I had hoped that the rain might wash everything clean, and it had. The city glowed, like a lovely woman fresh from her bath. But this woman, this Venice, still had her feet wet—the *acqua alta* had come again.

I opened all the shutters, took my time over breakfast, and afterward I cleaned all the food and drink out of the refrigerator and out of the cabinets. I kept only the canned goods and boxes and bottles that had never been opened, their seals still intact. In the midst of this Giorgio called, said the Young Master had conveyed my wishes concerning Zenia, and that he would of course comply. He suggested that I call him directly if I needed anything. I thanked him and assured him that I would. Just as he was about to hang up I realized that Zenia had always taken care of emptying trash and I had no idea what to do with it, so I asked Giorgio. He said to leave whatever I wished discarded outside the kitchen door, and he would pick it up himself.

That task finished, I felt again the sense of relief and freedom I'd felt before, when I'd realized that I wasn't sick or going crazy. Marc and I would take care of Paolo, I was sure we would! I wanted to see Marc, I had to fight down a strong impulse to run up to his rooms. I dressed instead, remembering to wear the rubber boots, and went out as usual.

On elevated wooden planks I walked across the high water, all the way to the Piazza San Marco. At the edge of the piazza I stopped, profoundly, strangely moved. I had never before seen the large space empty of people and pigeons. Yet it was not empty at all; it was filled with water. Water as still as a lake, its surface silvery, reflecting the domed basilica and the arched colonnades like a mirror. People walked on the wooden boards under the colonnades, pigeons roosted on tops of buildings, yet there seemed a vast silence. And a heaviness, a brooding, deep melancholy.

For long moments I stood there. My eyes saw beauty: the beautiful buildings, perfectly reflected in the water, should have been twice beautiful. But somehow, in spite of the evidence from my eyes, it was not beauty that I saw. I perceived something else. Sadness. Violation. That is what I saw of Venice when I looked not with my eyes, but with my heart.

Venice, Bride of the Sea. So seriously did Venice believe in the bride's role for herself, that for centuries each year in the spring there was a marriage ceremony: the Marriage to the Sea. The Doge, in his splendid robes and distinctively shaped golden *corno*, was rowed in the gilded ship of state, the *Bucintoro*, over the lagoon and through the gates of the Lido to the open sea. There, amid music and singing, the marriage vows were said, and with a flourish of trumpets the Doge cast the golden wedding ring and wreath of flowers into the ocean waters. Happiness! Rejoicing!

But Venice no longer had a happy marriage. Her groom, her Lord and Master, had turned on her. He invaded her. Over and over my Lord Sea now entered without invitation. The Bride, raped by her husband. This was what I saw, this was the source of my profound unease, this terrible wrong called *acqua alta*. And what I felt was the grief of violation.

To see the truth about Venice, you must look with more than your eyes.

THE WATERS RECEDED; my uneasiness did not. Marc and I went out to dinner. It was ironic that we felt we had more privacy in a public restaurant than we did at the palazzo. He tried once more to convince me to move to a hotel, and once more I refused. He grinned at that, reached his hand across the table and squeezed mine, and said that was what he'd thought I'd do, but he had to try. Then he gave me news: Zenia had left not only the Palazzo Corelli, she was gone from Venice. I expressed concern for her and Marc said not to worry, it had been Giorgio's idea. Giorgio had sent Zenia to stay with his cousin on a farm near Vicenza; the cousin was nine months pregnant and could use extra help now and after the baby came.

That was not all of Marc's news. He'd had a busy day. While I was philosophizing about the Bride of the Sea and playing student at the Accademia, Marc had been going through the storerooms on the top floor. He'd found nothing suspicious, only the usual discarded stuff, most of it covered with so much dust that it obviously had not been disturbed in years. Then he had gone to his bank and taken from the safety-deposit drawer an inventory of all the items in the Grand Salon. He'd told Giorgio that he needed to update the house insurance policy, and asked Giorgio to check the inventory against the Salon's contents—a job which my own experience told me would take at least two or three days.

"I don't know what else I can do," Marc said, leaning back in his chair.

"I guess we wait," I said. I also leaned back, more relaxed in Marc's company than I had been all day. The meal had been excellent, the after-dinner espresso had the proper body and bite. Altogether I felt well, and best of all, healthy.

"Cognac?" Marc asked. He smiled, and the light in his eyes came from more than the reflection of the flame of the candle between us on the table.

"You'll make me giddy." I, too, glowed. I felt the glow inside and knew it showed on my face.

"Ah, but I will also take care of you, if you become giddy!"

"In that case, yes, I would enjoy a little cognac."

Marc signaled the waiter. The restaurant he had chosen was new to me, small, secluded, elegant, quiet, in a house which presented a severe facade to its dark, narrow street. But inside it opened up into high-ceilinged rooms, surprisingly small for their height, all clustered around a courtyard filled with greenery. A tiered fountain in the center of the courtyard spilled water in silvery cascades. Tiny white lights, like stars, twinkled in the trees. Our table was next to a long window, which opened onto this loveliness. I gazed at the courtyard and sighed. When the waiter placed our cognac on the table I barely noticed. I was thinking that I should miss places like this one when the time came for me to go back to Boston.

Marc's voice was deep, with a trace of huskiness that sent a thrill pricking across my skin. "You are a golden woman, Clea. Your hair, so many shades of brown and gold, your tawny eyes . . . You are my lioness."

I turned my head. I looked at him. I wanted to say, And you are a Renaissance Prince, my Prince. But I could not. My heart went up into my eyes, but I couldn't say a word.

Marc didn't seem to need words from me. As if he had read my look, his eyes deepened, the pupils widened, a signal of growing passion. His mouth curved and I remembered, with a hot liquid rush, the feel and the taste of those well-shaped lips. He said, "Tell me, brave lioness—"

Marc did not get to finish. Our privacy was shattered. "Oh, no," I said. "How on earth did she find us here?"

Marc whipped around to see what I saw: a little old woman picking her determined way toward our table.

"Someone you know?" he quirked a dark eyebrow. I nodded. He said under his breath, "Well, this is a public place, but she couldn't have picked a worse moment as far as I'm concerned." Then, gentleman that he was, he rose as Maria Bonavita approached our table.

"How nice to run into you here, Clea," she said in English, her head nodding. White curls bounced around a little black hat that had gone out of style at least thirty years ago. She wore a shiny black dress all tiny pleats down the front, with a white lace collar, and black shoes and black stockings. In this outfit she looked like somebody's little Italian grandmother, which was at least a bit of a change, I supposed.

"Yes, it's such a surprise to see you, Maria," I said in English, for her benefit. "Maria Bonavita, this is my friend Marcantonio Corelli. Maria is visiting Venice for the first time, Marc. Her home is in the United States, in New Jersey."

"How do you do?" Marc said, using English as I had. "Won't you join us?" he invited, although ours was a table for two.

"Well, no, there really isn't room, is there? I just wanted to say hello to Clea."

"I can have the waiter bring another chair," said Marc valiantly.

"No, no." Maria rocked on her heels, looked Marc over thoroughly, then said, "So this is the boyfriend? He talks like one of those stuck-up English actors."

I wanted to shrivel and die. "Maria—" I began in a warning tone. But she interrupted me, she was on a roll.

"He sure looks Italian, though, a certain kind of Italian. Not jolly, like my dear departed Mr. Bonavita, like the other kind."

Marc, still standing, looked questioningly at me. I shrugged, helpless.

Maria was relentless. "Too dark," she pronounced, with one last sweeping gaze of Marc's form. Then she bent, peering at me over the tops of her glasses. In a stage whisper she said, "The other brother is much better looking, if you ask me."

That was too much for me. I hissed back, also in a whisper, "I didn't ask you, Maria."

Marc folded his arms. His mouth curved within his beard. He had decided to be amused.

"You're looking a mite peaked yourself, Clea," Maria said in her normal voice. "Been sick, have you?"

"Not really. I feel fine. I really don't think it's such a good idea for you to stand there talking, people are beginning to look this way. Let Marc get you a chair."

"No, no, I'll be on my way." Maria shook her head, the curls bobbed. "I just wanted to say hello because I haven't seen you in a while. But I'll be seeing you again, Clea. Real soon." With a swish of skirt she turned on her heels and trotted back the way she'd come. There had been a venomous note in her last words, almost a threat. I had to wonder why; perhaps she'd thought I was rude and wanted to get back at me.

"An unusual person," Marc observed, sitting down again. "Apparently she knows Paolo?"

"He's her travel agent," I said, reaching for my cognac. I took a healthy swallow and enjoyed its burn on the way down my throat.

"And how do you know her? Is she a friend?"

"I used to think so. I met her one day when she was lost, I gave her directions, and she's just stuck to me ever since. I know she's elderly and harmless, she doesn't even speak Italian, in spite of the fact that her dear departed Mr. Bonavita was Italian, so she's kind of lost in Venice, but..." My usual excuses for Maria trailed off, sounding lame to my own ears.

"But you don't particularly like her, no matter how you try, is that it?"

"Yes," I smiled at Marc, relieved that he understood, relieved that he had said what I dared not say. "Yes, that's exactly it. I confess I'll be glad when Paolo gets her travel plans together and she leaves Venice.''

"Paolo," Marc said darkly. He turned and gazed out of the window at the courtyard, but I doubted that he saw the cascading fountain or the lights that twinkled like stars. His elegant profile was stern, he had a brooding air.

"Let's not talk about Paolo any more tonight," I said. But the romantic mood of our evening had been broken, and we both knew it.

I WAS DREAMING the dream again. On one level, I was in a dream and telling myself to wake up. On another level, I was telling myself that this was not a dream, at all; that there really was someone in my room. I rolled my head on the pillow, my eyes screwed shut, in that state which is neither awake nor asleep. The movement woke me, and in that same moment an inner voice warned me: Don't move! Don't open your eyes. I didn't. I heeded the warning and lay still as a stone, hardly daring to breathe.

I could feel someone standing very near, feel the person's eyes on me. I told myself it was an illusion, there could not possibly be anyone in my room. For the past two nights I had not only locked the bedroom door, I had dragged the heavy boudoir chair in front of it; no one could have gotten through that door without making one heck of a noise. Nevertheless, I felt a presence, the same horrible presence that had dogged my recurrent dreams, dreams I had thought were drug-related and could not happen again.

Don't let him know you're awake! cautioned that inner voice again. My skin crawled but I didn't open my eyes. I was strangling on fear. Apparently satisfied that I still slept, the person moved. I heard a faint, scraping sound which came from near my right shoulder. The bedside table, he or she or it was at the bedside table. Then I sensed rather than heard motion. I felt the presence recede. I drew a long, deep breath through my nose, gathering courage, and opened my eyes. Looked to the foot of my bed.

A shape was there, a huge, dark shape. The ghost of Umberto Corelli, come to haunt me! That was my first thought. It looked unearthly, looming there with no face, at all. But no, it was moving slowly away from me, and my reason returned to tell me that there was no face because the shape was that of a man with his back to me, and he was walking straight into the wall. Into the wall opposite my bed, where there was no door. The black shape dissolved into more blackness. My eyes and my ears strained to make sense of what was happening. I dared lean up on one elbow to get a better look. I heard a sound, very slight, a smooth, swishing sound. Then the deeper blackness resolved into the normal dark of the room. I struggled against believing what I had seen. Then I heard a new sound, for me a frightening sound. It had been there all along but I'd been so focused on the intruder that I'd blocked it out.

Tick, tick, tick! I nearly leapt out of my skin. It was not very loud, this clock ticking, but there should have been no ticking at all; my travel clock, which I kept by the bed, was quartz and worked on a battery. My arm shaking with fear, I reached out and turned on my bedside lamp. Yes, there was the innocent-looking offender, the silly little cloisonné clock, the one Marc had had to pry out of my fingers on a night that now seemed eons ago. I remembered standing there, the light of one candle throwing hideous shadows on the wall of the storage room; remembered a sound, the heavy sound of someone's breathing . . . and suddenly I wasn't afraid. I was angry.

"Damn it!" I growled, throwing off the covers. "You were there, Paolo Corelli, you saw us with the clocks and you saw Marc kiss me, you saw the whole blasted thing, and now you think you can scare me out of my wits by putting this stupid clock in my bedroom!" I strode across the room as I muttered this, and began to examine the wall where the man had vanished. The floor was cold, I stood on first one bare foot and then the other, running my fingers along the wood panels.

There had to be a concealed door here, there simply had to be. My eyes had not deceived me, he had gone through this wall! While I searched with frantic fingers I glanced toward the real bedroom door to reassure myself that the boudoir chair was still in place—it was. And my head was clear, nobody was putting barbiturates, or whatever the drug had been, into my food so that I would feel drowsy and confused enough to doubt my own senses.

Slow down, slow down, I told myself, you won't find anything with fingers that flutter like moths. I folded my fingers into fists and stepped back to look at the wood panels of the wall. My hands were freezing, my feet were freezing—I was freezing. The wall looked just like my wall had always looked. If one of those panels was really a door, then the mechanism that made it work was very, very well hidden. Maybe I would have a better chance of finding it if my fingers weren't so darn cold. I went back to the foot of the bed, where I always leave my robe at night, and put it on. The blue wool flannel would warm me soon. I rubbed my hands together, located my slippers under the side of the bed and put them on, too. Then, hands warming in pockets, I approached the wall again.

For a minute I faltered. This was ridiculous, I felt like a middle-aged Nancy Drew. The ticking clock seemed to mock me. I went to the bedside again, picked up the pretty little thing and made a face at it, and thrust it under a pillow to muffle the sound. That was better. Nancy Drew or no, I tackled the panels one more time. I closed my eyes and tried to recall what Marc had done to open the secret stair from the first-floor reception hall to the basement. But I couldn't, I hadn't really seen him do anything. He had just pressed somewhere.... Methodically, beginning at the top, I pressed at intervals of about an inch along the molding. Nothing happened. The wall seemed solid as a rock. I tried the other side of that panel. Still nothing.

I stepped back and eyed the wall again. I looked over my shoulder, back at the bed, to get my bearings. It was this panel, all right, this was the one directly opposite the foot of the bed, where I'd seen him disappear. Why couldn't this be like in the creepy old mystery movies I'd seen as a child, where there's always a carving of a rose, or an eagle, or something obvious to press on?

That was when I saw it: one spot, almost imperceptibly darker than the rest of the wood, right in the center of the panel at about shoulder height. I glued my eyes to the spot, walked forward, and pressed with the palm of my hand where other hands had so often pressed that the wood was darker there. Smoothly, with that whispery sliding sound I'd heard, the panel opened. It did not swing inward, but slid to the side like a pocket door. "Bingo!" I yelled, then clapped a hand over my mouth. What if Paolo was still out there somewhere? I didn't want him to hear me, to know that I had discovered at least a part of his secret.

I both wanted and did not want to step onto the hidden stair. A part of me was afraid that if I stepped through the door it would close behind me, and I'd be trapped. I went back to the bedside table, wishing I'd had sense enough to go out and buy a flashlight back when Marc had said there should be one in the apartment. I knew there wasn't one in the whole place—I'd looked. But there was a candle I kept in the drawer of the bedside table for emergencies, and that would have to do. I lit the candle. Shielding its flame with my cupped hand, I returned to the hidden stair. I leaned through the doorway, candle at arm's length, craning my neck to see. The steps clung between the wall of my room and the next room, in a space less than three feet wide; they went up as well as down. I wanted so badly to explore that I almost itched all over. My lifelong cautiousness was suddenly a thing of the past.

I stepped through the opening and stood upon the first narrow step. There wasn't even a proper landing—these were primitive stairs, indeed. Which way would Paolo have gone, up or down? By my candle's wavering light, I considered. Both, of course. These stairs must go through the whole house, they must be how he had gotten around so easily without being seen.

As much as I wanted to do this by myself, I knew that I should not. It was too risky. I dared not confront Paolo Corelli alone, I was no match for him. He probably didn't yet know that Zenia was gone, probably thought I was drugged and would not awaken when he played his mean trick with the clock. Even now he might still be in the palazzo, doing... what?

I should get Marc. I wondered what time it was. I went back to the bedside table to look at my travel clock. It was not there. Curse that Paolo, he must have taken it when he'd left his fancy little gift. I dragged the ticking cloisonné clock out from under the pillow, hoping at least that it would have the right time. It said 3:45, which felt about right. I wrestled the boudoir chair back into its usual place and unlocked my bedroom door. I took the clock with me, since I could never sleep with it in the room anyway, and left it in the kitchen. I kept the candle for the little light it gave, and left my apartment. I went to wake up Marc.

I moved as swiftly and as silently as I could, not letting myself think too much about what I was doing or else I knew I would lose heart. Still, questions came into my head. What if I ran into someone, Giorgio or Rosa or, worst of all, the Lady? What if Paolo was loose in this part of the house? What if I got the wrong door? What if Marc didn't hear me knock?

The questions came, but I didn't allow myself to answer them, nor did I allow myself to look at all those dead Corellis who stared down at me from the walls. I went all the way to the end of the corridor and counted doors back—his bedroom should be the fourth from the end. I prayed I was right. I tapped with my knuckles, softly, but the sound was loud in that lofty silent space. One, twice, three times I knocked. Fortunately Marc was not a heavy sleeper. He heard me. He opened the door, pulled me inside and into his arms, without a word.

"I found something!" I whispered against the silk of his beard. His hands caressed my back, but for once I was too excited to respond to his touch. "You have to come and see, please, Marc!"

He was slow to catch on. He let me go, moved back, smiled lazily. Thick, untidy waves of his dark hair drifted down over one half-closed eye. "What? *Carissima*, you mean you didn't come here to finish the night with me?"

"No," I swallowed hard as at last I really looked at Marc. He was nearly naked, he wore only the briefest of white shorts. Even in my task-oriented state I couldn't fail to see that he filled them well. "I, I... for goodness sake, Marc, put on a robe or something, you'll freeze!"

"Not if you keep me warm, I won't."

"Really, Marc, I have to show you what I found. This is important."

"Cruel, cruel woman," Marc muttered, but he went back to his bed where he, like I, left his robe at the foot. I tried not to watch, not to be distracted, but it was impossible. His body was gorgeous, there was no other word for it.

"Don't you, ah, have some pajamas you could wear under that?" I asked as he reached for the robe. "I wasn't kidding, it really is cold in this place tonight."

Marc raised both eyebrows, looked up at the ceiling, and spread his arms in an exasperated gesture. I looked away, unable to bear the sight of dark hair spread wing-like across the broad planes of his chest, tapering down and down... and down.

He was more fully awake now, I could tell by his tone of voice. And he had opened a chest of drawers, so he must be putting on the pajamas I'd suggested. He said, "Clea, do you realize that three of the last four times I've been with you, you've been dressed for bed? And one of those times, so was I, and now I am again, and you're here in my bedroom. Do you think I have unlimited self-control?"

I sneaked a peek from the corner of my eye. He had on cream-colored pajamas, both bottoms and top—he was buttoning the buttons. Safe. I faced him again. "I never thought about it," I confessed. "I'm just glad you woke up when I knocked on your door."

"I was dreaming about you," said Marc, belting his robe and coming toward me.

"I don't believe you. And besides, I didn't come here to—to flirt!"

"Temptress!" said Marc, but he smiled and tousled my hair. "Now, what is this that you have found, that is so important you would come and wake me in the middle of the night?"

"I'd rather just show you," I said, and then, "Ouch." I had let my still-burning candle, forgotten, tip and it dripped on my hand. I righted it and Marc blew it out.

"I was wondering when you'd remember you were holding that thing. You looked so quaint, in that high-necked nightdress under your robe, with a candle in your hand. But I'll get a flashlight, shall I?"

"Yes," I agreed. "We're going to need it."

"WHEW!" Marc whistled, "You weren't kidding, you really did make a find!" He stepped through the opening and shone the flashlight up and down the hidden stairs. "How did this come about?"

"Those bad dreams I told you about, that I thought were part hallucination, induced by the drugs Paolo and Zenia were feeding me—they were neither dream nor hallucination, Marc. They were real. I dreamed someone was coming into my room, standing over my bed in the night. Well, someone really was and this time he brought a clock, one of the ones we took out of here weeks ago. I moved it to the kitchen. Anyway, tonight I wasn't drugged and I woke up and saw this huge black shape disappear right into the wall! It was Paolo, Marc, it had to be. And these stairs are how he has been getting around the palazzo without being seen. All that stuff about Umberto's ghost: the huge size, the dark shape, the sounds in the walls, all of that has been Paolo. I'll bet there never was an Umberto Corelli. Ghost stories are always told and retold in families, Marc. If there'd been an Umberto's ghost you'd have heard of him. I'll bet Paolo made up the whole story and planted it with Zenia. She told the rest of the servants, and pretty soon Paolo had the perfect cover-up!"

"You could be right." Marc rubbed the back of his neck. "The Lady seemed to know about the ghost, though, according to Giorgio. You think she's in with Paolo on this?"

"I've tried not to think that. But Marc, face the truth. She would do almost anything to be with her precious Paolo." There, it was out. Marc winced, as I'd known he would—being denied a mother's love is the deepest hurt, no matter the age of the child.

"Yes." Marc drew in a breath, his nostrils flared. Then he was ready to go on. "Well, how does this door work? How did you get it open?"

"Close it, and I'll show you."

Marc came back into the bedroom, tugged at the edge of the panel, and it slid into place. "Someone has been using this regularly, all right. The mechanism is well-oiled. All right, show me how you opened it."

I showed him. He closed the panel and opened it himself. Then he said, "Okay, I'm going down. I want to see how far and exactly where it goes. I have a hunch that these are the old stairs I told you about, the ones that were no longer much used after the grand staircase was built. You wait here, I'll be back shortly."

"Uh-uh. No way. I was dying to explore these stairs when I found them, but I didn't, I went for you. We're in this together, remember? This is my find—I go, too!"

"Not only do you look like a lioness, *cara mia*, you are as brave as one, too. All right, together we go. But I go first, and if I motion for you to stop or to go back, I hope you will do so."

"Okay."

The farther down we went, the more glad I was that I had not tried this alone. The stairs were so dark and narrow that they gave me claustrophobia, and their wood was so old and worn that they felt fragile underfoot. I told myself that if they would hold Paolo they would surely hold me, but still every step seemed precarious.

"Clea, come. Look!" Marc whispered. He made room for me on the step where he stood. Actually, it was a bit bigger than most of the steps, some sort of standing place if not exactly a landing. He shone the flashlight on two small holes in the wall at eye level, not quite round holes, more oval. "Do you know what this is?"

I shook my head.

"Come closer. Put your face to the wall and look through the holes."

I did, and then I understood. "It's a peep!" I exclaimed. For a moment I didn't know what I was looking at. Gradually I recognized the slender columns, visible in pale patches of moonlight, which shone into the reception hall through the louvered shutters of the windows on the back garden. Then I remembered something, and shuddering, I moved aside so that Marc could look.

"Fascinating!" he breathed. "I wish I'd known this was here when I was a kid!"

"I think your brother knew, or at least he does now. That day when you were showing me the palazzo, I saw eyes in the ceiling, Marc, human eyes among all those painted leaves and vines. I couldn't believe it, I thought I'd imagined it."

Marc turned his head and looked at me. "Someone was watching us?"

"I think so. Creepy, isn't it?"

"Yes," Marc agreed grimly. "Remind me never to tease you about your big imagination again! Well, we should continue on. Or do you want to go back?"

"No. I want to see everything."

The stairs went all the way down to the basement. But before they got that far, there was a door. An unbelievably ancient door, heavy wide boards black with age. "My god, I don't believe it!" said Marc.

"What?" I asked, huddled next to him.

"Put your hand on the door." I did—it was damp. "Now listen carefully. What do you hear?"

I listened. I said, "Water."

"It's the channel that goes from the canal to supply the fountain in the garden. That channel was a kind of service entrance, but it has been blocked off for years, like this door and the stairs. Paolo, if he is really the one who has done all this, has opened it up. Opened all of this up. That's how he gets in, Clea."

"Well, I'll tell you one thing, he has a heck of a lot more nerve than I do. If I had to come in this way and use these stairs, I'd rather stay out! Let's go on down to the basement and get it over with. He must have a place to hide things down there."

"He must, that's the only place left. He'll be using the vault. It's the obvious place, he must have opened the vault too. I had no idea Paolo could be so devilishly clever."

The vast underground chamber of the Palazzo Corelli was a place no one would wish to be by day, and it was worse at night. A thousand times worse.

"This isn't fun anymore," I whispered, hanging onto Marc's arm.

"I know, but we've come this far. You don't want to give up now without checking the vault, I know you don't."

"N-no," I agreed reluctantly. I bit my tongue and tried to ignore the rustle and squeak of rats all around us. "Marc," I asked in a quavery voice, "are you sure you know where you're going?"

"Yes, I'm sure. We're almost there."

The old vault of the banker Corellis was a room that had been enclosed by bricking up the arched space between two of the huge pillars. Once there had been a door, but no longer. "We sealed it by bricking in the door," said Marc. "See, those bricks are newer."

"I see. This isn't it, it's not Paolo's hiding place for the things he steals."

"No, it isn't." Marc rubbed the back of his neck. He played the flashlight again and again across the face of the bricks, reluctant to acknowledge the evidence before his eyes. "The vault is still sealed. He hasn't used this vault, nobody could. He's not here, Clea. If he was here earlier, he's gone now."

We were both terribly disappointed, and cold, and tired. We climbed back up the hidden stairs, which were steep and uncomfortable, and no longer an exciting discovery. Marc slid the panel closed and stood looking at it.

"What?" I asked, yawning. "What are you thinking?"

"That we have to find a way to keep this panel closed permanently. We can't have Paolo, or whoever it is, coming into your room again."

"You still don't want to believe that Paolo is doing what I said, stealing and all, do you?"

"No," Marc said, turning to me. "I don't want to. But I suppose I should."

"Yes, I think you should. But you don't have to worry about me, the solution is simple. I'll just change bedrooms and keep this bedroom door locked from the outside. Not tonight, though, I'm too tired. I'll do it tomorrow. I can put a chest or something out in the hallway in front of the door for good measure."

"Clever Clea," Marc smiled, ruffling my hair.

I began to shake, suddenly my legs would barely hold me. I didn't know what it was, some sort of aftershock. "Hold me, Marc, please hold me," I begged, opening my arms to him.

"*Carissima!* Brave lioness," he said. He held me. He picked me up in his arms and carried me to my bed.

Chapter Thirteen

Marc laid me gently on my mussed-up bed. "Do you want the robe off?" he asked in the softest of voices, as he removed my slippers.

"N-no," I said. My body still trembled. I saw his hand go to the belt of his own robe. "What are you doing?"

"I'm going to stay with you. I'm going to hold you, that's all, that's what you asked me to do." He shed the robe and lay down next to me.

"B-but, you said, about not having unlimited self-control..."

"I know what I said," he put his arm around me, fitted me against his side and with his other hand drew the covers up over us both, "and it's not important now."

"Oh. If you're sure..." I murmured. I felt so warm, comforted, protected and for the moment that was all that mattered.

Marc's arm tightened, then relaxed around my shoulders. After a few minutes in which I grew drowsy, he said, "The reality of what you've been through hit me like a ton of bricks. Just now, when you started shaking. I haven't had anybody coming into my room at night, threatening me in such an insidious way. I haven't had anybody drugging me until I was confused and disoriented."

''No,'' I said in a sleepy voice, as if it were the most commonplace thing in the world, ''you've just had someone sink your boat and try to drown you.''

''You know,'' he mused, ''that incident already doesn't seem real to me, either.''

I roused myself enough to turn my head and look at his profile, faintly etched against the darkness of the room. ''Have you done anything about that, tried to find out who could have done it?''

''No, but I haven't been idle, either. I've been working to find out who has sabotaged my business dealings. We haven't gotten very far, but I guess these things take time.''

''Maybe it was the same person. Maybe that's Paolo, too,'' I mumbled, drifting off again.

''Right now,'' Marc said, planting a soft kiss on my temple, ''neither of those things seems as important to me as finding out for certain who has been terrorizing you, and why. You may be sure that if it is Paolo, or if he has any part in it, I'll see him punished. My bank has a security firm that provides us with guards. I'm sure they have private detectives. I'll hire one to investigate Paolo. I promise you.''

''Thank you.'' I was barely awake, but I heard him and was grateful.

''Clea, *carissima*, I want you to make me a promise, and then I'll let you sleep.''

I opened my eyes, looked again at Marc's elegant profile. ''What?''

''Be patient, let the detectives do their work. Don't go opening up any secret doors, don't go, as you say, 'nosing around.' Act as if nothing, at all, has happened except that you've been ill and are now recovering. And for God's sake, when you're out of the palazzo, don't go to any more of those little deserted, out-of-the-way churches. Stay where there are people.''

''That's easy to promise.'' I snuggled, warm inside and out with the warmth of knowing that Marc cared for me. He really, truly cared, he was showing it in every way he could, in every way I could possibly have asked. I smiled to myself in the darkness. "I've finished with all those little churches, anyway. I'm doing the basilica now."

"That's good. Perfect. The basilica is never deserted, you'll be with other people all the time. I don't want you to be alone, Clea. Promise."

"I do, Marc. I promise."

WE SLEPT. For how long, I don't know, but I awoke to find Marc on his side, facing me, his arm flung protectively across my bosom. A strong tenderness welled up in me, as strong as I had felt for my babies, when I looked at that sleeping face. In that moment I did not want him to leave me, or me to leave him, ever.

Marc stirred. He opened his eyes, his wonderful, sensual lips curved in a smile. I smiled, too, and reached out to smooth the tumbling waves of his hair back from his forehead. "Good morning," I whispered.

He didn't speak. He simply folded his arms around me, and his lips over mine in a long, sweet kiss. I melted against him, moving closer, until our bodies melded, our legs entangled...and then his kiss became searching. He traced my lips with the tip of his tongue, seeking entry. I met his tongue with mine, and he was the one who yielded, I was the one who entered into the mysterious textures and depth of him. I wanted Marc, as I had never, ever wanted anyone before. Nothing else mattered, past betrayals and fear of intimacy dissolved in the magic of his touch. I burned with desire, strained with a need for union.

Our clothing became an impossible barrier. There were no words, our hands and eyes spoke more eloquently than words could have done. I felt Marc's gentleness and his strength and the surging force of his passion.

He entered me with one long, deep thrust, and held. I cried out, a sound I had never before made nor heard. A sound deep, elemental, the cry of perfect union. We were no longer two but one, his pleasure was my pleasure...and more than that. Through mounting waves of joy I felt an almost mystical rightness for which I had no name. Our mutual coming was fiery and sweet and devastating.

"LIONESS," Marc said, locking his fingers in my impossibly tangled hair. He had rolled off to the side, but his legs were still locked over mine.

I smiled. I knew my face, my whole body was flushed with pleasure. I still had no words, and I knew that did not matter to Marc.

He pulled me to lie across him with my head on his softly furred chest, and stroked my hair. When some of the heat of our bodies subsided, he began to talk. "You told me once, it seems a long time ago, that you were not normal. I've been wondering ever since what you meant by that. Do you remember? Will you tell me now what you meant?"

"Mm." I did not move my head as I spoke. I traced the circle of his navel with my finger. "I meant that I had gotten kind of, well, I guess the right word is phobic, about sex. I avoided intimacy. It may be hard for you to believe, and I'm not particularly proud of it, but in the last years of our marriage, making love with my husband wasn't an intimate act. I did it, but I felt . . . nothing."

Marc trapped my hand and stopped circling. I could see why—he was becoming aroused again. "I knew someone had hurt you. It was your husband, then."

"I . . . well, yes. I have a hard time even trying to think about it, much less talk about it. Because at least part of it must have been my own fault, and I felt so much shame. . . ." I hung my head and crossed my arms over my bare breasts.

Marc pulled me down into his arms. Once more, as he had all night, he simply held me. Held me until he felt the tension in my body begin to ease, and then he spoke. So softly, *sotto voce*. "Surely you know, *carissima*, now that we have truly been together, that I belong with you, and you with me. I knew, somehow I have always known since that first day when I met you on the stairs, that making love to you

would be different. As you are different. To me, you are
perfection. Being linked with you is not sex, it is commun-
ion, the most profound communication I have ever known.''

I raised my head and looked deep into his eyes. I nodded. My voice was husky. ''Yes.''

He placed his index finger on the indentation in my chin.
''I must say this, though the words do not begin to express
the depth I feel. I love you, Clea.''

''Yes,'' I said again. I could not do as he had done, I
could not say the words. Not yet. But I knew that if I could
not declare my love for Marc Corelli, I would never be able
to say those words to anyone.

BEFORE HE LEFT to get on with his day, Marc extracted from
me again the promise that I would do no investigation on my
own, that I would behave as if I were merely recovering from
an illness. He expected that his mother would invite me
again to lunch and hoped I would accept. He said he hoped
that his mother had no part in anything Paolo might have
done, but in case she did, he would not take Giorgio into his
confidence. It would have been much easier for us to keep
track of Paolo if we could have enlisted Giorgio's help, but
Giorgio's loyalty to the Lady was great. We could not risk
him knowing anything that he might pass on to the Lady,
for she might in turn pass information along to Paolo.

''I will see you again this evening,'' said Marc on his way
out of the door. ''I suppose I must have dinner with the
Lady, but I will come soon after.''

I did as I had promised. I spent what remained of the
morning in the Accademia library, in the reading room
where I had the company of several other people. In the afternoon I went to the basilica. There was more than enough
in that barbarically splendid place of worship to keep me
occupied every afternoon for at least a week. I came home
early, shopped for food along the way. It was still a relief not
to have to deal with Zenia, though I worried about her.
What would Paolo do when he found out she was gone?

Would he think that she had betrayed him? Would that put her in danger?

There was nothing I could do to help Zenia, but I could help myself. While a spicy concoction of beef and vegetables simmered on the stove, I moved all my belongings out of the Rose Room and into the Blue Room. The drapes and bedspread were a cold, rather drab shade of blue that I didn't like, but the ones in the Gold Room were too fancy, brocaded satin, which I liked even less. As a final touch I wound the cloisonné clock and left it on the bedside table in the Rose Room. There, I thought with grim satisfaction, let him come again and find this clock ticking away in a room all by itself! Then I locked the door from the outside with its long, heavy key, and put the key in the catchall drawer in the kitchen. The chest I intended to drag in front of the door to the Rose Room was too heavy for me to do it alone, I would need Marc's help.

He came after dinner as promised, and gave me a progress report. He had hired not one but two detectives: one to do a thorough investigation of Paolo Corelli, the other to try to find out, through less conventional means, what Marc's associate had not been able to ascertain, the reason for Marc's sudden business problems. Giorgio was about halfway through the inventory of the Grand Salon, and rather than finding objects that should not have been there, he had found a few missing, none of them particularly valuable. "Beyond that," said Marc, settling with after-dinner coffee on a love seat in the Morning Room, "all we can do is wait. Go about our own business."

"Yes, I guess so," I agreed. But I was restless, I plucked at the nubby fabric of my tweed skirt. I confessed, "I don't know what's wrong with me. I always used to be a patient person. Methodical, practical. So everyone thought, and they were right." I reflected for a minute, and then laughed. "Probably boring, too!"

Marc raised one eyebrow. "You, boring? I don't believe it."

I cocked my head to one side. It was hard for me to believe, too. I had changed, really changed. I said, "That was before Venice."

"Hm. Yes. Come and sit beside me, Clea." I went to him happily. He could quell my restlessness. He held my hand, lost in his own thoughts. He said, "This Venice, our Venice, is a strange place. Beautiful, and yet at times she has been so . . . corrupt. There is a dark side to Venice, Clea."

"I know. I've seen it. Felt it."

"The corruption is in my family, too. My mother . . . I fear for her. She is behaving strangely, as strangely as I have ever seen her behave. I don't know what to do. She talks of going out again. She makes plans."

"Surely that's more normal than keeping herself shut up in the palazzo all the time!"

"Perhaps. Perhaps my judgment is clouded these days."

We continued to talk, and not to talk, for a while. Eventually I asked Marc to help me move the chest in front of the door to the Rose Room. He said, "I have a better idea."

"Oh?"

"Don't stay here, at all. Come upstairs, stay in my room with me tonight. Stay with me every night, until this mess is brought to a close and we can make plans for our future."

"No." I pulled away from him. "I can't do that."

"Why not? I want you to be safe, I want to know that you are safe, and you will be, with me. I want to take care of you, Clea."

"I appreciate that, I really do. But you know that if I stay with you, if we sleep together again . . . you know what will happen."

"We will make love. And it will be even more wonderful than the first time, if that is possible." Marc's sensual lips curved, his aquamarine eyes sparkled. So tempting.

"I . . . I can't." I clasped my hands together, holding hard to my own fingers. A hint of desperation was in my voice. "One time is one thing, but to be with you every night is another. I can't do that."

Marc's fine nostrils flared, his eyes darkened, those were the only signs that I had hurt him. And his silence. I kept silent, too. At last he said, "Clea, is it so hard for you to trust a man that already you doubt the perfection of what we have together?"

I looked away. I said, "Yes."

"Well, then," Marc rose, "there is nothing else to do except to move that chest."

THE DAYS DRAGGED BY, completely uneventful. Nothing happened, nothing at all. I did not see Paolo anywhere, not in the palazzo, not in a shop or a street or a *campo*. I did not see Maria Bonavita, and I began to hope that she had gone on with her trip, at last. Eugenia Corelli did not invite me for lunch, but she, at least, was doing something. I saw her, moving like a great, gaudy ship, down the stairs, in the garden. She looked right through me, as if she did not know me, at all. Perhaps Marc was right; her failure to recognize me, to speak when I spoke to her, did not seem normal. Little Rosa trailed after the Lady like a terrier mistakenly called into duty as a watchdog. I was so hungry for meaningful activity that I felt like volunteering for watchdog duty in Rosa's place; but of course I did no such thing.

Marc dutifully came to my apartment and reported to me every night. Private investigation was a slow and painstaking business, he said, be patient. He, at least, has his business to occupy him. He was physically wary of me, he did not touch me. In our silences I would catch him watching me, with a look that said he wondered if he had spoken his heart too freely, too soon.

Of course, I had my work, too, but art and architecture could not hold my attention. My mind wandered. Unwilling, and unable to stop myself, I thought about Marc. What held me back? Not the lingering aftereffects of a bad marriage. Marc had erased those, he was making me trust again. What I ought to be doing was trusting more, and yet I was not. Again, why?

The answer came on an idle afternoon as I walked back to the Palazzo Corelli. I didn't trust *myself*, Marc had nothing to do with it. I didn't trust myself because I still couldn't remember what had happened in those missing moments on the day of my husband's death. No one had drugged me then, there was no Paolo to blame. And, too, there was the matter of the anonymous note. There had been no more, surely that note had been only a hateful prank? But my past was still very much a part of me; I couldn't shake it off, and I hadn't made my peace with it. I didn't know how. When I didn't even trust myself, it was no wonder I could not commit myself to Marc.

Better not to think about my own past problems. Better to think about the mystery that was here, the mystery that Marc and I had at least a chance of solving. Daily I chafed against the delay. I wanted to do something, shake Paolo somehow, force him into some rash act, a confession. When I was able to be completely honest with myself, I admitted that what I really wanted with Paolo was revenge. He had made me suffer, and I wanted to make him suffer in return.

I could not do any of that, I knew. Marc's approach was the correct one. Since I couldn't concentrate on my work, I sat in the library of the Accademia and wrote letters. In my apartment I made phone calls, I began plans for Christmas. That was not enough. There had to be something more I could do, something that touched the Corellis, something that would help Marc.

I had it! Greatly daring, I picked up the telephone and called my banker in Boston. I told him about a villa I had seen and might want to buy: the Villa Corelli-Leone-Polcari. I understood it had been under contract, but the contract had failed. I wanted to know why the contract failed, what was wrong with the villa, which seemed to me only in need of restoration. More than that, I wanted to know if there was any reason I should not do business with the owner, Marcantonio Corelli of Venice.

My banker said, "I'll get back to you."

"Soon," I urged, "I have a feeling the villa won't stay long on the market and I've fallen in love with it." When I hung up I realized I had told him the truth. I really did want to buy the villa. And maybe, just maybe, my banker would be able to learn something from his side of the ocean that would be useful to Marc. At least, I would know what was being said about Marc in international banking circles.

On Thursday of that slow, inactive week my children called. They were both at my parents' house. In the United States it was Thanksgiving, and I had forgotten. Both my son and daughter were busy, happy, healthy, and they missed me. I missed them, too, but my own country seemed a million miles away. With a pang, I realized after I hung up the phone that I did not want to go home. I did want to see the children, but not there. I would have to remake the Christmas plans, they could come here to me. Boston, the whole United States, no longer seemed like home. Nor did Venice seem like home, not quite. I felt homeless, rootless.

When Marc came that night, a glimmer of understanding forced its way into my consciousness: where Marc was, that was home for me. I hung suspended by my own inability to commit, to declare for him the love he had already declared for me. Suspended by a thread whose essence was my inability to recall a lost block of time, a time of direst consequences.

"We've learned something about Paolo," Marc said. We sat over coffee and a cheesecake I'd made as part of my effort to fill up time. Marc went on, "It's not much, but it's a beginning."

"Tell, tell!" I urged. "Anything is better than this nothingness I've felt all week."

"This cheescake is very good," Marc said, moving a bite around on his tongue appreciatively.

He was teasing me for my impatience, and it was good that he could tease, an improvement over his coolly polite manner for the past several days, but I didn't care. "The heck with the cheesecake, Marc. Tell me!"

"All right," Marc agreed, grinning. Then the grin disappeared. "You've heard of *La Familia*?"

"The Family? In the U.S. I think we call it the Mafia."

"One and the same. In Europe it's more like a network than a family, but they're just as powerful and just as much devoted to activities that are unlawful. My private detective thinks Paolo has linked up with *La Familia* through his travel business."

"That could explain a lot, couldn't it?"

"I suppose so. The detective is still working on it, we'll know more next week."

"What will happen then?"

"I'm not sure. It has occurred to me that a travel business would be a good cover and a good opportunity for Paolo to be involved in a smuggling ring. I haven't yet suggested that to the detective. I'd rather see what else he finds out on his own first."

"Um." My impatience flared up again, and I pushed it down. "That makes sense. Marc, do you think Paolo may have gotten wind of your investigations? Disappeared? I haven't seen him all week."

"I have. He's in town. I think, judging by my mother's state of agitation, that he has been here in the palazzo. But of course I can't prove it. I told Giorgio I was concerned about the Lady, and to keep a sharp eye out for Paolo. Giorgio knows from experience that Paolo can overexcite her."

Marc fell silent, thinking. I finished my piece of cheesecake, hardly tasting it. I had my own thoughts, and they were not about Paolo or the Lady. Marc broke the silence. "Clea, I want us to do something together."

"What?"

"There is a carnival Saturday night. It's the night before the first Sunday of Advent, a celebration that is as important to us here in Venice as Mardi Gras before Ash Wednesday is elsewhere. Traditionally everyone, especially the old families, takes part. We wear masks and dominoes, get out the gondolas, all that.

"For years the Lady has not gone to this carnival, she has stayed in the palazzo and I have stayed with her so that the servants could go. This year, she is going. She has already brought all the old masks and dominoes out of storage, she has them scattered all over the Grand Salon—I've seldom seen a more bizarre sight, some of the masks are truly strange. She makes one choice one day and another the next. I can't dissuade her, I tried. She is determined to go. She insists she is going alone, with Giorgio to pole the gondola. I must go, try to keep an eye on her, since there is no telling what she might do in the carnival crowd. I want you to go with me."

"I'd love to. You're probably worried over nothing, you know," I said to reassure him. Then I remembered that, even to my inexperienced eye, the Lady Eugenia Corelli had seemed to be acting abnormally.

"I don't think so, but I hope you're right."

"I have my own mask. I bought it to wear to a street carnival while you were away last month. I'll show you."

The mask was as beautiful and fantastic as I remembered. "You look like an exotic bird," Marc said. "With your distinctive hair all covered up like that, you look like a totally different person."

"Well," I said gaily, "that's the point of a mask, isn't it?"

"Yes. But I think I prefer you to look like my lioness." Marc's voice held a note of yearning that struck at my heart. The usual composure of his features dissolved before my eyes into that astonishing vulnerability he so seldom let show.

"Marc, I—" my voice caught in my throat, but I went on "—I know I've been a—a disappointment to you. I don't mean to, but I don't seem to be able to help it." I gulped, my courage all but deserted me. "There's something from the past hanging over me, something I can't, I don't dare explain.''

''Come here to me, Clea. Please.'' He held out his arms.

Marc was sitting in the straight chair at the table, turned out to face me as I stood with my mask in hand. I went to him. He did not rise, he put his arms around my waist and buried his head against my belly. A child's gesture, deeply moving in a grown man. His voice was muffled by my skirts. ''I told you once that there is nothing so terrible that you cannot say it to me. Tell me, *carissima*, remove this barrier that keeps us apart!''

I dropped the mask on the table. I took his head in my hands and raised his face. The agony I saw there was no greater than my own, but the fault was wholly mine. Words came out of me, I heard myself saying them and could not stop. ''I think I may have killed my husband. My mind is a blank for the time in which he died. I cannot remember. This, Marc, is what keeps us apart.''

The agony on Marc's face was replaced by shock. I snatched my hands away. My mind closed down, and so did my voice. I was no longer capable of speech. Marc implored me to explain, to say more, but I could not. I could only shake my head. Tears started, and I ran. I ran from him, into the Blue Room, and I closed him out. I closed out the one person in all the world to whom I might have opened myself. I was hopeless. I wanted to die.

Chapter Fourteen

What should I do? Should I pack my bags and leave, take myself out of Marc Corelli's life before I could do any more damage? In the black, small hours of the dead of night I started to do just that. I began to pack and I did pretty well until I came to my handwoven wool cape, that wonderful garment which held in its very fabric some of the mystery that is Venice. I remembered buying it in the narrow, dark street from the strange old woman. Smoothing the cape's softness under my palm, I enjoyed its colors, yellow deepening to gold and all shot through with a blushing pink—the colors of a Talisman rose. I thought of Marc, and the ridiculous excess of all those yellow roses. I could not leave; I did not want to leave.

Then I must do as Marc had asked, I must explain about the lost minutes, the blank space in my memory when my husband died. Yes. I would write it all down, that's what I would do; writing would be easier than trying to tell him face-to-face. But writing was not easier. All through what remained of the night I wrote and crossed out and tore up pages, threw them away, started again. The more I wrote, the more I doubted myself until finally, exhausted, I gave up. I pushed my half-packed clothes to one side of my bed and fell in a heap on top of the covers. I slept.

Near dawn, struggling from the depths of sleep, I thought I heard sounds. The intruder, Paolo, in the Rose Room? I was too wrung-out to care. The locked door and the heavy chest in front of it would stop him. If, in fact, I had really heard anything, at all. I slept again.

I next woke to broad daylight and a distinct rapping on my salon door. "Just a minute!" I called out. Marc, I thought, it must be Marc! And I was instantly wide awake, pulling on my robe and running to the door in bare feet. My visitor, however, was not Marc. It was Giorgio who stood there with his long, rather mournful face.

"Good morning, Giorgio," I said, holding my robe together under my chin. "I guess I, ah, overslept. What can I do for you?"

"The Young Master asked that I give you a message before you leave the palazzo this morning. He wishes you to meet him in the Grand Salon at three o'clock this afternoon."

"Oh. I suppose I can do that. Did he say why, Giorgio?"

Giorgio rocked onto his toes and back on his heels. He cleared his throat, looked away from me and back again. Clearly my question made him uncomfortable, but he answered. "I believe it has something to do with the ball at the Palazzo Corleone tomorrow evening. The ball for the carnival."

"Ball? I know I said I would go with him to the carnival, but I thought it was a street carnival. I don't know anything about a ball."

Giorgio cleared his throat again. "It is a ball for all the oldest families, every year there is an invitation. The Lady has said that she will go. I told this to the Young Master at his breakfast this morning, and he then asked me to give you this message, to meet him in the Grand Salon."

"All right. I'll be there."

"And there is one more message, *signora*. This one is a note which was delivered here for you just a few minutes ago."

He extended an envelope and I took it, saying, "Thank you. Good day, Giorgio."

The envelope was creamy, heavy paper. My hand trembled as I held it, black spots appeared before my eyes as I looked at my name written in blue ink in an old-fashioned, spidery backhand. I took a deep breath and closed the door; went with a halting step to the Morning Room and sat down at the table. I put the envelope down and stared at it until I could breathe evenly. I had seen this writing before, on cheaper paper, in another world. Delivered by hand, Giorgio said. The writer of the anonymous note here, in Venice?

"Oh, God," I moaned. I did not have the courage to open it. Not yet. I left the envelope lying on the table while I opened every shutter in the apartment, letting in the bright, sane light of day. I made a pot of coffee, but nothing to eat; my heart was in my throat, I felt as if I might never be able to eat again.

With fresh, hot coffee to fortify me, I returned to the table, sat down, and decisively took the envelope in hand. The paper of the flap was thick and resisted my tugging fingers. And I noticed, with a quickening of my heartbeat, a crest embossed there. I pulled out a sheet of folded paper. My heart pounded harder as I saw that spidery blue writing which covered the page.

"Ahh," I sighed, letting go my fear, feeling suddenly boneless. My ability to reason was restored to me. The note was from Maria Bonavita, my annoying but harmless old friend! No danger here, I had let myself get all bothered over nothing. The similarity of handwriting was no more than coincidence: hers was a style of penmanship which thousands of women her age must have in common, just as they had in common a preference for blue ink. My own grandmother, when she had been alive, had used blue ink and that backhand style of writing.

I smiled and shook my head at myself. My big imagination, Marc would have said. I read the note and felt an even greater relief. It said that she was sorry to have to leave Venice without seeing me one last time, but her reservations for Hong Kong had come through. She was to sail not from Venice but from Naples, and had to be on her way immediately. The note closed with the conventional sort of thanks for my friendship, and a wish that the two of us might meet again in Boston one day.

Such a lot of fuss over nothing, I thought. If I hadn't been so tangled up last night in things of the past, I probably wouldn't have jumped to the conclusion that Maria's note had come from the anonymous letter writer. The power of suggestion! Maria's leaving was actually good news. I wouldn't have to feel guilty around her anymore! Suddenly I was so hungry I could eat a horse.

AS I CLIMBED THE STAIRS just before three that afternoon, I tried not to think about the way I had run from Marc and closed my door against him. Life goes on, I told myself, even the most seemingly insurmountable problems can be solved. I squared my shoulders and went in through the immense double doors, which stood wide open.

At the far end of the Grand Salon a long refectory-type table had been set up in front of the fireplace. It looked, as I approached down the length of the blue-and-gold rug, like the world's most exotic garage sale. The table was piled high with jumbles of clothing in rich fabrics and colors. Pawing through the sumptuous mess was Marc, in his usual dark-suited severity. His back was to me.

"I come at the appointed hour," I said, forcing a smile to my stiff lips, attempting to be witty. I always felt a little awkward in this room; today I felt like a paragon of awkwardness.

"So you have," said Marc, glancing over his shoulder. He did not smile. "Thank you."

"Ah," I crossed my arms, hugging myself, "what's this about a ball?"

"*Un ballo in maschera por carnivale,* a masked ball for the carnival," said Marc in a mixture of Italian and English.

"I know what it means," I said with some irritation. "I take it we're going?"

"Yes, unfortunately. I do not like these balls, but my mother is determined to go, so we must go, too. These are the costumes. I'm looking for something that will suit you."

"I can do my own looking, thank you," I said, stepping up to the table. In the profusion piled there, a gorgeous shade of rose caught my eye. I reached for it. As I pulled the rose garment from among several others, the quality of workmanship of all these clothes impressed me. "Marc, these aren't just costumes! These gowns are old, they're priceless!"

"I suppose some of them are very fine," Marc conceded. "Not all are old, though. For instance that pink one you have in your hand...that is not for you, Clea."

I finished pulling the rose gown free and held it up. It was the size of a small tent, three of me could have fit inside. Ruefully, I smiled. "I see what you mean. But I do like the color."

Marc smiled, too. The smile touched his eyes, the aquamarine ice began to melt, but then he looked away and resumed his search. "That was the Lady's, she wore it when I was a child. I remember. You will have to wear one of the truly old gowns, I think. You are a rather small size, perhaps something from a much earlier century will fit you."

"I did lose weight, all those weeks when my stomach wasn't right, but I've never thought of myself as being small. Why don't you let me find my own dress, and you find yourself something to wear? If I have to have a costume, then so do you." I sorted through the piles of wonderful things, loving the feel of velvets and satins, the crispness of old lace, the excitement of finding a collar encrusted with pearls, a skirt embroidered in gem-studded gold.

"I have chosen my costume. It is there, on that chair," said Marc with a toss of his head in that direction.

I went to look. Black. Of course, I thought, Marc would wear black. But that was the domino, the long, full cape. I moved the domino aside and saw what else Marc had chosen: knee breeches of pale gray velvet and matching stockings, black shoes with enormous silver buckles, a long vest of silver brocade, a full-sleeved shirt with a lacy jabot and cuffs. A jacket of dark green velvet, so long that it was almost skirted, and nipped in at the waist with silver buttons. Sitting on the arm of the chair and looking sinister was a black mask attached to a black tricorn hat with a veil in back that would hang down to his shoulders. "You will look wonderful in these clothes," I said, meaning it.

"Mmm," said Marc. No doubt he, like most men, hated to get dressed up, but I was beginning to enjoy this. He turned. "What do you think of this, Clea?"

"It's the wrong period to go with these seventeenth-century clothes you'll be wearing," I said, reaching for the dress he held up, "but actually, I love it." The dress was either a copy of a medieval style, or very old itself. Feeling the fragility of the fabric, I thought the latter. Juliet might have worn such a dress on the balcony as she waited for her Romeo. It was a deep amber velvet cut low and square across the bosom and falling full beneath, with long narrow sleeves that came to a point. Very simple, yet the color and the size were perfect for me. I had to admit that Marc had a good eye.

"You will need a domino, and a different mask. The one you showed me last night would not suit this dress, I think," said Marc. He began to sort through the dominoes, piled like black shrouds at one end of the table. "We keep all these things from one year to the next, one century to the next," he said. "The masks and dominoes are a part of Venetian life."

"I know," I said, "sumptuary laws and all that. People had to wear the plain cloaks when they went out in public, to hide their splendid clothing. Surely the masks and dominoes had the effect of making the city a more democratic place. At least you couldn't tell someone's rank by the way they dressed in public. If a woman had wanted to go out alone, wearing the mask and domino would let her get away with it."

"Yes, and criminals and all sorts of unsavory characters could wear the same disguise."

"You're certainly in a dark mood this afternoon," I observed. Marc held up and rejected one domino after another. Apparently many Corellis had been taller than I.

"And I wonder who could be responsible for that?" he asked softly, while he shot me a glance cold as ice from under his dark brows, a glance that burned, as extreme cold burns. I flushed and turned away.

"This one should not be too long for you," he said. Marc dropped the voluminous cloak around me and for a moment I felt his hands strong upon my shoulders. The domino was surprisingly heavy. It reached to my ankles and was so full that I felt lost among its folds. "Now the mask," he mumbled.

I turned back to him. I had a physical pain in the center of my chest. I wanted so much to make everything right and I could not. I said through my pain, "I'll find a mask. You can go on with whatever else you have to do."

The masks were on yet another table, the round one Giorgio had set for us here in front of the fireplace when I'd first met the Lady, all those weeks ago. I was glad that I wore the domino, I felt that it protected me somehow, and I had no desire to take it off.

I went to the table and scarcely saw the fantastic shapes of the masks, I saw only the blank holes of their eyes. My own eyes were wet. I wasn't crying, not exactly; yet my eyes were wet and I didn't know how they had come to be that way. I picked up a mask, a black one affixed to a hat and veil like the one Marc would wear, and I put it on. I hid my wet eyes and my face, which threatened to crumple on me at any minute. In the mask I felt better. I wished that I were a Venetian of long ago—they had found a grand way to hide.

Marc had not left the Grand Salon, in spite of my suggestion. With the mask obscuring most of my vision, I felt rather than saw him join me. "That mask is not for you, that is a man's mask," he said. His hands moved through the strange half faces on the table while I admitted to myself that those were tears on my face, inside my mask.

"I like this one," I said stubbornly.

"What game are you playing, *carissima*?" Marc asked in a gruff whisper. "You, who have accused the Corellis of having secrets? You run away, you close your door on me. Now must you hide your face from me?"

I raised my chin. I felt the veil attached to the mask's tricorn move against the back of my neck. Marc's face was inches from mine, his vivid eyes stared at me through the eyeholes of my mask. "The masked ball was your idea, not mine," I said.

"Actually it was the Lady's, and no good will come of it, no more than any good has come of any of her ideas that I can remember. I do not want to go, but someone must watch her and the responsibility is too much for Giorgio. This comes at a bad time for us, Clea."

"Yes, it does," I agreed.

"Perhaps you would rather not go with me. Perhaps you would prefer to close me out of your life completely, as you closed me out of your room last night."

"I thought of that." I took two steps backward, the domino swaying against my ankles. "I thought of leaving Venice, I even started to pack."

"Well, then, what stopped you?" Marc advanced two steps.

"I—I don't want to go," I said miserably, backing further. "I thought perhaps I could explain, I could write it all down in a letter. But I couldn't, I—I got all tangled up..."

Again, Marc advanced. The intensity of his feelings burned through the air, reached me through the heavy cloak, through the mask. Anger. It was anger that I felt from him. I had never known his anger before, and it was devastating.

When his voice came it was low, controlled, and held an edge of threat. "I will never force you to anything, Clea Beaumont, but there is a part of me that wants to snatch you up and carry you to my room and keep you there until you let out this secret of yours that is poisoning you. Not for a minute do I believe that you killed your husband in cold blood. Either you are very much mistaken about the manner of his death, or you had good reason to do whatever you did. But you must tell me, of your own free will. Until then you can hide your true feelings from me, with or without a mask, I do not care."

Marc wheeled. He stalked away, the thick rug absorbing his angry stride. I did not move until I heard the ring of his heels on the bare wood of the threshold and knew that he had left the Grand Salon. Then I took off the mask and wiped my wet face with my fingers.

He had a right to be angry, and I was a fool.

I went back to the round table and its many masks. All those empty eyes stared up at me. They were as empty as my life would be without him. One mask drew me, and I reached out for it. It was a cat's head, a golden cat with sequins round its eyes and long, mischievous whiskers on its cheeks. Like most of the others, this was a half mask, my own mouth and chin would show beneath those whiskers. Not a lioness, but a cat still, a relative of the lioness. Yes, this was the mask I would wear to the ball, to the carnival. But would Marc ever again call me his lioness?

I WENT TO MARC'S ROOMS, I knocked on his door. First his sitting room, then his bedroom. There was no answer. Either he was not at home or he would not open his door to me. I looked at that implacably shut door and understood how he must have felt when I had closed my own bedroom door on him. I was getting what I deserved.

The Palazzo Corelli had never seemed more oppressive than it seemed to me tonight. Worse than oppressive, it seemed evilly haunted, as if every malevolent and corrupt spirit of that family had overpowered shades of the more benevolent and now walked the halls. I fled down the stairs and into the safety of my own apartment, but even there I could not escape. My own walls, even in the Morning Room, seemed to heave and sigh ill will. I could not stay inside. I flung on my wool cape, ran down the stairway and through the vaulted shadows of the reception hall, out into the garden.

There I spread my arms and inhaled a deep breath of night air. But there was no freshness in it, the night was oppressive, too. The air had weight, was almost palpable. Ominous, heavy. I will walk, I thought, until I walk off this heaviness. I started for the gate.

A shadow rose up out of the darkness. I stifled a scream, and bolted. As I reached the gate a hand grabbed my shoulder.

"Clea?" The voice was Marc's. "You should not go out alone, especially not at night!" No longer angry, full of concern.

I slumped against him in relief. "It's such a strange-feeling night, I couldn't stay inside."

"Yes, I felt it, too. I believe there is a storm brewing, although the weather forecast said nothing of it. I could not stay in my own rooms, either."

"I know. I was there, I mean I knocked on your door and no one answered."

"You came to see me?" Marc's arm went around me, he turned me within its circle, and I looked at his face in the light of the lamp on the gatepost. His expression was both watchful and hopeful.

"Yes, I did," I said, swallowing hard. I would keep my resolution to tell him everything. "We could talk here, I suppose. We seem to have done a lot of meaningful talking in this garden."

"So we have." We went to one of the stone benches and sat side by side. "Now, *carissima*, tell me whatever you want to say."

"About my husband, what happened on the day he died. I had received an anonymous note in the mail which said that my husband, his name was Chet, was a criminal. I intended to confront him with the note, because I thought it might be true. We had grown very far apart—I've told you that—I scarcely knew him anymore. I had been planning to get a divorce when I could support myself, I'd been working on my art-history degree so that I could get a paying job. And when I got that note I decided I'd had enough, I would show him the note and ask him if it was true. Even if it wasn't, or he denied it, I thought I would go ahead and tell him I wanted a divorce." I paused to catch my breath.

Marc nodded encouragement.

I went on. "Chet was in his study. I gave him the note, and he read it, and he was enraged. His face turned purple, he started to get up from his desk ... And that's all I remember. After that, there is nothing but a blank space in my mind. A horrible blank space. The next thing I remember is Chet slumped over his desk, his face in a pile of papers, and I had the anonymous note in my hand again. Then I called 911, the emergency number, and the rescue squad came. He was dead. I knew he was already dead."

"Obviously he had a heart attack. You didn't kill him. How could you ever think that you had, Clea?"

I shook my head, feeling no relief from this confession. "I had the note in my hand and I didn't remember taking it back. What if I stood there and watched him die, deliberately let him die before I called the rescue squad? Or what if I somehow goaded his anger, pushed him into the heart attack?

"Later I burned that note, I destroyed it, and I never told anyone about it. I felt guilty, Marc. I still feel guilty. I don't think I ever wished Chet dead, but the fact is that I wanted out of the marriage, and with him dead I didn't have to divorce him. There was money, Marc, a great deal of money I didn't know he had. Later I thought, what if during the time I don't remember, he told me yes, he was a criminal and he had a lot of money from his criminal activities? What if I wanted that money and I pushed him into a heart attack so that I could have it? And then, because I couldn't consciously stand the thought of doing such a thing, I just conveniently forgot?''

Marc took my hands. "You wouldn't do that. I know you, Clea. This great secret that you have been so closely keeping is not so horrible as you think. You had a shock, you witnessed your own husband having a heart attack, and you could do nothing to help. His agony must have been a terrible sight, that is why your memory had blocked it out.''

"B-but the note . . .''

"From what I know of you, *mia cara*, it is far more likely that you retrieved that note in order to protect him. Even in a state of shock, you would not let such an accusation fall into the hands of strangers.''

"I don't know." I huddled, bowed, in my cape. "I just wish I could remember.''

We were silent then, Marc waiting for me to say more if I wanted to, and me too miserable to say or do anything. Finally Marc asked, "Was he a criminal, Clea? Is that why you left your home and came here?''

"No!" I snapped my head up. "I just wanted to get away. I don't know if Chet ever did anything illegal or not, he was a lawyer, for heaven's sake. I never had another of those notes. I liquidated all his holdings, I haven't touched any of that money yet, there was plenty of insurance money. If he did anyone wrong I'll make restitution.''

"Hey, be calm, I wasn't making any accusations." Marc put his arm around me.

"I know you weren't. Don't you understand yet, Marc? The problem is me. I don't trust myself. I was very unstable when I came here. I was getting better, or at least I thought I was, and then there was all that business with being drugged. I was so relieved to figure out what was going on that I almost let myself forget that there is one very crucial blank space, loss of memory, whatever you want to call it, that drugs played no part in. I almost let myself forget that I forgot—Ha!" I laughed, semihysterically. "Forget I forgot, that's funny!"

"Hang on, Clea," Marc warned, gripping me tightly, "this is not as awful as you seem to think!"

"Yes, it is," I insisted, "because until I can remember what really happened when Chet Beaumont died, I'm not going to trust myself. I can't, can't make any kind of commitment to anyone...."

"Shh." Marc pulled my head down to his shoulder. I felt his fingers stroking, working their gentle way through the curls of my hair. "Don't say any more. I understand now what you've been getting at, why you have been so upset when I talk of loving you, when I want to make plans for our future. I do not care about your blank space, *carissima*. And when our current problems are over, when we have lived through tomorrow night with the Lady and whatever horrors that may bring, when we know more of the truth about my half brother, then I will persuade you to let go the doubts of yourself."

"I hope so," I said. But around us the very air of Venice hung heavy. The Palazzo Corelli brooded above us. Behind us the wicked little Pan spewed his filth into the fountain.

Chapter Fifteen

Preparations for the carnival went on under skies that were veiled in black like widow's weeds. The clouds seemed low enough to touch, they seemed to roil of their own volition, without wind. The murky canals, too, roiled, of whatever menace crawled in the muck beneath. It was neither cold nor hot; an unearthly, ominous stillness gripped Venice. The very texture of the air made my flesh creep.

All day Saturday I kept to my apartment, I saw no one. Somehow the hours passed. Rosa came to my door with my clothes for the ball cleaned and pressed. I bathed without the pleasure I usually took in my bath. Perhaps I had caught Marc's apprehension about the evening, or perhaps I had only caught the weather's ominous mood; at any rate, I did not enjoy dressing myself in the lovely gown of amber velvet as I should have done. I wondered how old the dress was, wondered for whom it had been made. It fit me so perfectly that no alteration whatever had been required. Had she had a good time at her ball, this *Signora* or *Signorina* Corelli, in her amber velvet gown?

I put on the golden cat mask. That made me smile—my lips curved saucily under the upswept long whiskers of gold wire. The sequins around the eyes twinkled, the little ears on top of my head were perky. The indentation in my chin, my own chin, added to the impish cat look. I liked this mask. I pulled the black domino over my shoulders and stood back in front of the mirror to get the full effect. If only my children could see me now, I thought, they'd never recognize their old Mom! I wished I had a camera. Then I took off the mask and the domino and waited for Marc to come for me.

He was early, I didn't have to wait as long as I'd thought. When I opened the door, he almost took my breath away. I looked him over as thoroughly as any man ever undressed a woman with his eyes.

"Come in, *Signor* Corelli," I said mischievously, "and allow me to be the first to tell you that you look absolutely ravishing this evening!"

He raised one dark eyebrow and made a sort of self-effacing grimace. "The proper response must be 'thank you,' but I feel like saying something else entirely! However, you, Clea, are lovely. I was right about the dress, wasn't I? It suits you well."

"Yes, you were right, but don't let it go to your head. You're early, aren't you? I thought we weren't to leave for another half hour."

"That's true. I expected to have to wait while you finished dressing, but you are done already, I see. I've brought you something, Clea. I thought it would go well with that dress. Let's go to your room where you can sit in front of the mirror. I would like the pleasure of putting it on you myself."

"Sounds a bit dangerous, but okay."

The long mirror, which hung over the dressing table in the Blue Room, was old. It gave back a wavering reflection, as if one were underwater. Marc dropped his domino and sinister-looking mask on the bed. In his hand he held a slender black box. I followed his reflection in the mirror as he approached me where I sat at the dressing table. It was like watching a costume film. Though Marc's hair was short and thus out of period, his beard compensated. His legs in knee breeches and stockings were splendid. The brocade of his long vest rustled slightly as he walked toward me with the box in his hand. He opened it and placed it before me on the dressing table.

"Oh, how beautiful!" I exclaimed. Inside the box on a bed of white satin lay a large pear-shaped deep yellow topaz attached to a chain of braided gold. "Have you raided the family coffers to adorn me for the evening?"

"No, *carissima*." Marc reached over my shoulder and took the necklace in hand. "I bought this myself today. It looks old but it is new, and it is yours. My gift to you, Clea." He fastened the chain around my neck. The pear-shaped topaz gleamed as it nestled in its place, just above the hollow between my breasts. Its color and spark gave light to the amber velvet of the low-cut gown. "Perfect," Marc murmured, "I knew the jewel would be perfect for you tonight, Clea."

"Thank you," I whispered. He stood behind me, holding my shoulders in his hands. He moved close, so that my back rested against his thighs and I felt the stirring of his manhood. He did not move, nor did I. We looked at ourselves in the old mirror. "We look like an old portrait," I said. I felt a little strange. Were these beautiful people real?

"A handsome couple," said Marc rather hoarsely. Even in the wavy reflection of the mirror I could see his eyes darken with the depth of his feeling. He bent his head and placed a kiss, gentle and hot, in the curve where my neck met my shoulder. A thrill rippled through me from head to foot, a silver shiver of liquid fire.

I gripped Marc's hands, which were still on my shoulders, as his lips went to my cheek, my temple. "Stop," I breathed, "no more, please. I'll melt, right here!"

Marc chuckled, a wonderful, warm, sensual sound. He moved back and I stood up and turned to him, my fingers on the topaz he had given me.

"The necklace is beautiful," I said. "And just wait until you see my mask! You're going to like it, I know you will."

"WHAT DO YOU MEAN, we're not going with her?" I asked Marc. "I thought that was the point, for us to keep an eye on Eugenia tonight."

"Yes, but from a distance. After she told Giorgio that she was going to the ball at the Palazzo Corleone, I offered to accompany her and she refused to hear of it. Then I said I would go anyway and take you, and she sniffed and said very well, but I would have to hire a gondola as she was taking ours. So I really don't know, she may have other plans. At any rate, we'll wait here by the stairs until she comes down. If we stay back in the shadows she won't notice us. Our gondolier is waiting outside, and as soon as Giorgio leaves with the Lady, he will pull up to the steps and we'll follow them."

It was rather exciting, lurking in the shadows of the reception hall. In our long black dominoes we were like shadows ourselves—especially Marc. His mask completely covered his face. He looked just like the specter of Mozart's father in *Amadeus*. He inclined his head to me, and I imagined a smile behind that somber visage. "You keep that bright cat's face of yours well back out of the light, *carissima*," he said. He rested a gentle finger briefly on my chin.

"I will," I whispered.

Moments ticked by, and then we heard a rustling on the stairs. Giorgio came first, dressed in the splendid old livery of the Corellis, green and gold. He wore a handsome white wig with a little pigtail in back, tied in a dark green bow. At the foot of the stairs he turned, his hand extended in order to assist the Lady.

She came slowly, majestically down the stairs. Her black domino, so voluminous that it could have sheltered a whole brood of children, flapped open to reveal a slash of blood-red satin. Her mask was much like Marc's, it was attached to a tricorn with a veil in back, but the face of it was white, with exaggerated black eyebrows and bright red lips. She moved across the cracked mosaic tiles of the hall with a slow grace incredible for one of her size. On this night Eugenia Corelli seemed more myth than woman, too large to be quite human.

The Grand Canal was alive with gondolas. No vaporetti, no motorboats to spoil this night. Each gondola bore fluttering ribbons in the family colors; even our hired gondola, as it was ours for the evening, had ribbons of green and gold and our gondolier wore green and gold ribbons tied around his upper arm. People cloaked and masked walked and capered along the *fondamenta*. Light blazed from the long windows of every palace and building. Music filled the air, all kinds of music yet somehow the sounds did not clash with one another. I was enchanted. I forgot the oppressive weight of the certain-to-come storm, forgot Marc's concern for his strange mother. This was going to be a glorious evening, I was sure of it!

Eugenia did go to the ball. The Palazzo Corleone was a grand house, far grander than the Palazzo Corelli. We danced in a hall at the top of the palazzo, with great marble columns, which rose to a barrel-vaulted ceiling painted with clouds and winged cherubs and half-naked gods and goddesses. We accepted crystal flutes of champagne from white-wigged servants in the Corleone livery of deep burgundy and silver. Marc was a good dancer and an attentive companion. He introduced me to a great many people, all of whom were politely curious. Slim, elegant women with long, aristocratic Italian noses eyed me with barely concealed jealousy. Marc never left my side. And both of us stayed, always, where we could see Eugenia Corelli.

She had, of course, caused a sensation. The full-face mask was apparently to be worn only outside, with the domino. Once in the palazzo both Marc and his mother had removed that mask and donned another, smaller, which covered only the area around the eyes. Marc's was simple, black; Eugenia's was red, covered with sequins. Her dress was either a masterpiece or a disaster, depending on one's point of view. It was cut low enough to reveal the mountainous tops of her too-white breasts. Unlike the shapeless caftans I had always seen her wear, this dress clung faithfully with its blood-red satin to every rolling inch of her torso. It had balloon sleeves and a huge, bell-like skirt supported either by her own flesh or a mass of petticoats, or both. Pearls were woven into the elaborate loops and braids of her black hair. In her pudgy white hand she carried a black lace fan, which she wielded well, coquettishly. Once or twice I saw Marc wince as she flirted broadly with the men who, for whatever reason, clustered around her.

"I think she's just having a good time," I said to Marc during a break in the dancing.

"She's too excited, I'm sure she's drinking too much," said Marc. I thought he was anxious over nothing, and told him so. We danced again, to a waltz whose swirling steps caught us in a pattern that carried us far to the other side of the ballroom. And when we came again to the place where we had started, Eugenia was gone.

"Damn!" Marc swore under his breath, "We've lost her! I was afraid something like this would happen."

"She's probably around somewhere, we only have to look for her," I said. I wasn't worried, not then. But a woman of Eugenia's size didn't get lost in a crowd . . . any crowd. We looked for Giorgio, who with his relative height should also have been easy to spot. He was nowhere to be seen. I said, "I expect Giorgio has taken her back to the Palazzo Corelli. She must have been tired, that's all. Give her a few minutes, and we can call."

"If she has gone back to the palazzo, then there is no problem. But if she has gone out into the streets... We must get our cloaks, Clea. We have to go out into the streets ourselves, after her."

I hurried down the grand staircase after Marc. It was not yet midnight, and I felt like Cinderella forced to leave the ball before time. As he placed my dominio hurriedly around my shoulders I grumbled, "I think you're making a mountain out of a molehill, Marc. What, exactly, are you so afraid that Eugenia will do?"

He fixed me with a hard gaze. "Let's just say that she has been known to lose control of herself in public, to the extent that she has been brought home from many a carnival by the police. Afterward her remorse is so terrible that she is suicidal, and I have to deal with the consequences. This has not happened in a number of years. I do not want it to

happen again." He ripped off the small black mask and
stuffed it in a pocket, and clapped the tricorn hat with its
sinister face on his head, stopping all argument.

"Oh," I said meekly.

Marc seemed to know his way through the lower reaches
of the Palazzo Corleone and its extensive rear garden. I ran
after him with some difficulty, as the folds of the long black
domino kept getting tangled in my legs. I was out of breath
when we reached a street on the other side of the garden,
and I hadn't the slightest idea where we were. Marc looked
back to be sure I followed, and we were off again.

Street lighting is sparse in Venice, and for the carnival
there were torches burning, stuck in old sconces along the
walls, which must have been there for hundreds of years for
just that purpose. The torches gave more light, but it was an
uncertain, flickering sort of light that made unpredictable
shadows. And they gave off a lot of smoke, adding to the
heaviness of the still oppressive air. The rollicking crowd,
however, did not seem to care. For all its jollity, there was
something eerie about the sight: all those figures in long,
black cloaks, their garish, often gruesome masks seeming to
float bodiless along the dark streets.

"Marc," I called, "slow down. I can't keep up with you."
When I gained his side I asked, panting, "Where are we? I
don't recognize anything around here."

"North quadrant," Marc said. His mask was like an echo
chamber, and in spite of myself I shivered at the sound of his
voice. "The Palazzo Corelli is in that direction." He gestured and I looked hard in that direction even though I knew
that in these streets, in the dark, I would never find my way.
"If she's out here she won't go toward home, she'll go in the
other direction. Come on."

"Great," I grumbled. This wasn't fun anymore. Marc
held my hand and pulled me along, but soon I had to claim
the hand back from him; I needed both hands to keep the
domino from tripping me up. We crossed a narrow back
canal on an arched bridge and went into a street that was no
more than a twisted alley. I didn't like this, not one little bit.

We came at last out of that scary place only to be engulfed by a boisterous crowd, which caught us up and swept us along like leaves in an eddying stream. I fought bravely to keep up; and then a figure caught my eye.

Off on the edge of our crowd, moving along at a fair pace, was a very large person in a voluminous black domino. "Marc," I yelled, "that's her! That's Eugenia!" and I took off after her, working my way with elbows and determination. I kept my eyes fixed on the black bulk that was the Lady, I didn't doubt that Marc had heard me or that he would follow.

"Eugenia, wait, wait!" I cried, struggling toward her. Suddenly we were alone, in a pocket of silence. She turned, and I saw my mistake. There was no white face on this tricorned and veiled mask, only a black face, like Marc's but more sinister, with a sneering line of mouth. A hand shot from under the domino and caught my wrist in a grip of steel.

"So," the voice said from its echo chamber, "I have you now, and more easily than I thought. What a pretty little cat you are! No, don't struggle, Clea. I'll only hurt you if you do."

I was not yet as alarmed as I would be soon. "I thought you were your mother," I said. It was Paolo, of course. "You may as well let me go, Marc is right behind me."

"Oh, he is? Look around, Clea. I don't see him, do you?" I looked, anxiously. Marc was nowhere to be seen. The wave of celebrants that had swept us up must still be carrying him along.

"Well, he'll soon miss me. He'll be here any minute," I insisted.

"Let him come. It won't matter. This is the opportunity I have been waiting for. You won't get away from me again, Clea Beaumont. I've tracked you and Marc all evening. I knew exactly where you would be because I knew Marc would follow after the Lady once I had persuaded her to go to the Corleone's ball. I didn't think I would intercept you until farther up the street—I have some helpers planted there. I suppose Marc will get away now, no doubt he will turn back to look for you. But it won't matter, because you and I will be long gone.''

I pulled against his steely grip on my wrist, and opened my mouth to scream. Instantly Paolo's other hand was over both my mouth and nose, and he jerked my arm painfully around at an angle behind my back.

"Don't make a sound, and don't fight me, or I'll break this arm. I can, and I will. I mean it. Nod your head if you understand."

I nodded avidly. He wasn't allowing me to breathe, and I was getting panicky.

"All right. That's better. You behave yourself and you won't get hurt."

"What do you think you're doing, Paolo Corelli?" I hissed, as soon as I could breathe again.

"You think you're pretty smart, you think you've out-witted me," Paolo growled. He picked me up and carried me as easily as if I were a child, and kept up a fast pace as he talked. "You found the secret panel, I know you did because you locked that room. Left the clock for me to find. Got rid of Zenia. You must have figured out that we were putting something in your food?" He raised the pitch of his voice in a question, but I wasn't going to give him the satisfaction of an answer. I was too busy, anyway, trying to get my bearings. Where was he taking me? He ducked into a dark space that was no more than a hole in a wall, and I shuddered, forced to cling to him.

"That Zenia, I never should have relied on her. Never mind, she's not a problem now." We came out of some kind of tunnel onto one of those awful side canals. Paolo dumped me in a flat-bottomed boat and climbed in himself in a swirl of black. God, what a nightmare vision he was!

I gulped. "W-what do you mean? Zenia isn't here any-more, she went to the country."

"Uh-huh." Paolo began to pole the boat. "Thought she could get away from me. She screwed up. I don't like that, I don't allow people to screw up. I killed her, of course.

They'll think it was an acccident. Those country people are so dumb. Giorgio will probably get word of it tomorrow. You're the first to know. You like that, don't you, Clea? You like to know everything."

I wrapped my arms around my knees, shivering from the awfulness of all this. Poor Zenia!

"You're going to know a lot pretty soon. Consider yourself lucky, Clea. Not as lucky as you would have been if you'd let us scare you into leaving the palazzo, and not near as lucky as you'd have been if you'd taken up with me instead of Marc. But you're such a curious woman. That's why you're wearing a cat's head, isn't it, Clea? Because cats are curious, they put their little pink noses into everything. You know what they say about cats, don't you? Answer me, Clea."

Oh, yes, I knew. I said in as strong a voice as I could manage, "Curiosity killed the cat."

Paolo laughed. It was a hideous sound, made more so by the mask. He turned that grim visage and looked down at me, and laughed again, all the while poling the boat in as leisurely a manner as if we were lovers slipping down a canal for an idyllic afternoon.

I closed my eyes. I didn't even want to know anymore where he was taking me.

Eventually the boat's motion stopped. I opened my eyes. We were in a dark place, too dark for me to recognize, but there were walls around and overhead. We seemed to be in some sort of a channel under a building.

"I have to tie your hands now, and we have to take that pretty mask off so I can gag you. It wouldn't do to have you making any noise, attracting attention." Paolo took strips of cloth from the bottom of the boat—they were none too clean. The one he bound around my mouth had an ugly smell. I breathed through my nose, and prayed I wouldn't vomit.

"Up we go!" Paolo lifted me out of the boat and onto a narrow, slimy ledge. I was thankful I'd worn flat shoes with my medieval-looking dress; in heels I'd likely have fallen and broken my neck right there. He instructed, "Now you just walk along right behind me. There's no point trying to get away, there's nowhere for you to go, so you'd better follow me."

I followed him. This was a dank, evil-smelling place. From somewhere above I heard a rumble, a familiar, threatening roll. Thunder. The storm had at last come, but for me there would be no relief. None, at all.

We left the slimy ledge for a passageway equally dank and evil-smelling, but at least it was not slimy. The passage was so low that Paolo had to bend over, and I could barely walk upright myself. The thunder rolled again, but I saw no corresponding flash of lightning. The only light in this place came from a flashlight Paolo kept low to the ground, and it didn't help me much at all.

The passageway was short. Paolo stopped to unlock a door, and once through the door he swept his light around us. My heart leaped with hope—these surroundings were familiar. Big brick columns joined into arches, spaced widely apart, and all around the rustle and squeak of rats.

"Know where you are now, eh, Clea?"

I tried to speak, forgetting the gag. He laughed at my effort and I glared at him, nodding my head.

"Yes, this is the underground chamber of the Palazzo Corelli. We came in along an old channel that brings water from the canal to that fountain in the garden. They used to deliver stuff through there, too, in the olden days. It's been closed off, everybody has forgotten it's there, but I found it and opened it up. Just like I opened up the old staircase. Pretty good trick, huh? I told you I could get in here anytime I want!"

He wasn't smart, but he was cunning. I gave him that.

"Now this, this is my best secret. Might as well get some light on the subject. See," he reached behind a pillar and flipped a switch. "I've put lights in here and everything. Look here, Clea. What do you think of that?"

He whipped off his mask and untied my gag so that I could speak.

"It's the vault," I said.

"No, not the family vault. This is my own vault, I made it myself. Well, I paid somebody to make it, which is the same thing, and nobody knows about it but me. Wait till you see inside!"

Paolo's eyes glittered, he was like a huge, gleeful child. A gleeful, mad child—the expression in his eyes and the way his hands shook were not at all normal. He worked a combination in a door that looked like a slab of concrete set in the bricks, which filled one of the arches, and the slab swung open. Inside was his loot, his treasure trove. He rubbed his hands together, gloating, then came back for me and dragged me in. There were paintings and small statues of bronze and marble, priceless old manuscripts, assorted pieces of jewelry, and one object I recognized: the gold salt cellar I'd seen in the Grand Salon.

"This is why you wanted me to leave the palazzo," I said, "because you were afraid I'd find your stuff. And I did see some of it."

"Yeah, that's why. But it's not the only reason."

"What more could there be?"

"May as well sit down and wait. She'll be along soon. She thinks I botched the job, so now she wants to do you herself. I may as well untie you, I know you won't get away now. Marc doesn't know about my vault, he never comes this far back into the chamber."

"What are you talking about?" I rubbed my wrists, restoring circulation.

"You'll find out." Paolo leered. With his twitching fingers he caressed the objects he could reach. "Pretty great stuff I got here, huh?"

"Yes." I encouraged him to talk. "I admit I didn't know you were so clever."

"I don't steal it. Other guys do that. I just keep it until they have a buyer, and then I send it out wherever it's going. I book one of their couriers on one of my tours. It's a good sideline, and I've made lots and lots of money on it. Made some powerful friends, too. Powerful enough to ruin my big brother, the so-legitimate heir!''

So, that was it. ''So your friends are behind Marc's business difficulties. Did they also sink his boat and try to kill him, or did you do that all by yourself?''

Paolo's face darkened. He cracked and cracked his knuckles. ''I did that, but it didn't work out. I don't know what went wrong. I wanted to get the horse back, the bronze horse. He's hidden it in his bank, no other place it could be, and they'll never let me in there as long as Marc is alive....'' He lapsed into brooding, demented silence broken only by the sound of cracking knuckles.

I was too weary to keep him talking. I sank down on the floor of the vault. Paolo paced back and forth, stopping from time to time to finger one of his treasures. He tried once to taunt me, saying, ''I liked to watch you sleep,'' but I paid him no attention.

Then, all of a sudden, everything happened at once. At first I simply could not believe my eyes. I saw her from away off, as she came out of the unlighted part of the underground chamber. I scrambled to my feet and went to the door of the vault, peering out, disbelieving. The white hair, the little hat, the sensible black shoes, the blue polyester suit. ''Maria Bonavita!'' I gasped. My mind tumbled, and almost snapped. I looked back over my shoulder at Paolo, and what I saw frightened the wits out of me. He was afraid of her, I could see it in his eyes. And if a man like Paolo feared Maria...! I could not begin to comprehend what that meant.

She came on, nodding her head, white curls bobbing. Behind her came someone else, moving with slow, majestic grace. A stalking mountain of blood-red satin, and I could have sworn that Maria did not know Eugenia Corelli was there. I held my ground, I bit my tongue.

Maria advanced confidently, her sensible shoes making little sound on the floor of hard-packed earth. When she was close enough she peered with her bright little eyes first at me, and then at Paolo. ''So he finally caught you, did he, my dear? I must say it took him long enough." She glared over my shoulder at him.

My voice, and my heart, both caught in my throat. Wordlessly I stared just past Maria's ear and watched Eugenia glide closer.

Maria said, "I'm going to kill you, Clea Beaumont, for what your husband did to my husband. I would have done it sooner, but this excuse for a man behind you there insisted you had to be out of this palace first, and the Family agreed with him. Well, my revenge is more important. I'm not listening to any of them anymore." She pulled a little gun out of her purse and set the purse carefully on the floor. The gun looked like a toy, small and silver. But it was not a toy, it was real. Deadly.

I found my voice. "You *did* send that anonymous note, it *was* your handwriting!"

She nodded her head, the curls sprang up and down.

"W-what did my husband do?" I asked, a note of pleading in my voice.

"Your husband, Chester Beaumont, handled certain deals for my husband, Girolamo Bonavita. They call it money laundering. We were never in New Jersey, that was a lie. My dear departed Mr. Bonavita was a Family man in Boston. A minor member of the Family, maybe, but he was everything to me."

I noticed Eugenia moving ponderously but silently closer. She watched Maria with a predatory gleam in her eye, she was hearing every word. And now I saw Marc! He moved silently and swiftly through the shadows. Most likely, I thought, he could not see Maria; Eugenia's bulk must hide her from his view.

Maria continued to speak. "Mr. Chester Beaumont found out that he'd been handling dirty money, and he said he wouldn't do it anymore. He'd made a bundle off my Girolamo's dirty money, too, his own hands weren't all that clean! But Mr. Chester Beaumont was going to tell. My dear Girolamo couldn't stand that, couldn't stand to be a failure, and he was afraid what would happen if your husband told. You see, Girolamo Bonavita was really a weak man, afraid of a lot of things. He should have put out a contract on Chester Beaumont, but he didn't. He killed himself instead. They wouldn't even bury him in the church because he was a suicide. Then your husband died before I could have my revenge.

"I tracked you, Clea Beaumont. The Family helped, and of all the worst choices you could have made for yourself, you came to Venice. I had a real good contact in Venice— that boy behind you there. That bôy who is my husband's bastard. Oh, yes, I've known about him for years. Only Paolo turns out to be not too bright and not so much help, after all. So I've got to do the job myself. At least he got you here tonight, like he said he would." Maria lifted the gun.

Eugenia hoved into view. "You!" she spat, her great rich voice clanging like a bell. "You miserable, ugly, rude little woman. How dare you even to speak his name?"

Maria, startled, stumbled back. She squeaked, "What name?"

"Girolamo Bonavita! So you, you poor excuse for a female, you were the wife my Girolamo left me for. Me, the Lady Corelli!" Eugenia launched herself at Maria. Marc leaped forward to intervene. I didn't know what Paolo was doing, I hadn't heard a peep out of him. Everything was happening so fast that I barely had time myself to comprehend that dear departed Mr. Bonavita must have been the Lady's lover, and Paolo's father. And Maria must have known about Paolo before she had come to Venice, known about the relationship and used it.

"Get away," Maria was yelling, "get off me!" But Eugenia was bigger than three of her and Eugenia in her fury seemed not even to notice that Maria had a gun. Nor did Marc, he was focused on his mother, trying in vain to pull her away from the smaller woman.

I was worried about that gun. I tried to judge my chances of breaking into the fray and wrenching it from Maria's hand. She was putting up a good fight, kicking and screaming and squirming. I darted forward.

Marc yelled, "No, Clea, stay clear!"

In that one moment, as she was going down under yards and yards of red satin, Maria's eyes snapped toward me. She didn't have time to aim, but she pulled the trigger. She shot me.

At first I didn't realize what had happened. I felt the impact, like a blow to my shoulder, but there was no pain. I still wanted to go after the gun when Maria disappeared under Eugenia's bulk. Then I heard something behind me. Paolo! I whipped around, and my shoulder stung. Paolo had decided it was time to leave, but with his customary greed, he wanted to close the vault first. I stood in the way. He pushed me. My shoulder pierced me with hot pain and I cried out, but I lunged at Paolo, grabbed his domino like a leech, and hung on.

"Marc," I yelled, "don't let him get away!" And then everything went black.

I WAS ASLEEP, and I struggled to wake. I had dreams, bad, bad dreams. I couldn't wake up. Someone was in the room with me, and I couldn't wake up. I panicked. But I was drugged, there was nothing I could do, and so I slept again.

Sleep was not so bad. This was a good sleep now, deep and pillowy and comforting. Sleep was good because then there was no pain. Why should there be pain? I didn't know, it didn't matter. Sleep was good. I slept.

I drifted in a world of images, some pleasant, some not so pleasant. Gradually I realized I was neither awake nor asleep, I was somewhere in between. I saw my children. I saw a handsome bearded man, a good man, I loved this man but oddly I couldn't remember his name. The name came to me: Marc. Yes, Marc. And another man's face came into my vision, a beefy face, once boyishly charming but no longer. Chet, that was Chet.

The scene inside my head shifted. I gave Chet the note. He read it. He rose from his desk chair, his face purpling, and then he sat down again, hard. He muttered obscenities. He grasped at his chest. I ran toward the desk, reached for the phone. He was sick, he was having a heart attack, I had to call for help. "Not sick!" he insisted angrily, his face now a deep shade of red-purple, and he pushed my hand away from the phone. Pushed so hard that I fell against the edge of the desk and drove the corner of it into my hip bone. I had had that bruise for a long time after. The sudden pain dazed me, I saw spots before my eyes. I heard Chet slump heavily forward, his head hit the desk. I called his name. I shook him, and he didn't respond, at all. He still had the note in his hand, that awful note that had upset him so much it might have killed him! I snatched it back, and frantically dialed the phone. 911.

I OPENED MY EYES. Saw white walls, and lots of sun. My shoulder hurt. I remembered. I remembered everything, then and now. Everything. I turned my head. "Marc." He was there, he took my hand.

"Welcome back, *carissima*." His smile was all the welcome I would ever need, anywhere.

"Why am I in the hospital? It wasn't such a bad wound, I barely felt it."

"My brave lioness!" Marc bent over and kissed me softly on the lips. "You barely felt it, yes. You fought like the lioness you are and kept my half brother from getting away. And then you lost consciousness. When I finally was able to get you here to the hospital, they said the bullet was still inside of you and had to come out. You had surgery, Clea, that's why you are here. But you are all right, thank God. You are going to be fine. I thought I would go insane when we were separated that night. When I couldn't find you in the street I thought that if you lost me, you would go back to the palazzo. So I went home, and just as I came in the door I saw the Lady going through the secret door to the underground chamber. I followed her, and you know most of what happened after that."

"Mmm-hmm." I shifted in the bed. There was pain, but it was bearable. "Come and sit here by me."

"With pleasure."

"How long has it been since the surgery? How long have I been sleeping?"

Marc frowned. He held tightly to my hand and it was a moment before he raised his head and looked into my eyes. "Too long. The doctors were worried. They think you may have had some allergy to their anesthetic. But they watched you very closely, I made sure of that. They were sure you were not in any danger. You slept for almost two days, *carissima*. It is Monday afternoon now, and you were shot early Sunday morning."

"That's all right." I raised Marc's hand to my lips and kissed his knuckles. "I had interesting dreams, interesting...memories. I'll tell you in a minute. First, I want a drink of water, and then I want to know about the others, what happened to them."

Marc poured water into a glass from a carafe on my bedside table, inserted a straw and bent it for me, as if he had been nursing all his life. Then he sat down on the bed again and said, "Mrs. Bonavita is in jail. Paolo, he—he went crazy. He locked himself inside that vault, and he was like a gibbering idiot when he got out. The Lady, I'm afraid, my mother..." he looked away, gripped my hand tightly, then looked back at me. There was great sadness in his eyes. "My mother is dead."

"How? Marc, she saved my life. Maria Bonavita would have killed me, for sure, if your mother hadn't followed her down there and gone after her the way she did!"

"I suppose it was all too much for the Lady. She didn't know that Paolo was doing what he was doing, hiding stolen goods in her house. She really thought he had been coming there out of love for her. I left him in that vault, I couldn't watch both him and Mrs. Bonavita at the same time. I took her gun after you collapsed, picked you up and held the gun on her, told the Lady to come with us, and we all went upstairs. The Lady kept mumbling about Paolo, that he didn't really love her, and about that—what was the name, Girolamo?—Bonavita. When we got upstairs I called an ambulance first, for you, and then I called the police.

That little woman Bonavita is feisty, Clea, I had to keep the gun on her all the time or she would have gotten away. I didn't have time to think about my mother for quite a while. When the police came they had to arrest Mrs. Bonavita first, and then I took them underground to get Paolo out of the vault. I was pretty sure he would have let himself out by then, but he hadn't. He was a mess, Clea. He'll be in jail or in a mental institution probably for the rest of his life.''

"There's no doubt of that," I said. "Did he confess that he killed poor young Zenia?"

"No!" Marc rubbed the back of his neck, still a more loyal brother than he himself realized. "Are you sure? How do you know he did that?"

"He told me himself, Marc."

"I suppose I'll have to tell the police," he acknowledged, and I nodded my agreement.

"Your mother, Marc," I reminded him gently when he seemed to lose his train of thought, "tell me what happened."

"Yes." Marc shook himself away from thoughts of Paolo. "When I finally got back upstairs and went to look for her, I couldn't find her. Then I remembered her private study. That's where she was. She had taken out all those goblets you told me about, with the jewels, arranged them all around her on the table. And she had poisoned herself. She had cyanide. I don't know where she got it or how long she'd had it—years, probably. She often said she would kill herself, and I did believe she meant it, but I didn't think she had the means to do it. As I said, I think it was all too much for her. She just didn't want to live anymore."

"I'm sorry," I said. "She was a tragic figure, really. Larger than life." I reached for Marc, to put my arms around him, but that was not a good idea for my shoulder. I winced in pain. I held both his hands instead.

A nurse looked in on us, smiled, and went away.

"Marc," I said, "I love you."

"Ah, Clea. I had begun to wonder if I would ever hear you say those words." His smile was beautiful to behold.

His kiss was heaven to feel. "I love you, *carissima*, you know that. After all you have been through, I feel most humbly blessed that you would tell me now that you love me. I was so afraid, when you did not wake up for so long, that I would lose you."

"No chance of that. You aren't going to lose me unless you want to, Marc, not ever. I can tell you this now, because I remembered. I remembered everything right here in this hospital bed. And you were right. I didn't stand by and watch Chet die. I did try to help him. I don't know why I had blocked it out of my mind, but it doesn't matter now. All that matters is that I'm alive, and I love you."

"Clea, *mia cara*. Then you will not leave Venice?"

"No, I will not leave Venice. In fact, in just a little while I'm going to chase you out of here so that I can call my children and tell them they are coming here for Christmas."

"Your children. I always forget that you have children. Do you think I have to ask their permission to marry their mother?"

I glowed. A hospital bed would not have been my first choice of places to receive a proposal, but somehow now it seemed just right. I said, "First I think you should ask their mother."

"Very well." Marc went down on one knee beside the bed. "I believe this is the preferred position. Clea, will you marry me, and stay with me always?"

"We must first take time to properly mourn Eugenia, the Lady, your mother."

"Of course."

"Then yes, Marc, I will marry you and stay with you always!" This time I did reach for him, pain and all, and he came to me and folded me in his arms.

MARC LEFT AND I slept again. I would have to call the children later, I was too muzzily tired and happy to do it at the moment. When I woke the room was full of yellow roses, dozens of them, far too many, a ridiculous profusion. I laughed.

Marc returned. He had in his hand one perfect Talisman rose. "I had to look many places to find this rose, but you see I remembered. Your favorite, the Talisman rose."

"Marc, you are the most ridiculous, romantic man I have ever known!"

"Perhaps," he grinned. "I am also a puzzled man. You had a most strange telephone call, Clea. I have had your calls routed to me until you get out of the hospital, and so I answered it. I told the man my name and he seemed surprised. He is your banker. He said you want to buy the villa."

"Oh, my goodness! I had forgotten all about that!"

"Well," said Marc leaning over me, his eyes dancing, "you can't buy it because it's not for sale!"

"No?"

"No. The villa is not for sale because I have renamed it the Villa Clea Corelli. You see, I am going to give it to my wife as a wedding present."

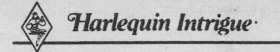

Harlequin Intrigue

A SPAULDING & DARIEN MYSTERY

Make a date with Jenny Spaulding and Peter Darien when this engaging pair of amateur sleuths returns to solve their third puzzling mystery in Intrigue #171, ALL FALL DOWN (October 1991).

If you missed the first two books in this four-book A SPAULDING AND DARIEN MYSTERY series, #147, BUTTON, BUTTON, or #159, DOUBLE DARE, and would like to order them, send your name, address, zip or postal code along with a check or money order for $2.50 for book #147 or $3.25 for book #159, plus 75¢ postage and handling ($1.00 in Canada) for each book ordered, payable to Harlequin Reader Service, to:

In the U.S.
3010 Walden Ave.
P.O. Box 1325
Buffalo, NY 14269-1325

In Canada
P.O. Box 609
Fort Erie, Ontario
L2A 5X3

Please specify book title(s) with your order.
Canadian residents add applicable federal and provincial taxes.

IBB-1AR

Coming in March from

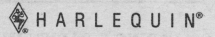
HARLEQUIN®

LaVyrle Spencer's unforgettable story of a
love that wouldn't die.

SWEET MEMORIES

She was as innocent as she was unsure . . . until a very special
man dared to unleash the butterfly wrapped in her cocoon and
open Teresa's eyes and heart to love.

SWEET MEMORIES is a love story to savor that will make you
laugh—and cry—as it brings warmth and magic into your
heart.

"Spencer's characters take on the richness of friends, relatives
and acquaintances."   —*Rocky Mountain News*

SWEET